D1527365

A Monkee
By My
Side

Jerri Keele

DEDICATION

This book is dedicated to
all loved ones who have passed before us,
to the mentors, the idols,
the ones who inspired, encouraged, and loved,
and allowed us to love them back.

All proceeds from this book benefit
The Davy Jones Equine Memorial Foundation.

ACKNOWLEDGMENTS

I extend my sincere thanks and appreciation to the following individuals and groups for their support and guidance:

Brian Keele, my loving and supportive husband,
who stands by all my wild ideas and projects,
who endures forgotten dinners, distracted conversations,
and less than stellar housekeeping.

Colleen Gruver, the best friend I could ever have,
the most enthusiastic, patient, and detailed proofreader
and editor, who tirelessly encourages and supports me and
lets me bounce those same wild ideas around.

Andrea Gilbey and Ginny Fleming,
who both lend their unending support and encouragement.

The Jones Girls (Talia, Sarah, Jessica and Annabel)

All of my supporters at NaNoWriMo.org
(National Novel Writing Month)

All of my supporters on Facebook

THE MONKEES® is a federally registered trademark of
Rhino Entertainment Company.
There is no affiliation, endorsement or
connection between Rhino Entertainment Company
and this book or its author.

NOTE: This is a novel of fiction, a work of fantasy.

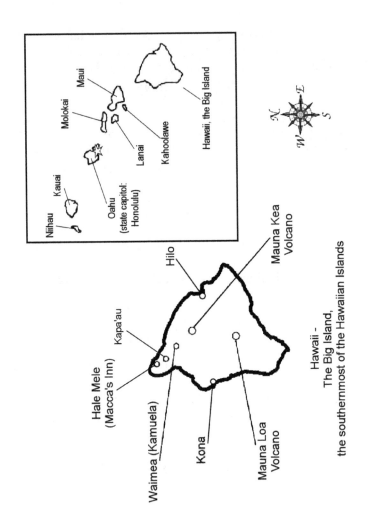

Niihau

Kauai

Oahu
(state capitol:
Honolulu)

Molokai

Maui

Lanai

Kahoolawe

Hawaii, the Big Island

N
W E
S

Hale Mele
(Macca's Inn)

Kapa'au

Hilo

Mauna Kea
Volcano

Waimea (Kamuela)

Kona

Mauna Loa
Volcano

Hawaii -
The Big Island,
the southernmost of the Hawaiian Islands

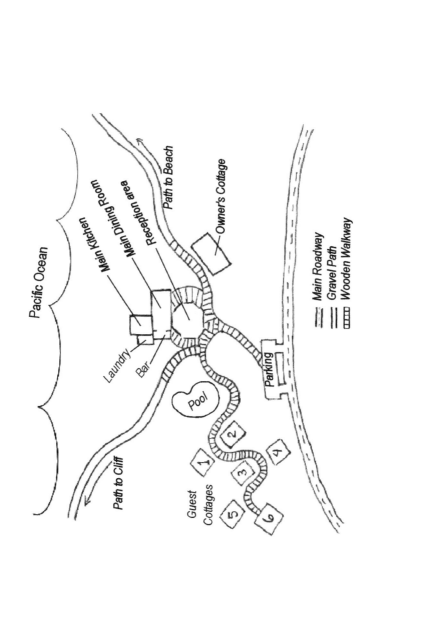

Pacific Ocean

Main Kitchen

Main Dining Room

Reception area

Path to Beach

Owner's Cottage

Laundry

Bar

Pool

Path to Cliff

Guest
Cottages

1

2

3

4

5

6

Parking

===== Main Roadway
===== Gravel Path
▫▫▫▫ Wooden Walkway

Prologue

We were quickly working our way through the early months of winter, but it was a winter unlike most of the rest of the country was experiencing. The seasons in Hawaii barely registered change. There was the occasional day when I wore long pants, but those were few and far between. And while Davy wasn't there quite as often as I'd gotten used to before, he still seemed to shimmer into the picture just when I needed him most.

On one such day, I was standing at the computer in the reception area working on the bookkeeping when Sam appeared leading a beautiful German Shepherd dog by a nylon rope.

"Oh, what a gorgeous dog, Sam." I came around the desk to stoop beside it and offer my hand for sniffing. "Is it yours?"

"No, Miss Macca. I found her digging in the trash out back. She has no tags, and none of us recognize her from the area."

"Oh dear," I exclaimed as the dog accepted my hand and gave it a few licks. Her warm tongue lapped at my fingers and wrist, and I gave her a pet on the side of her face with my dry hand. "Where do you live, sweetheart?" I asked her, holding her lovely head between my hands. She simply scooted closer to me and laid her large head down on my leg as I squatted next to her.

"I cannot take her home, Miss Macca. No pets allowed." Sam handed his end of the rope to me. They both looked so sad.

Never one to turn away an animal in need, I stood and led the dog to my cottage, calling over my shoulder, "No problem. I'll take care of her and try to find her owners too."

Once inside, the dog sat obediently while I got a bowl of water and rescued Chester's bowls to a higher level. The feline jumped to the top of the bookcase and voiced his displeasure.

"I expect you to be more hospitable, Mr. Chester."

All I got was a hiss in response from the big orange cat who had bravely traveled across the Pacific Ocean with me to experience this adventure here in Hawaii. And although he was grumpy at times, I know that the fresh air invigorated both of us, the tropical foliage provided hours of entertainment as he hunted for bugs and small critters, and the constant flow of people to give him pets put him at his happiest.

Setting the larger bowl on the floor in the kitchen, I gave a short whistle and the dog hesitantly came over to lap at the cool water. I ruffled her fur and opened the refrigerator. Inside was a bowl of leftover brown rice. "I don't have any dog food yet, but perhaps you'd like some of this?"

I fluffed up the grains and set the container next to her on the floor. She sniffed once and then wolfed it down in three bites.

Davy shimmered into the room and stood peering at the dog with a puzzled look. He walked around to one side of her, then the other, and then stooped down to her level. She licked his face. "Susie!" He dropped to the floor next to her, saying the name over and over again. "Where have you been, my luv?"

"Wait... what?"

Davy and the dog both shimmered out of the room, and I stood there with my mouth hanging open in shock and disbelief.

"No, no, no, no, no, no. You come back here! Both of you!"

I called to Davy a few more times and my irritation grew as he failed to reappear. A little pop sound in my head reminded me of our secret word that would summon him if I needed. "Goldfish!"

"No fair." He shimmered in. "There's no emergency!"

"No emergency? Do you know that it was Sam who found the dog and brought her in? Who is Susie anyway?"

"Susie was my dog in the sixties. And... she's a he." He was nearly bouncing before me. "And now I gotta go. He's waiting."

He was like a little kid who wanted to get back to playing with his dog.

"Okay, but..."

"I'll bring him back in a few. I promise."

I shooed him away. "Fine then. I look forward to seeing..." But he was gone before I could finish my sentence. I glanced up at Chester and chuckled at the degree of disgust on his face. "You'll live, big guy." His response was a growly-grumble. I reached up and smoothed his cheek. He settled quickly but stayed on top of the bookcase.

Later that night as I settled into my bed, I realized I'd never asked Davy why he'd given his boy dog a girl's name.

ONE

Innkeeping

My name is Macca Lennon Daydream Liberty, and I am the product of two aging hippies who never aged enough for my liking before they were taken away shortly after my tenth birthday. They had been loving parents, and they named me after their heroes, Paul McCartney and John Lennon of The Beatles, and Davy Jones of The Monkees.

My Uncle Wally and Aunt Fran continued my rearing in a loving if not quite the hippie-ish manner. Aunt Fran passed before I graduated college, and it was Uncle Wally and me on our own for a while. Upon my graduating with a business degree, Uncle Wally informed me that he had inherited an inn on the Big Island of Hawaii and had gone off to enjoy what he considered would be the adventure of a lifetime.

It was devastating then to hear of his passing and my subsequent inheritance of the inn itself. It was those early days here in Hawaii where I discovered my first dead body, floating in the pool. It had turned out to be the dastardly doings of my neighbor, the owner of a much larger hotel resort complex. He had then tried to push me off a cliff in order to take over the inn that he felt was rightfully his. If it hadn't been for Davy Jones' interference, I would not be here today... soon to discover yet another dead body.

Did I mention that Davy Jones was a ghost from the sixties? Yeah — *that* Davy Jones. Of The Monkees. He popped into my life on a day when I had nearly given up on existing, having just heard of the passing of my sweet Uncle Wally. My parents, Jude and Willow, had asked their fellow ghost to intervene on their behalf, and although Davy was sixty-six years old when he passed suddenly in 2012, he was able to change his appearance at will. Therefore, I had that adorable twenty year old Davy — the one in black pants and a red eight-button shirt, white boots, and a haircut better than any that Justin Bieber could have ever imagined. He was more talented than the Beeb as well. Who makes up nicknames for themselves anyway?

At first though, he was quite the pest, following me around, constantly yammering on, doing stand-up comic bits, singing, dancing, playing guitar, and just being so darn sweet and cute that I often wondered if I should check my blood sugar. But soon he grew on me to a point where I could not imagine life without him. We'd shared one beautiful kiss in the early days of our friendship, but it had been fairly chaste since then, although I'd occasionally wondered if a ghost and a human could fall in love. And despite my protests at the time, he'd become my frequent — and beloved — companion these days. Some days it was weird, but most of the time he was a welcome friend.

My previously mundane life had become a scene that might have worked had Shirley Jackson written *The Haunting of Hale Mele* instead of Hill House... and if Stephen King had helped her... along with George R.R. Martin... or something. Hell, maybe if Neil Gaiman had been tossed into that mix too? Me? I'd rather have lived in an old Agatha Christie or Mary Stewart novel myself. Safer stories, and the women swooned a lot. I'd never swooned. What was a swoon anyway?

Hale Mele — "House of Song" — was mine though, and I loved her as a parent loves her child. My uncle had indeed had visions for the inn, and I promised him in my heart that I would do my best to continue working toward his dream. Our family had always been kind and loving toward all creatures and the earth itself, and I found no reason to change the results of the nurturing I'd received for most of my life.

The inn consisted of seven bungalows, each with a small living room, combined kitchen and dining room, two bedrooms, and a bathroom. The main building housed a small reception area where guests checked in, a tiny gift shop, a dining room and bar, and a quite nicely appointed professional kitchen where the husband and wife team of Kalei and Lani created magic in the way of luscious and local food six days a week. To the west of the main building were the six guest bungalows, separated just enough to give each guest plenty of privacy. A small pool was between the main building and the bungalows.

The seventh bungalow was situated on the other side of the main building, to the east, and it was mine. The biggest difference besides the location was the fact that there was an expansive deck on the backside that provided a beautiful view of the lush vegetation and the sea beyond. While I had the main bedroom, the second bedroom was technically Davy's, yet he never seemed to need it much. Uncle Wally had installed a wine fridge in the kitchen though, and it was our favorite feature. There were few nights where we didn't sit out on the deck with a glass of wine and watch the sky turn to coral, then to lilac, and lastly to midnight blue.

There is no way on this good earth that I could run this inn without my new "family" of employees, because that's exactly what they had become — family. Kalei, the big man with the long braid down his back, and Lani, his tiny wife with nearly-black hair hanging down her back and the softest doe eyes you could ever see, were experts in the kitchen and in the dining room. Ming, tiny but tenacious, was my sweet clean-freak. She was in charge of keeping the bungalows and the rest of the inn tidy and doing the laundry. Bennie, about my height and with dark hair, eyes, and skin, was my right-hand, my assistant manager. He took care of bookings and made sure the guests were comfortable, as well as helping with the accounting, but any time I mentioned his name in Davy's presence, my bestie would break out in song, namely an old Elton John tune about *B-b-b-b-bennie*. Shy Albert was Mr. Greenthumb and happily took care of the grounds. I was fairly certain he preferred plants over people. Lastly, Surfer Sam, complete with longish blond hair and a deep tan, was an important "floater" in addition to his duties of taking care of the tiny gift shop and the bar. He was happy to fill in wherever we needed help.

When I inherited the inn, I also inherited a very wise soul in the way of Winston, an African grey parrot named after Winston Churchill and taught by a previous owner to recite nearly every famous quote by the historical Prime Minister of Great Britain. Winston had also, sadly or not, come to be the resident comedian at times, often rivaling Davy I might add, much to the latter's delight. Davy spent inordinate amounts of time teaching the bird to sing "Daydream Believer" and to recite really bad (and very old) one-liners. I tolerated both of them though, because love prevails over bad jokes. Mostly. Winston had full access to the inn and the skies above but preferred our company. He slept in his cage at night, but the rest of the time he would flit around the inn to greet and entertain people. He'd often spend many hours inside my bungalow, and poor Chester had finally come to accept him, begrudgingly I might add.

More than a year ago, I'd been handed a tidy sum of money from the estranged wife of the man who had tried to kill me because he believed, incorrectly I might add, that the land my inn was on was rightfully his. It had been deeded to his sister after their father's death, while he had received the bright, shiny, and hugely successful massive hotel complex up the road. I had met with a financial advisor recommended by my attorney Alex Baldwin —no relation to the Baldwin family of the silver screen he told me — and the money had been invested in such a way that I could only draw out enough at a time to finance upgrade projects now and then.

I was expanding the parking area to accommodate more vehicles and also installing solar panels to provide energy in a more environmentally efficient manner. We switched all of our lighting to LED bulbs and installed eco-friendly ceiling fans in the main rooms of each bungalow as well as in the common rooms. I chose fans with blades that resembled pale ecru palm leaves. I knew Uncle Wally would have been proud of all of these endeavors.

The decision to have parts of the inn renovated one area at a time was not an easy one for me. The steps and path between the parking area and the inn were torn out and replaced with materials that were not only sustainable but also locally harvested. I'd contracted with a local company that specialized in greening the state. Section by section, the old wooden walkways and railings were being greened as well using sustainable bamboo. It was costly, but the durability in the long run would eventually prove to be cost effective. While so much was torn up already, I also took the opportunity to have our rainwater catchment system upgraded.

As the daughter of hippie parents, it had always been my dream to go green. I'd started with my car — an economical Smart Car I'd named R2

5

— and I was now in the process of greening my inn. It was the responsible thing to do. My "to do" list of greening was lengthy, but I wanted to stretch the money, and so I made the decision that it would be done just a little at a time. The only other thing I needed to do was to exercise great patience. For me, this was the most difficult.

So it was daily that I was not only dealing with the operational decisions for the inn but the contractor projects as well. It could be tricky too because we had to work around guest schedules. I couldn't have a torn up walkway in an area that would be needed by a guest in order to get to their bungalow, so I was constantly comparing our reservations to the next stage of the upgrade. So far there hadn't been any horrible timing conflicts, and we put little tent cards in each bungalow to explain our project to our guests. The response had been nothing short of amazing to me. The acceptance of the fact that we must help our planet was shown by glowing online reviews and also guest satisfaction survey cards that had been left for us.

The staff was quite supportive as well, especially Ming, whose cleaning supplies had been exchanged for more environmentally conscious materials. This included 100% cotton towels and bed linens. Most important to Ming was the use of non-toxic natural cleaning and laundry supplies. In fact, we'd even implemented the use of distilled vinegar as a disinfectant. While she hated the odor at first, it did indeed dissipate within minutes. For freshening the air, there was nothing better than flinging open every window in every bungalow as she cleaned once a day, but there was also homemade potpourri in each bathroom. We had spent several evenings creating our natural bits — dried peels and petals, baking soda, and essential oils, all combined in cute little mismatched diffuser jars I'd picked up at rummage sales and thrift shops. I'd come to love haunting the various deals in the area; the old saying that one man's trash is another man's treasure was indeed correct. As long as a little vinegar and elbow grease were applied, they were like new.

In the common areas we employed unscented organic soy candles at each dining table and the bar, not so much for air freshening — for much of the building was open to the elements unless shuttered during a storm — but rather for an environmentally conscious way to light the mood.

I found myself wandering the grounds and buildings frequently to see what areas could be improved upon. As a result, I kept thinking ahead to having some days off for a little R&R. So far it hadn't been feasible, but I knew there would come a time when it would fit into the schedule. I daydreamed of visits to the tourist spots we were always suggesting to our guests. Kilauea, Parker Ranch, Kona, Waimea, and the green sand beach at Papakôlea. I'd love a day of shopping, dining, and touring art galleries. I'd even consider a day out on a fishing boat! I hadn't been on a boat since I was a small child and missed the feeling of freedom while floating upon the vast open sea. It's always good to have that occasional reminder that we are all just tiny specks in the universe, and the power of the ocean was a perfect way to jog one's memory.

I was actually able to escape the inn, however, for a few hours when I attended the Merrie Monarch Festival with Kalei and Lani. Well, Kalei and I attended with Davy shimmering in to join us; Lani actually participated. The Merrie Monarch Festival is the annual week-long festival featuring an internationally acclaimed hula competition, an arts fair, hula shows, and a parade through Hilo. A complete surprise to me was that the lovely and petite Lani was indeed a talented dancer in the Hawaiian tradition, performing dances handed down by ancestors. Each dance tells a story which the dancer then retells with fluid movements and lovely accompanying music. Although her dance troupe had not yet won, they were thrilled each year to participate.

I had been awed by the performances, both group and soloists, and especially tickled when Lani's troupe took the stage. I clapped so hard that my hands felt bruised at the end of the day. It was then I got an idea. On the ride home I presented it to the couple.

"Lani, you were so wonderful, so beautiful! I had an idea though..." My words were met with total silence; I'm sure they were thinking it was going to be yet another of my half-baked ideas so I charged on. "What would you think about providing a special dinner every Saturday night and including a little entertainment: you... dancing?"

The silence lengthened and I thought for certain my idea would be quashed. Kalei, his hands on the wheel of their family car, kept glancing at me in the rearview mirror, then giving a sideways glance to his wife. I saw Lani's shoulders rise and fall as she took a deep breath before turning to me, a grin on her face. "I would be honored."

In the mirror, I could see Kalei's grin reach his eyes. "And perhaps a less touristy luau? More traditional fare from our history, yes? It's actually just a very large backyard cookout, like our family does for birthdays and special occasions."

I squealed. I admit it. It doesn't happen often, but there it was. The elusive squeal, sometimes followed by the giggle snort. I clapped my hand over my mouth, and we shared a good chuckle. Davy simply grinned and shook his head at me, and I ignored him. Kalei, Lani, and I spent the rest of the ride home tossing out ideas and setting up the framework for this new weekly event at Hale Mele.

TWO

Critters

I was refilling Winston's food on his perch under the bird's watchful eye. "Yummy." I smiled as I closed the food storage bin. He cocked his head and peered at me with one beady eye. I reached up and gave the soft feathers of his chest a few strokes. Suddenly he stretched his wings and made such a ruckus that I worried he'd awaken any guests trying to enjoy a sleepy morning during their vacation. It was then I heard a squawk from the highest trees surrounding us. Winston squawked back; the distant squawk replied. Back and forth it went as I shaded my eyes to try to see what kind of bird the visitor was. I didn't have to wait long, for soon it appeared on the perch next to Winston, all fluttery feathers. It was a beautiful deep blue parrot of some kind, nearly purple, with a dark band across its nose reaching from one eye to the other. The bird was slightly larger than Winston, with a shiny black beak and bright green wings.

"Winston, have you got a new friend here?" He bobbed his head up and down, the newcomer mimicking the moves as I chuckled. "I'm going to have to put the two of you to work if I'm expected to feed you both now, you know," I teased. "Do either of you have experience as maids?" They stared at me blankly. "Security guards? How about attack birds? You attack the food bowl and I'll just keep filling it."

I noticed, however, that the new bird had a band around its leg. I pulled my phone out of my pocket and snapped a photo of the two of them perched there like old friends. "Will you let me touch your pretty ankle bracelet, New Guy?" I slowly reached toward the piece of plastic. Winston nuzzled his friend's head. The blue parrot angled its head to watch me as I twisted the small leg band. I snapped a photo of the number imprinted there and then slowly pulled away just a little. I gave New Guy's chest feathers a little stroke and he preened for me.

"You're sure a nice little new guy, New Guy." And with that, New Guy stretched his wings again and seemed to float back up into the trees. "Sorry Winston. Didn't mean to chase your friend away." Winston hopped up onto my shoulder, gave my cheek a rub with his beak, and then followed his friend into the tree. "Send a postcard when you can," I teased before turning back to my innkeeping tasks.

I awoke the next morning to the sound of loud chattering. Peering out the bedroom window, I saw Winston and New Guy perched on the railing of my deck, apparently deep in conversation. I'd nearly forgotten about the photos I'd taken. I showered, dressed, pulled out my laptop, and uploaded the photo for a search. Similar images told me this New Guy was actually a female Derbyan parrot. So Winston's got a girlfriend! I found a listing for a parrot club here in the islands and whipped off an email including the photo of the leg band. I just wanted to make sure New Guy/Girl wasn't lost. As I snapped the laptop closed, I realized I was ravenous and trudged to the kitchen.

Davy shimmered in, all cat-that-swallowed-the-canary grins. I was immediately suspicious of The Pest, for I'd seen what he drew his excitement from in the past.

"What?" I grumbled, making coffee and toast. Tea be damned; I needed a hefty caffeine infusion.

He was nearly vibrating, almost jumping up and down like a six year old kid. "I have something to show you."

I dropped the teaspoon I'd been using to stir my cream into my coffee. "What?" I asked again, rather exasperated.

"No. You have to see." He bounced.

I watched him from the corner of my eye. "Really? You can't just... send a letter or something?" I was tired, cranky, and a little unsettled with the new development in the way of a ghost dog. How does one explain that to guests?

He bounced more. I tossed the spoon into the sink and downed the coffee, nearly scorching my mouth and throat. Turning to the bouncing pest, I sighed. "Show me, but I'm warning you, I'm not in the mood for much of anything."

He grabbed my hand and pulled me ahead, out the door, down the walk, and down the stairs to the beach. It was quite a hike normally, but being in the sour mood I'd found myself, it was a trek of epic proportions on this morning, and I grumbled the entire way. At the bottom, on the last bit of stairs, he stopped and swept his arm wide, as though ready to take a bow before a Broadway audience. There before me was a beast of beauty like I'd never seen. A horse, a deep bay with black mane and tail. His striking beauty was the first thing I noticed before noting strong features and seemingly powerful muscles.

"Ohhh, absolutely beautiful!"

"His name is Glory-Gunn, but I call him Glory."

"He's huge!"

Davy smiled proudly, running his hand over the horse's massive body. "He's 16 hands!"

"Where did he come from?"

Davy grinned. "He followed me home."

"I really find that hard to believe." I was shaking my head and considering the million stairs we had just traipsed down.

"He did!" He looked down at the sand, scuffing his bare foot in it and looking very much like a guilty child. "I just had to show him the way first."

I slapped my palm to my face. "Another ghost?" I nervously glanced up and down the beach, thankful to find it deserted as usual. "We... this... I..." Yep. I was basically speechless.

"But he's like Susie! Everyone can see him, and he doesn't do the disappearing act until he's hidden. Like in the trees."

I shook my head. I shook it harder. It changed nothing. The horse was still there, with Davy hanging onto its lead like a kid with a new bike. Oh great.

"Please?" He begged. "Please can we keep him? I promise to feed him, Mum." Now he was getting on my last nerve.

"I am NOT your mother. And it's a good thing this beach is small and secluded. Oh, and you're responsible for him." I turned on my heel and went to work, grumbling the entire way, and the entire day. People steered clear of me, and for this I was grateful.

That night Davy and I were having a light meal of pizza and salad. Lani had given me a round of dough she'd made that morning, and I simply rolled it out and loaded it with tomatoes, mushrooms, olives, peppers, shaved zucchini slices, and mozzarella. Davy was tossing some spring greens with a light roasted garlic dressing and caramelized onions. I hadn't yet decided to fully forgive him for adding more complications to our lives with a horse-ghostie. True, I couldn't blame Susie on him for the dog had arrived on his own. But a horse? I kept doing a mental face-palm every time I thought about my simple life that had become so complex.

"Tuppence for your thoughts?" he asked in a very gentle voice.

"What's a tuppence? Not sure my thoughts are worth it."

"It's a figure of speech. Not worth a pound nor a dollar."

"I'm worried about the..."

"Horse?" He supplied the word that wouldn't roll off my tongue, and I simply nodded. "Wot's to worry about?"

I made a derisive sound in the back of my throat. "Well for one thing, what happens if someone reports a horse on the beach? This isn't really a place where wild horses roam, now is it?"

"There are wild horses in Waipi'o Valley." He sounded once again like a child trying to convince his parent.

"Yes, a long way from here, and they don't wander out this far." Stubborn streaks aside, we both knew that we'd already gained a new pet of the ghostly equine variety. I sighed and admitted defeat.

With so much going on, I revisited a habit from my college years and had begun writing in a journal again. Of course, all I had was an orange and white composition book, but at least I had pens — lots of pens. I began to write in the journal whenever I felt stressed and had a spare moment. The problem with this plan was that oftentimes stress precluded the spare moment part of that equation, but I was trying. I hid the composition book in such a unique little hidey hole that I was sure even Davy couldn't find it. I had a stack of my aunt's old *Ms. Magazine*s on the bookshelf, and I chose the edition in which the cover sported the question "How Late Can You Wait to Have a Baby?" I figured it was an innocuous enough cover that he'd never look there.

So, after the initial appearance of our dear Glory, I pulled out the composition book and began to scribble. It wasn't a long passage, but I felt altogether at ease when I closed the book and slipped it into the designated copy of *Ms. Magazine*.

Ghosts

What the hell. Just when I was learning to deal with having a sidekick who is invisible to most of the general population, a ghost dog comes along. But this is one different ghost! Others can see him. I mean, ALL others can see him! Why is Susie's visibility different than Davy's? It's certainly a puzzle, and Davy has no answers for me. I wonder if it's based on desire? Susie wants people to see him because he wants attention, playmates, and food maybe? It's possible. I may never know the answer. For now, I just tell guests that he's a bit aloof and hides occasionally. What really happens is that he disappears and goes who knows where!

He's a lovely dog — a medium-sized German Shepherd. He has a really good disposition too. I wonder if that is because he used to be Davy's dog back in the sixties? I love watching them take walks along the beach together. That dog loves to chase the waves.

Today, dear Davy introduced me to a new ghost named Glory-Gunn, or Glory for short. A big beautiful beast of a horse, and ever so gentle and sweet. Just after we'd met he was already nuzzling my hand for a massage.

So now we have an orange cat named Chester, an African grey parrot named Winston, a German Shepherd named Susie, and a big bay horse named Glory. What's next? Or maybe I shouldn't tempt fate and ask that question. And why was a boy dog named Susie? And... is New Guy/Girl a ghost Derbyan parrot or a real one? Tune in tomorrow (or whenever) for the latest in the continuing melodrama that surrounds Hale Mele.

When I pulled my journal out of its hiding place the next day, this had been scrawled at the bottom of my last entry:

Dear Macca,

Firstly — Watch your language.

B — So I'm a sidekick? I thought I was a primary player. Sigh.
3 — Susie and I have a good history together; he's a loyal friend.
Lastly — I didn't realize you're a stalker. Watching me on the beach?
Yeah. You love the little Manchester Cowboy. Admit it.

Love,
David
(little happy face with its tongue sticking out)

It was several days before I received a reply to my email about the Derbyan. The numbers on the leg band were unlisted and unknown, and there had been no reports of a lost Derbyan. Great. Yet another mouth to feed, although she'd seemed to be able to fend for herself. I decided to put a notice in the local paper about a found bird. She had become a frequent visitor, all chummy with Winston these days.

I soon discovered that, unlike Winston, New Girl whistled. I caught a few bars of what sounded like "I Shot the Sheriff" more than once, and another several bars of something very close to the reggae feeling of "So Much Trouble in the World."

"So, New Girl, someone taught you Bob Marley? Whistle something else for me then."

She whistled more of "I Shot the Sheriff," and Winston accompanied her with his exaggerated head bobbing. If I'd had a video camera I'm sure we could have gone viral with that one, but that was not my aim. I just wanted to find out if this girl had people looking for her.

"Hey Miss Marley, are you a one-hit wonder then?"

She whistled the same tune over and over again. I chuckled and then stroked Marley and Winston's soft feathers.

The days were filled with all the exciting and breathtaking tasks of keeping an inn running. Wait. I can't lie. It's quite mundane and boring, frankly, but when we all worked together, the inn seemed to almost keep itself... in guests and demands. My Uncle Wally's legacy though made me want to make it even more successful.

I hadn't had any nibbles on Marley's "parents" so she just sort of morphed into another resident of Hale Mele. Pretty soon I could open a petting zoo. Winston had an appointment with Dr. Josh, our local veterinarian, for a check-up, and I called to include the young Derbyan as well. When the day for the appointment came, I put Chester's carrier on the deck in front of Winston's perch and helped him inside. He was such a good little guy and went in willingly. Marley was a little less enthusiastic, but Winston seemed to encourage her to join him, and in the end it only took five minutes to load them both. Davy shimmered into the passenger seat of R2 just as I was loading the birds, so he braced the carrier on the floor between his feet.

"Thanks for coming with me." I smiled at him.

"Someone has to chaperone between you and Dr. Josh," he teased. Dr. Josh and I had indeed shared a couple of dates, but any relationship we might have had was made difficult not only by my long hours at the inn, but also by the ghostly presence around me most of the time. It wasn't that Dr. Josh could see Davy, but more that I felt uncomfortable dating someone and knowing I had a secret audience.

Julie Lucas had been one of the vet techs for Dr. Josh for years. I noticed a lovely rock on her finger today though, and I saw the occasional loving glance at the good doctor who seemed quite ready to return her devotion. A tiny part of my heart gave up all hope of ever having any kind of a love life.

"What a beautiful ring!" I reached for her hand to admire it.

"Thank you." She blushed so prettily. The 13-year-old in me wanted to scratch her eyes out, but the feeling passed quickly.

"When's the date?"

"Sometime around Christmas we think. That's the slowest time for Josh's practice." I saw Dr. Josh blush just a little before she continued. "We do hope you'll be able to come!"

"I wouldn't miss it for the world." I made an effort to add some extra enthusiasm because they deserved it. It wasn't their fault that things didn't happen between Josh and me.

In the end, both Winston and Marley were deemed healthy and received their vaccinations.

"Beautiful female Derbyan parrot," Dr. Josh murmured and then looked up at me. "I'd estimate her age to be around five years," he added, "and we can put a poster up on our Most Wanted board for you if you'd like." Their Most Wanted board was a large framed display in the waiting area where people posted notices for lost or found animals. The local vet offices shared their Most Wanted items weekly.

"I'd love that. I don't mind keeping her, but I'd hate to think that someone is missing their baby," I mumbled as I pulled up Marley's photo on my phone to share with them for posting. Dr. Josh looked into my eyes for a very long moment then, and I admit I squirmed a little. He really was gorgeous, and who doesn't love a man who loves animals, right? I heard Davy clear his throat behind me and stifled an embarrassed chuckle. Busted.

A couple hundred dollars later, we were back in the car and heading home.

"I guess you won't be needing a chaperone any longer." Davy was trying not to smirk.

"Shut up." And he did.

The two birds happily reclaimed the perch at home and chattered away to each other and to anyone else who might stop by and listen. They were probably gossiping about the doctor and his techs.

I don't like seafood flavor. I heard a voice as I fed Chester that night. *I thought you'd have figured that out by now.*

I looked around but we were alone. "Huh? Who said that?" The voice had been that of a male, with a clipped English accent, but very unlike Davy's. The timbre was deeper, the language more like that of the queen.

Mee. Oww.

I looked down at Chester sitting by the window, his eyes squeezed. He began licking his paw and then grooming behind his ear — over, down, repeat.

"Chester?"

The cat yawned. Great. Now I was hearing things? I rubbed my hand over my face, trying to dislodge the fear that I truly was losing my mind. Placing the bowl of flaked cat food on the floor, I watched as Chester sniffed it, turned up his nose, and returned to his place in the sun by the window.

"I'm outta here, you... cat." I put my hands on my hips and glared down at him. Davy shimmered in just inches in front of me. "It was YOU, wasn't it?" I accused.

"Whoa! What'd I do now?"

"You were trying to trick me, right?"

I could see him pondering this a moment, a grin spreading slowly across his face.

"Well?"

"Whatever it is you think I did, if it was a good one, I'll take credit. If it's just enough to piss you off, then it wasn't me."

I gave that a moment of thought and decided it was too much effort to interpret. I turned on my heel and marched off to the reception area to work on the morning's duties that I hadn't yet had time for due to the vet visit. Davy followed behind me, chattering incessantly about good practical jokes and evil tricks and the difference between them, and which one was it that I was accusing him of. I ignored him and found great pleasure in that simple act.

Bennie and I were working on the invoices and bills in the deserted dining area while Davy bounced around the room, still babbling, but he had moved on to the subject of Broadway shows and his time in New York City. I'm sure I'd have found it interesting if I had not been attempting to check invoices against receipts and shipping labels. Not wanting Bennie to think I'd gotten more crazy than I already was, I chose not to answer Davy or to remark on his comments and stories. Remarkably, it never seemed necessary; he just went on and on. A couple of times though, I couldn't help but smile at some of his old jokes and dry delivery of such. He truly did have a sharp sense of humor. Or *humour*, as he might spell it. Davy popped his head over my shoulder to peer at the invoices I was shuffling and whispered "*B-b-b-bennie*" a few times. I swatted at him, much like you'd swat a gnat.

With the bills done, I left Bennie and caught up with Ming who was cleaning the reception area.

"How is your day going, Ming?"

Davy continued to chatter as he wandered behind me.

"Very well, Miss Macca. I left you the inventory changes in your inbox." She smiled, indicating the little cubbyholes below the reception desk where we could leave notes for each other.

"Thank you! I'll be sure to pick it up." My inbox usually tended to be the one most filled, and while I'd made a point to ignore it earlier this morning, now I couldn't delay any longer. I grabbed the stack of papers and headed to my bungalow, Davy amazingly keeping up the chatter behind me. He'd followed me all day. Once inside our place, I turned to face him and he bumped right into me, his head having been bent as he picked at his nails.

"Oi! Turn on your signals when you're about to stop there, Babe!" He chuckled.

"Does your throat ever get dry or sore from talking so much?" I teased. "Or does ghosthood make ailments go away?"

He chuckled, making that raspy sound that was so endearing, and began to tell yet more stories and jokes, most of which I was able to tune out as I straightened our little bungalow.

I turned on some music, my mp3 player on shuffle, and "Bennie and the Jets" was first to play.

"You did that on purpose," I exclaimed, hands on hips.

"Mayyyyybeee," he drawled it out, a twinkle in his eyes.

I shook my head and muttered under my breath as I went back to my house cleaning chores.

THREE

Flying

After dinner was prepared, eaten, and subsequently cleaned up one evening, we sat on the sofa to chill. But chilling never lasted very long when Davy was around.

"I've got it," he proclaimed. "Let's rendezvous at 4 a.m. at the bottom of the beach stairs! Be there or be square, in those immortal words of dear Mork," and he shimmered away.

What kind of an invitation was that? I didn't even get a chance to RSVP. There was no embossed card. And I'm fairly certain there'd be no rubber chicken dinner waiting for me. Ooo, there's always an upside. I shook my head and decided to get some sleep before my ridiculously early appointment with a ghost.

At 3:45 a.m. I had all the lights ablaze in my bungalow. I don't know why exactly. Perhaps it had something to do with the fact that it was the middle of the night and only the dead were active. And me. Chester slunk off to the cool dark recesses of my closet to sleep, I assumed.

Humans are weird. If I only had thumbs...

That voice again. Definitely British... posh almost. I tried to shake the sleepy cobwebs from my mind.

After a quick shower, I pulled on my outfit from last night because who dresses for a 4 a.m. rendezvous unless they have unsavory intentions? I was wearing my white tank top and an ankle-length tie-dyed tiered gauze skirt in graduating shades of blue to white. My mother had made it for herself when I was six, and I had carefully tended it all these years, occasionally replacing the elastic at the waist or mending any seams or tears. It wasn't fragile really, but I tended to wear it around the house a lot, so it was well loved.

I started to put flip flops on my feet but then realized there wasn't much point; it's hell to walk in sand wearing flips. I opted for bare feet and quietly headed down the path and the steps. Pulling up short on the deserted beach, I peered both ways down the sand and saw no one, so I just walked down to the edge of the water, hiked my skirt in *Lucy Stomps Grapes* style, and let the foamy surf tickle my toes. I felt rather than heard the pounding on the sand and turned to look southwest.

"Oi!" Davy shouted as he and Glory galloped toward me, keeping to the hard-packed wet sand. I felt my face break into a grin. The horse was gorgeous, especially in motion, and Davy looked perfectly at home atop him. He trotted the last few yards and came to a stop directly in front of me. Davy was dressed only in jeans, and he had a bareback pad on Glory and a bitless bridle. I held my hand out and Glory gave it a nuzzle before licking the salty spray from my palm. Davy bent at the waist and reached his arm out to me.

"Really? What if someone sees us?"

"That's why I chose this time, just before sunrise. I don't think I've ever seen anyone down here before 9 a.m."

I reached up to him and we grabbed each other's upper arms as he swung me up behind him. I arranged my skirt around me and put my arms around his chest.

"Hold on, Babe," he called to me over his shoulder. He turned the horse in a circle and we headed back up the beach at a slow pace. I loved the feeling, and we weren't even going fast! It had been a long time since I'd ridden a horse, and I'd forgotten that feeling of the strength of the huge equine combined with that sense of freedom. Davy was remarkably silent, simply existing with Glory and me.

The sky was still rather dark, but the half moon high overhead cast a surrealistic silvery glow. I got lost in my thoughts, remembering a horseback ride long ago in the Griffith Park hills with Mom and Dad. They had taught me the basics at a very young age, but I never had the time, nor did we have the funds, to pursue anything further than the occasional pleasure ride, and it was always with Western tack and never bareback like now. I much preferred this way! The memory was wonderful, and it was not accompanied by the melancholy that such remembrances usually brought to me. Instead, I was happily making new memories. *Thanks Mom and Dad*, I thought and received a warm *You're welcome,* in my head.

I smiled and impulsively kissed Davy's shoulder, then rested my head on it as Glory's hooves splashed in the surf. I looked up when I heard Davy make a clicking sound with his tongue, and Glory responded by picking up speed. Soon we were sailing along the surf and sand. Glory's gait was remarkably smooth and I only bounced a little. I tried rocking along with Davy as he rode, sort of melting into the bareback pad.

"You're getting it," he tossed the encouragement over his shoulder. I found that if I visualized being glued to Glory and matched Davy's rocking we were in perfect tune. What a rush! I felt my heart pounding, my stomach filled with lovely fluttery butterflies. I loved watching Glory's beautiful mane flowing in the wind. His ears were perked, occasionally turning one or both to listen for Davy.

"It feels like flying!"

The wind tossed Davy's laughter back to me and I held tighter to him. At the end of the short beach we slowed and turned in a lazy circle before stopping. I reached back and gave Glory's flank a gentle pat and a caress; he snorted in reply. We rode back and forth along the beach and then wandered into the thick vegetation. The sea to the east of us was lightening, with hues of pink and purple dancing on the horizon. The sky became a watercolor canvas with yellows and oranges running into the pinks and purples. Davy stopped Glory and we watched as the sun pushed up into the early morning sky.

"Awe inspiring," I murmured and Davy nodded. Glory stomped his foot a few times, anxious to move, but Davy held him fast until the sun had completed its floor show. It was a Glory-ous start to the day!

But later that morning I found myself barely able to keep my eyes open. We had ridden for a little while longer after the sunrise, and then we had stopped and given Glory a good brushing. He arched his neck and kept turning so that we'd brush his happy spots. He was as big a ham as Davy, and I found myself laughing at the absurdity as well, for we were brushing a ghost horse. Try explaining that.

After my morning duties were done, I rewarded myself with a brief nap and awoke refreshed and able to tackle what was left of the day. As much as I loved my morning with Davy and Glory, I made a promise to myself that 4 a.m. wake-up calls were going to be few and far between.

FOUR

Homeless

Davy and I drove down toward Hilo the following Sunday, having heard of a homeless encampment just off of a bit of farmland. I could see it as I crested a hill. Tarps had been stretched between old out of use public buses that had been transformed into shelters. I was so impressed with the idea that I had decided I could help some by providing food periodically. We all need to do our part for the less fortunate and this was one way I could do it quite easily.

I parked R2 at the edge of the property. People milled around, chatting with others and picking up trash. It was nice to see that they took pride in their humble yet temporary shelter. A large picnic table had a plastic tarp draped over it. I opened the small hatch to the Smart Car and pulled out a box and a couple of bags. Kalei had baked extra loaves of bread for me and provided a lovely hummus dip as well. I had cooked up a large batch of pasta salad and egg salad too. People stopped what they were doing and watched for a moment. I could see smiles spread across their faces.

I arranged the bounty of food on the table and added some paper goods.

"Hello!" A young man with long blond hair approached me and helped with the second load of bags that contained fresh fruit and vegetables along with a huge box of Lani's special oatmeal cookies with dried cranberries instead of raisins.

"Hello! My name is Macca. I heard that you could use a little extra help here."

"It's nice people like you that make the sun shine even brighter. We thank you! My name is Chad. Welcome to Hale Maluhia! That means *House of Peace*, roughly translated."

He gave me the shaka sign and I smiled back at him. "Here," he continued, and picked up my hand, manipulating my fingers into their favorite sign of greeting, chuckling at my reluctance. "It's okay... It's sort of *hang loose* in a friendly way. And thank you for the fantastic food! Surely you'll dine with us?"

I joined him back at the table as others began to mill around. Chad welcomed them to fill their plates. It didn't seem like they needed any warning about making sure there was enough for everyone. I was quite impressed with the sense of community they shared. Each looked out for the others, helping to fill the plates of the children and also of those less fortunate with various disabilities that kept them from being able to reach or use both hands. I helped two lovely adolescent girls fill their plates with bread, egg salad, and pasta.

"Thank you, miss." Their voices were the mere whispers of individuals not wanting to draw attention to themselves.

"Call me Macca, please." I touched their beautiful faces gently.

"Thank you Miss Macca."

I chuckled. I was amazed at how many polite people there were on the islands. I was rarely just Macca but rather Miss Macca. At first it had made me a little uncomfortable, but now I was used to it. It was simply an expression of respect.

We sat on the ground and ate a little. I could see Davy shimmering about, walking in and out of the buses and the little tented areas. He had a wide grin on his face and seemed to be enjoying himself. I noted a small boy following him silently, in awe.

"Hi," the boy whispered.

"Hi." Davy grinned. "My name is David. What's yours?"

"I'm David too!" His reticence began to drop away.

Davy stuck his hand out and the boy tentatively put his out as well. I watched as the sweet man taught the boy how to properly give a handshake. Then the boy David showed Davy how to do the shaka greeting. It was quite touching, and I found I could not help but smile.

The following week we came with twice the amount of food, and twice the amount of people, meaning Kalei and Lani joined me. The big man Kalei seemed so comfortable dishing out the food and speaking with each person, whether they be native Hawaiian or recently arrived from elsewhere; birthplace and ethnicity mattered not to him.

Chad arrived immediately, helping us set up a buffet line and organizing others to get tables, drinks, eating utensils, and napkins set up.

"How have you been this week?" he chatted with a seeming comfort as we all worked together.

"Doing well. How about you all?"

"Oh, just the same, thanks. And it's always better to be just the same rather than having a step backward, yeah?"

"Definitely." I smiled and handed him serving platters for placement on the makeshift buffet table. "And if everyone pitches in every day, we'll all be living in a better world, right?" He stopped what he was doing, grinned, and gave me the hardest high-five I'd ever had, then turned it into a quick brotherly embrace.

"Damn straight, sistah." He did a little happy dance. "And you just keep preaching it. Someone is bound to hear that beautiful voice of yours!"

My cheeks warmed as I went back to setting up pots of food, serving utensils, and dishware. Chad was so cute — that adorable little brother that so many girls wished they'd had. He was protective, yet gave room for fun and flirtation. He was responsible yet still had that bit of play and spark in him. "How has it been this week with the deluge of rain?" I asked him as I folded utensils into the napkins.

"These old wrecks have proven to be mighty leak-resistant!" He gestured to the converted buses. "We're doing GREAT!" He was always about four amps up in emotions from where I usually was at my peak. But he was such a kindhearted man, always making sure the people in the encampment got their fair share.

My mind was filled with thoughts to record in my journal that night but I fell asleep before I could say much.

Homelessness

As it is across the country, we have a severe homeless problem here in Hawaii. We're no different than most other states in that respect. There's an encampment called Hale Maluhia within driving distance from home. The government took old buses and converted them into shelters. They're parked on a donated piece of land, and the camp dwellers have stretched tarps between the buses and around some of them as well so that they are protected from the elements. They have organized meetings, and they try to teach the children as well.

The children. It's heartbreaking. I would give them all homes if I could. But at least I can help by bringing a load of food once a week. Although it's a charitable donation, I do it because we must all come together to deal with the issue of homelessness. After all, it could happen to anyone.

The next day I hesitated before opening my journal, wondering if Davy had invaded my privacy once again, and sure enough, there it was.

Dear Macca,

Have I told you lately how special you are and how much I love you?

Love,
David (his trademark flower)

I gave up trying to hide my journal after that and just left it on my bedside table. This actually turned out to be more convenient anyway. "Thanks Davy," I called to wherever he may have been at the time, and I heard a voice in reply.

"You're welcome, Babe." I had to laugh.

FIVE

Guests

We had two sets of guests scheduled to check in today, and Bennie and I were hard at work readying their tourist packages and adding those personal touches to their bungalows. Mr. and Mrs. Peters were newlyweds arriving for their honeymoon. We had booked them into cottage number 6, the farthest from the common areas. I placed fresh local flowers in mason jars in their bedroom, living area, and bathroom, with a small spray of fragrant herbs in the kitchen. They had expressed interest in Waipi'o Valley and Volcano National Parks as two of their top priority destinations, so I gathered that extra information for their welcome package, placed it in the standard green pocket folder adorned with our logo, and tied it with a bit of raffia. I placed this on the table beside a plate of freshly baked macadamia nut cookies, Lani's signature. I noted that Ming had already set out the welcome gifts we had for newlyweds which included scented soy candles, fragrant soap, and an iced bottle of champagne in a bucket.

My next stop was cottage number 4 where traveling companions Ms. Hammond and Ms. Clark would be staying. Based on the telephone conversation I had with Ms. Hammond when she called to request additional electric fans be available in both bedrooms and the living room, I determined them to be in their late fifties. While she thought her request would be considered unusual, I assured her that we'd had that request many times as not everyone was comfortable when the temperatures rose beyond the seventies. I found this to be particularly true with women of menopausal years, and I suspected Ms. Hammond and Ms. Clark might fall into this category. I made certain the three efficiency fans were clean and in place as requested. In addition, they'd asked about beaches and shopping, so I included extra information on those locations in their packet. Their cookies were in place, and a bottle of white wine was chilling in a bucket. This was the standard welcome package we'd developed over the months.

As I hurried back to the reception area, I saw our first new guests arriving. Surmising the middle aged women to be Ms. Hammond and Ms. Clark, I welcomed them to Hale Mele and led them to Bennie at the front desk. Sunny Hammond had short graying hair cut in a bob. Adele Clark had light brown hair that looked soft and curly. Both of them were of average height and weight and seemed to talk to each other nonstop in a joking manner. Their humor was dry and sarcastic, and I found myself grinning and getting a kick out of listening to the banter. Both were waving brochures of some sort in front of their faces. This confirmed my guess at their menopausal ages and explained their request for fans. Bennie quickly checked them in. His friendliness and his cute looks always endeared him to the older ladies such as Sunny and Adele. His dimples never smoothed out as he let them tease him.

"Wooo, it's hot, isn't it?" Adele made the declaration to anyone who would listen.

"Fortunately you can cool off in the pool, or the wide Pacific ocean which is down the stairs. Also, your electric fans are in place and ready to go."

"Oh, aren't you a dear," Sunny nearly purred, and I detected a slight southern accent.

I reached to the basket behind the counter and pulled out two bamboo handheld fans and extended them to the grateful ladies. "Portable fans," I grinned.

"Oh Sunny, look!" They both waved their fans like good southern belles might have back on the plantation.

Once they had checked in, I left Bennie at the desk to wait for the next guests and showed the women to their bungalow, carrying two of their bags while they handled their smaller carry-ons. I opened their door and set the bags down in a corner then handed each of them their keys. I showed them around, and each woman quickly chose her bedroom without any squabbling.

"Do you travel together a lot?"

"Oh dear." I could see Adele thinking for a moment. "We've been traveling together for nearly thirty years."

"Every year we have a vacation away from our husbands and kids — they're all grown now anyway, except our husbands who are perpetual children," Sunny added. I moved their bags into their respective rooms, and they laughed with each other as I pointed out the welcome package.

"Oh, I think we're going to have a dandy time here, don't you Adele?"

"Yes indeed. But then again, don't we have a dandy time wherever we go?" They chuckled in that comfortable style of old friends. "Oh look!" Adele pulled the bottle of wine out and read the label. "What a nice touch!"

"And these too!" Sunny had already taken a bite out of one of the macadamia nut cookies. "Heavenly!" She rolled her eyes.

"You'll love our food. We take dinner reservations, but lunch is buffet style every day."

"Fantastic!"

"Should we go ahead and make a reservation for tonight, Sunny?"

"I think so. I'm tired from traveling. A quick trip to the store for some supplies, a lounge around the pool, and that's about all I'm good for today."

"Me too." Adele yawned. "And maybe a nap too!" Both ladies laughed so comfortably with each other. Sunny switched on the fan and hovered in front of it.

"Don't Bogart the fan, Adele," Sunny chided playfully and nudged her friend to make room so they could both enjoy the cooling air.

"I'll leave you ladies to settle in then. If you need anything, you can call the front desk or pop in. In the evening we don't have anyone at the desk, but if you call it will be redirected to someone who can help. Usually me."

The last thing I saw was both of them hovering in front of the fan. "Woo! I'm havin' the hot flash from hell, I tell ya," Adele hooted. I grinned and shut their door behind me.

Bennie was on the phone when I returned to reception. I wandered into the kitchen and added the Hammond/Clark party to the dinner reservation list.

It was only a couple of hours before we welcomed our next guests checking in, the newlywed Mr. and Mrs. Peters. While Bennie took care of the mechanics of checking them in, I engaged them in easy small talk. "We're so happy to have you join us, Mr. and Mrs. Peters."

"Oh, thank you." Mr. Peters smiled broadly. "But please, I'm Anthony, and this is my beautiful new bride, Imani." Anthony was very tall, well over six feet. His skin was a warm medium taupe and his hair was quite dark and worn extremely short in a natural style. He carried his trim frame proudly.

"And I'm Macca." I gestured to my right, "And this is Bennie. We have a small staff here, hoping to make it feel more like a home than a hotel."

"I've heard so many great things about this place." Imani spoke with a lovely voice which matched her medium brown skin of pure silk. Her dark hair was close cropped and she wore very large gold hoop earrings that accentuated her long and graceful neck. I wondered idly if anyone had ever likened her to the grace and elegance of a majestic giraffe. Probably not; she might take it as an insult, although my thoughts were far from such intentions.

"Oh, really? From reviews?"

"Actually, no. My parents stayed here last year and could not stop raving about the place," Imani continued. Davy shimmered in beside me.

"Ohhh," he sighed in my ear. "She's rather gorgeous, no?" I nodded twice — once for him, once for Imani. My life was not simple.

"If I may... what were your parents' names?" Because now I really wanted to know who we'd made such an impression upon.

"George and Althea Barron." Imani proudly smiled.

"Oh my gosh! The Barrons!" Realization hit me. The Barron family, party of two, had been so lovely and thankful for all that we did to make their stay enjoyable that they had ordered several pizzas to be delivered to the staff after-hours.

"That was a great day," Bennie jumped in. "We all sat around the bar eating pizzas they'd ordered and sharing cold beers on a wickedly hot day." He was grinning, and the Peters and I were immediately sucked into his mood. "It was the first day I'd ever tried a taco pizza. Who would have thought, right?" Bennie's face was so serious, but I could only guffaw and give him an affectionate squeeze on his arm. "No?" He became less enthusiastic and backed down quickly from his initial exuberance.

"No, you're fine," I tried to assure him. "It's just that there are more... shall we say, *limited* pizzas on the island?"

His face showed confusion, then the idea registered and a huge grin erupted, nearly splitting his face in half. "Oh yes! We like our pizzas a certain way. Ask us about pineapple," he laughed.

"And spam," I added with a grimace. The Peters matched my grimace and laughter.

"Well, we are so happy to have you join us," I told them, "and please, thank your parents for referring you to our inn."

With the streamlined registration process complete, Bennie and I each hefted two suitcases and led our new guests to their bungalow. We set the bags down in the master bedroom. "There's a packet of information on the sites you asked about, and..." I was about to clue them in to the comped champagne when Imani beat me to it, in her own way.

"Oh look, Anthony, champagne! How lovely! Thank you, Macca. Mom was right, and this is going to be a fabulous honeymoon." When she looked adoringly up at her new husband, I took that as our cue to leave them alone.

"You're welcome, and I hope you enjoy your stay. Just ask any of us if you need something," and we made a quick getaway.

Taking over for Ming on her day off, I was slowly making my way through each bungalow once the guests had gone out for the day. Seeing Adele, Sunny, Anthony, and Imani all out by the pool, I knew that bungalows 4 and 6 were cleared, so I zipped over to number 4 first and quickly scrubbed, vacuumed, changed linens, and tidied. It was amazing to me how the use of efficient tools and an actual plan made clean up so easy. Before I'd inherited the inn, I'd hated housework and would put it off until things were so filthy that it took me longer than it should have. Now, I still hated the housework, but I had less time within which to hate it. Or something. Wait, what? My thoughts wandered like this each time I had to clean the bungalows, and I sometimes cracked myself up. Yes, I'm easily amused.

With number 4 complete, I hurried to number 6 and went through the same routine. By noon I'd cleaned all six cottages and was working on the common areas while laundry was being processed, and by two that afternoon I was sitting at one of the cafe tables by the pool and sipping from a glass of Kalei's iced tea while flipping through a hotel management magazine. I could hear Adele and Sunny bantering and laughing at each other's jokes; those women made me smile.

"I'm 59 years old and I'm still getting pimples, Adele! What the devil?"

"I know; nature is so cruel. We have to go through our monthlies and give birth and deal with blasted husbands and then the ultimate finish: menopause."

"It's horribly unfair, I tell you."

"In my next life, I'm coming back as a man."

"Oh, I don't know about that, Adele." I peeked at her and saw her wrinkle her nose. "All those dangly bits?"

Adele burst out laughing. "We've got our own dangly bits! Once perky, they now hang to our waistlines."

"If we still had waistlines..." Their guffaws were contagious. I even saw Anthony and Imani chuckling.

And speaking of Anthony and Imani, she looked fantastic in a tiny black strapless bikini, and he was stunning in yellow board shorts.

"Miss Macca?" Sam appeared at my side, Chester in his arms. "I'm sorry to interrupt your break, but I just found Mr. Chester trying to sneak into the kitchen."

I set my magazine down and took the cat from him. "Chester! Bad boy! You know you're not allowed in there. I'll have the health inspector shutting us down if you don't knock that off."

Blah, blah, blah. I heard the words in my head, but they weren't my thoughts. Where was that coming from?

"That's it. You're grounded, young man." I rose and directed my words to Sam. "Thank you for grabbing him before he could get us in trouble." I smiled and headed to my own bungalow. As I passed Winston and Marley on the perch, he had to add his two cents.

Baaaaaddd kitty. Bad, bad. I'm a pretty bird. I'm a good boy.

Marley whistled "I Shot the Sheriff"... again.

"Mind your own business, Winston, and you stay out of the kitchen too!" I marched to my bungalow and plopped the cat on the sofa, then closed the sliding door to the deck. "You stay here until you can behave like a proper inn-cat!"

Whatevah...

Who said that? I looked down at Chester. Was I imagining a cat channeling a hostile teen now? I went back out to the pool and gathered my empty iced tea glass and my magazine. I glanced over in time to catch

Anthony and Imani locked in a passionate embrace; I noticed Adele and Sunny surreptitiously watching them as well while trying to hide behind magazines. Each of the women had smiles that reached their eyes. It was heartwarming to see people so much in love.

As I turned, Davy appeared right in front of me. I jumped and shrieked a little. I made believe that I was swatting a bug away as all the heads at the pool turned to peer at me in wonder, and then I stepped around the diminutive ghost and headed to the bungalow, said ghost hot on my heels.

"I have to show you something! It's so cool, man!" Once inside, I turned and he bumped into me yet again. "Whoa, hand signals, Babe. Put your blinker on or something!"

"First, stop following so closely, and second, what have you come home with now? A ghost koala? The Loch Ness Monster?"

He knitted those thick eyebrows together and considered me for a moment. "No, but either of those would be cool, don't ya think?"

"No!"

He shrugged, undeterred. "Actually, just watch what I learned to do!" I set my magazine and empty glass down on the kitchen counter and turned to give him my full attention. He shimmered a bit, his image wavering out and then in again. He was now wearing a short-sleeved shirt in a wild orange and white pattern with matching shorts and no shoes. "Wardrobe change!"

I couldn't help it; I chuckled. "I admit, that's pretty cool."

He shimmered in and out, returning as MonkeeMan, complete with thick black eyeglass frames missing the lenses. He waggled his eyebrows and took a superhero stance, arms akimbo and chin up. He shimmered out once again and returned as Grandma Moses. Now I was laughing loudly, and of course he was eating it up. Anything for an audience. The next wardrobe change was an adorable pink bunny suit complete with floppy ears, but it was the bald-headed suit-wearing costume that had me doubled over. He took several bows before shimmering back to the orange and white beach outfit. That I could live with.

"It seems I can pull from any piece of clothing that I've previously worn... sort of. It's complicated. It has to be something I wore in the era of the body I choose to 'wear' at the moment. In other words, you won't find my fifty-year-old body dressed in this outfit." He chuckled and pointed again to the orange and white, which was very 1960s.

SIX

Plans

Sunday sure comes around quickly every week these days I thought to myself as Kalei and I were loading the big pot of pasta into the jump seat of R2 and nestling it next to the industrial sized container of brown rice salad, the fresh fruit bowl, and multiple loaves of bread stuffed into a basket. Lani came running up with a box of oatmeal chocolate chip cookies.

"Don't forget these!" She slid them onto the floor of the passenger side.

"Thank you, Lani! I wouldn't have been forgiven had I shown up without those!" Kalei and Lani usually followed me to Hale Maluhia, the homeless camp, but on this Sunday they had a family commitment and had made their apologies.

"I wish we were going with you." She had a far-off look in her eyes and a huge chunk of wistfulness in her voice.

"Family comes first." I smiled, trying to cheer her up. She had been quiet and sullen for several days, and Kalei had offered apologies for his wife's lack of her usual enthusiasm. I had brushed it off, but deep below the facade I was worried for her. "And besides, Chad has been gathering plenty of helpers for us. We'll manage just fine."

As predicted, Chad was waiting for me as I pulled up, and he'd recruited several people to help set up the food on the rickety picnic table.

"How are you on this fine sunny day?" he asked me.

"I'm doing well. And how are you?"

"Great, as always."

I saw Davy shimmer into the area between two old buses. He looked around and then waved at me before continuing to scan the grounds. I knew he was looking for the small boy he'd previously befriended. Davy's face lit up when he spotted him sitting on a blanket with his dad as they enjoyed the feast we had brought. However, the younger David was unaware of his older counterpart's appearance, being so deeply enthralled with the cookie in his grubby little hand. I saw Davy grin and shake his head in amusement. Cookies and children were a natural, and I was certain he had seen that as well.

"Please..." Chad pulled me out of my reverie. "Come join us." He had a plate of food and was heading for a small patch of grass where three older people sat, a woman and two men eating their meals.

I grabbed a cookie for myself and sat cross-legged beside them. The damp grass was cooling on this warm day.

"I'm Makala." The older woman with a long gray braid smiled as she plucked petals from a pile beside her and wove them into a small lei which she used to gesture to the men. "This is Joe and Kai."

"Very nice to meet you all." One of the men, Joe, had struggled to get to his feet as I approached, but I had waved him back down as I plopped next to them. "And please, we're all just friends. No formalities, okay?"

"Yes, Ma'am." Joe showed one front tooth missing when he smiled.

"And definitely no 'Ma'am' please." I grinned, trying to set them at ease.

"Oh, he's most gentleman man I met," Makala looked at Joe with exaggerated doe eyes as she spoke, and he shifted uncomfortably and blushed.

"It's easy being a gentleman with such a pretty lady like you, Makala, and Macca too."

And now it was my turn to blush.

Kai cleared his throat and spoke. "What am I, chopped spam?" I giggled at his joke and admired the twinkle in his eyes.

I gently touched one end of the lei the older woman was constructing. "This is so lovely, Makala! Do you sell them?"

"Mahalo! Yes," she nodded. "I sell them to tourists. It helps buy little things we need."

"Makala has been here the longest," Chad spoke between bites of rice salad. "She's like a mom to many of us, except to Joe and Kai. I think they enjoy the little competition of vying for her attention, don't you guys?" His grin was infectious, and the older men soon joined him.

"Chad, you're just a young whippersnapper." Kai smirked, then turned abruptly to the elder woman. "Is that the right word, Makala?"

"Damn straight that's the right word," Joe interrupted, laughing in a gentle raspy manner. Then he grew serious. "Actually, Chad here is an okay guy for a Marine."

"You Air Force vets are just jealous of us Marines. Hoo-Rah."

"Oh Hoo-Rah yourself." They teased back and forth and I found myself feeling so very much at home.

"Behave yourselves, you two," Makala scolded gently. "Miss Macca-Roon is with us."

I let out a loud guffaw. "Macca-Roon?"

"That's how everyone has begun to think of you, because you bring cookies." Kai grinned. "We love cookies."

I had to laugh again. "I could tell. Well, the real cookie is Lani. She always makes sure to bake plenty of extra for you all."

"I may have to give her a hug next time she comes," he smirked.

"She's married to that big native who comes with her, Kai," Joe warned. "Better watch yourself."

I was enjoying the comfortable banter and the warm family feeling. It was times like these that made me realize how alone I was in the world. I considered my employees to be family, but it wasn't quite the same. Still, it was more than I could have hoped for when I moved here.

"So, you're both veterans?" I asked Chad and Joe. "Chad, you look too young to have already served."

"I'm older than you think, I'm sure," he laughed.

"Chad signed up when he turned eighteen and served for five years. Believe me, he's still a young whippersnapper."

"Hoo-Rah." Makala made playful fun of them.

"Don't diss the Marines, Makala." Chad smiled before shoveling another spoonful of salad into his mouth.

"He's got shell-shock, you know," Joe confided.

"Hey!" Chad gently kicked him with his outstretched leg. "So do you, old man!"

"We wear our PTSD proudly." Joe laughed and wiped his eye, his tone dripping sarcasm.

"It is what it is." Chad winked at me. I appreciated their way of handling their situation, the self-deprecating humor and gentle teasing with each other.

"Hey, Sarge." Kai had a mischievous twinkle in his eye.

"Never... EVER... refer to a Marine like that," Joe rebuffed him then calmly turned to me. "Chad speaks from experience. I'll vouch for that."

I knew of the plight of veterans young and old, but this was the first time I was actually seeing it first-hand. "Does the V.A. do anything to help you?"

"The V.A. doesn't seem to have the money or the desire to help." Joe's joking manner slipped a little. "Once a month I see a therapist and get a meal. Six years of faithful service and that's the extent of my benefits."

"Joe served in Vietnam," Chad added. "It was an unpopular war."

"And Iraq wasn't?" Joe reached over and gave the younger man a friendly and supportive thump on the back.

"What war is really popular? And actually, do we want war to be popular?" I smiled gently when I asked.

"Good point." Joe turned to Makala. "She's one smart *wahine*, yes?"

Makala smiled warmly at me, that motherly aura about her. "Indeed she is."

"I guess that confirms it then." Chad touched my arm. "Welcome to our family."

"Oh my." I swiped at the sudden tears that threatened to spill from my eyes. "Thank you. I couldn't ask for a nicer family to be welcomed into."

"Ha!" Makala set her plate down. "You wait until squabbling begins over last cookie; you think differently then. You might even run to volcano."

"Don't you worry about me. Now that I've found you, I'll never abandon you."

I shared my day's happiness with Davy later that evening as we stood together at the kitchen counter in our bungalow chopping bits of tomato, olives, and basil for our pasta salad. I heard myself chattering away wh en I noticed something crawling behind the toaster. Never missing a beat in my relaying of the day's story, I pulled a paper towel off the roll and tore it in half. I used one piece to squash the spider that was taunting me on the window sill.

"What was that?" Davy asked.

"A spider."

"You killed it? Why?"

"He started it!" I used my petulant child voice I'd spent so many years cultivating.

Davy set his knife down and eyed me, exasperation evident on his face. "And how do you figure he started it?"

"Well," I bit my lip, "I have an agreement with bugs and things that belong outside. I won't go tromping in their bushes if they don't go invading my home. It's been in place for years."

"Did you get this agreement notarized?"

"Yep." I nodded emphatically as the silliness invaded our space. "And served it in triplicate."

"Very well then." He picked up his knife again and resumed chopping tomatoes. "You've done your part. Clearly there was a violation of terms by Mr. or Mrs. Spider there." He waved the knife in the general direction of the spot once inhabited by the spider. "I just hope his or her children have another parent at home, you know?" Glancing sideways I saw his cheeks puff as he tried to hold back a giggle.

"I'm quite sure there are millions of aunts and uncles. It's a great big hairy scary spidey world out there."

On Monday morning I put in a call to Alex Baldwin, my good friend and attorney.

"Macca! So good to hear your voice, and I was just thinking about you."

"Oh?"

"I was reviewing your file and we really need to sit down and discuss the inn's future."

"What do you mean?"

He cleared his throat and I could tell that he was about to bring up a sensitive subject. "You need to set provisions for the inn. If something should happen to you, and all that..." He left it hanging there.

"Oh." My demise, he meant. What would happen to the inn? I hadn't given it much thought, especially after nearly losing my life more than a year ago. I was momentarily ashamed. "What do you suggest?"

"Suggest? It's entirely up to you, my dear."

"Let me give it some thought," I stalled. I already knew the best thing to do, but it was something I would need to discuss with the parties involved. "In the meantime, what do you know about the homeless camp south of here, off the road to Hilo?"

"Only that it exists, it's peaceable, and the police never seem to have an issue with the campers. In fact, the local police often visit to hand out treats to the children."

"But, isn't there something more that can be done to help all of them, not just the children?" My words were gathering steam as the ideas rushed out. "What does the state provide for the homeless?"

"The buses, for one. Other than that, I'm not certain. Why are you asking?"

"I've begun to take food out there once a week, but it just doesn't feel like it's enough. I want to explore other means of assistance, and I'm willing to get involved."

"Let me look into it while you think about the inn, and we can meet together, say, Wednesday?"

Oh boy. "That soon?"

"Macca, I'll be blunt. You need to have a will drawn up. What would become of your employees if something should happen to you?"

"I know. I know. Okay, Wednesday." I sighed, and we set a time for him to come out on Wednesday.

Later that afternoon, after the lunch rush but before the dinner preparation needed to begin, I called a meeting.

"My attorney, Alex, has pointed out that I haven't set up any provisions should something happen to me. I don't have any family other than the six of you." I looked around at Kalei, Lani, Bennie, Ming, Sam, and Albert. "Would you all be interested in sharing the ownership of the inn in the event of my death?"

Lani gasped. "Are you ill?"

"No, no, no," I chuckled. "I'm perfectly fine. But he is right. What if Mr. Sikes had been successful when he tried to push me off the cliff? What would have happened to all of you?"

Sweet innocent Sam put his fingers in his ears and sang, "la la la la la..." causing us all to laugh, thus breaking the tension that had filled the room.

"Oh, believe me, I'm going to try to stick around for decades, just to drive you all nuts with my renovations and demands," I teased. There was a chorus of denials that I was driving them nuts, but at least it got us to talking. Nearly twenty minutes later, they had all agreed that they would be honored to continue running Hale Mele on my behalf, but they made me promise that it wouldn't happen for at least fifty years. A sudden vision of all of us, gray-haired and doing the same tasks we did now, made us all laugh.

On Wednesday Alex arrived for lunch, and we enjoyed the buffet before settling down to discuss.

"I've been in contact with a remarkable man who is doing great things to bring awareness to homelessness and veterans' issues here on the island. His name is Dylan Kimura and he was a professor at Hilo Community College, but now he dedicates his time to the issues of the less fortunate."

"Oh, that's perfect! Where is he located?"

"He still lives in Hilo and has a small office there as well, not too far from here. I've already contacted him, and he suggested you give him a call and the two of you can meet and have a discussion. He's eager for any assistance too. And you'll like him. He's intelligent and forward-thinking... a lot like you."

"Thank you, Alex. You've gone above and beyond, and I really appreciate it."

"Now, onto the business of... well, your business," he chuckled.

"I had a meeting with my staff and I'd like to leave the inn to them in the event of my death."

He smiled. "I figured as much, and considering your staff, I think that's an excellent idea. I'll draw up the paperwork and take it through the proper channels."

"Thank you, Alex." I breathed a sigh of relief. "That was easier than I expected."

"Oh, we're not done yet. It will take a while for it to all be set up, but we'll get it taken care of."

When all of our business was done, I walked Alex out to his car. On the way back to my bungalow, Davy shimmered in and did a little hop and skip to get in step with me.

"That was a pretty cool thing to do, Babe, leaving the inn to the kids." I thought that was cute how he referred to them as kids, and I smiled and just let him rattle on, which I knew he would. "Did I tell you about Glory today? We were racing the waves breaking on the shoreline, and birds were flying next to us! It was like we were truly sailing through the sky. Fantastic feeling, I tell ya."

I smiled and let him go on and on about giving Glory a good brushing afterward. Do ghost horses really need brushing? I never got a chance to ask because he launched into a story about his early days on Broadway, and I just let him ramble. I reached my bungalow, stepped inside, and shut the door firmly behind. Yeah, I know; it was purely symbolic because he just kept coming, as if the door never even existed.

"So I told the director that I had to give me fans what they wanted." I tuned him out because I had actually heard this story before. I sat at my computer and took some notes on the discussion I'd had with Alex. I also checked on the inn's bank account and scheduled a couple of bills to be paid, all the while with this sound like a buzzing bumblebee in my ear. Don't get me wrong; it's actually quite comforting... most of the time.

SEVEN

Luau

We were busy preparing for our first Saturday night event, our very own small-scale but more authentic luau. I was helping Kalei and Lani with the food and set up. The feast was beginning to be laid out, and my mouth watered at the sight of it. In the large grassy area between the rear of the kitchen and the paths to the beach, we had spent a full two weeks digging a good-sized hole, thus creating our very own *imu*, or underground Hawaiian oven. Kalei had christened it a few times, using the oven for pork and various types of fish — some wrapped in leaves and others just simply roasted alongside sweet potatoes — but today we were using it for all of that and more.

Albert and Sam helped mind the *imu* while Kalei dashed in and out of the kitchen. There was lomi lomi salmon, an array of fresh vegetables and fruits, and a poke, which is raw marinated tuna. And since Kalei prided himself on offering a variety of vegetarian and vegan meals, he pulled out all the stops by roasting and stir-frying several vegan main dishes that would delight even a hungry non-vegetarian.

Dessert, however, had me hooked by simply tasting it with my eyes: macadamia nut cream pie, coconut ice cream, and pineapple cake. For accompaniments to the meal, Lani was the taro and cookie expert. She provided the cookies, poi, and taro bread — lovely purple loaves with crisped tops. We had tried to use as many traditional serving dishes as we could round up in the storage shed, and Lani brought many others from home as well. There were koa bowls of poi, monkey pod bowls of fruit, and one prized platter from a milo tree. All were lined with leaves from taro and banana trees. If I closed my eyes, I could imagine this feast taking place on the beach hundreds of years ago.

I caught Davy pinching a piece of fresh pineapple, and he had the decency to look guilty when I caught him with his right cheek puffed out as he stuffed the wedge inside his mouth.

"I'b dot noing 'nything," he declared, barely able to form words around the huge obstacle he was busily chewing.

I stifled a grin and went back to assisting with the placement of the food. Just before the dinner hour was to begin, I scooted back to my bungalow and changed into a sarong that Lani had chosen for me — a lovely sleeveless dress cinched at the waist and hips, but not overly revealing. It was rather like a tank top and fitted skirt that reached nearly to the knee and with luscious fabric in a tropical floral screenprint and a deep blue background. I felt so grand... and so Hawaiian, even if I wasn't a native. Even Davy got into the mood, wearing a vintage red Hawaiian print shirt and dark slacks. I realized suddenly that it was only vintage because it was the same one he'd worn on one of the television episodes in the sixties. I stifled a laugh, which came out as a snort, and he winked at me from across the room.

Guests began to arrive, and many of them had dressed accordingly as well which pleased me. The buffet was a hit and soon the banquet table was needing replenishing. Lani and I jumped into action and quickly refilled the serving dishes.

By sunset our guests were relaxing with tea, coffee, and after-dinner cocktails. Kalei stepped out from the kitchen and together he and I cleaned up the tables while Lani ducked out to change into her dance costume. She had chosen a simple costume for this because we were stressing a non-commercial, down-home, casual atmosphere. She returned to the kitchen while we were cleaning a bit and I clapped my hands excitedly. Davy was in the corner, grinning like a fool at the sight of her. She wore a sleeveless knee-length fitted dress made of a soft yellow print that draped softly around her hips but flared out toward the hem to show her movements. Her hair was out of its usual braid and hung loosely down her back, a headband of maile leaves encircling her head, and a floral lei around her neck. Lani's wrists and ankles were adorned with rings of kukui nuts, and she was, of course, barefoot.

We had commissioned Makala from the homeless camp to make both the lei and the headband for her, in addition to a large basket of similar leis for our guests. I had insisted on paying her what a commercial florist might get for the order, despite her protests. "For the good of the camp." I'd urged the money into her hand and received a hug and a kiss on each cheek, so now I felt even more touched looking at the lovely Lani.

Glancing to my right I saw Kalei's eyes glisten. In two strides he was taking her hands and giving her a kiss. Lani quickly looped leis around each of the employees' necks, and I hurriedly took a tray out to the dining room to clear the last of the empty cocktail glasses.

I dimmed the lights and stood in the doorway between the kitchen and the dining room in time to see Lani strike a dance pose as Kalei pushed the button for the music to begin. I knew they'd chosen music by Israel "Iz" Kamakawiwo'ole, a modern Hawaiian legend, for the show. The first was "Hawai'i Aloha," and Iz's melodious vocalization was accompanied by his ukulele.

A beautiful breeze ruffled Lani's hair as she began to dance the dance of her ancestors, in the style of what they call *Auna Hula*. Her hips swayed slowly, imitating the music, but it was her arms and hands that had me mesmerized. The fluid movement illustrated the story being sung, her gestures so accurately describing the rise of the sun, the dance of the waves upon the shore, and the wind in the tall trees. And although the song was almost always sung in the native tongue since the time it was written in the 1800s, Kalei had previously shown me the rough translation:

O Hawai'i
O sands of my birth
My native home
I rejoice in the blessings of heaven
O Hawai'i, aloha

Happy youth of Hawai'i
Rejoice! Rejoice!
Gentle breezes blow
Love always for Hawai'i

May your divine throngs speak
Your loving people
O Hawai'i
The holy light from above
O Hawai'i aloha

God protects you
Your beloved ridges
Your ever glistening streams
Your beautiful gardens

I felt my heart swell with love and pride for Lani and for my newly adopted home of Hawai'i. The music ended and she bowed modestly, her face glowing with happiness as well. Kalei brought the big basket of extra leis and followed Lani from table to table as she placed one of the heavily scented floral wreaths around each guest's neck. She included the children using specially made shorter leis, and she whispered to the parents, "Do not worry; these are made so that the string will pull apart if needed." I saw parents' eyes shine with happiness at this little personal touch that eased their worries about having something roped around their child's neck.

Lani put a short gathering of ti leaves around her waist for the next number, which departed from the hula competitions she danced in, for it was more of a combination of Hawaiian and Polynesian. This faster dance was accompanied only by drumming. Kalei turned the music back on and we saw her slowly begin to shake her hips to the rhythm, gradually gaining speed until her "grass skirt" was nearly a blur to the fast beat of the drums and sticks. The guests clapped and hooted their delight!

For her final dance, Lani chose to perform a style called *Kahiko Hula*, a truly ancient art that was accompanied only by chants, drums, and other percussion instruments. Kalei had a stick and a coconut shell sitting in a wooden base. Lani picked up a large gourd that had been hollowed out.

Kalei began to chant and hit the shell in a rhythm that I found quite dramatic. His clear voice chanted in his native tongue as he punctuated the words with his drumming. Lani danced, occasionally hitting the gourd. When Kalei stopped chanting, Lani began "answering" his chants while doing intricate moves with her feet, arms, and the gourd.

Tears pricked my eyes and I swiped at them quickly. I felt Davy put his arm around me and rest his head against mine. It was just so moving. I had a brief moment of wishing I'd been born a Hawaiian as well. There was so much pride and awe in their performance, and every move was so precise, each having meaning that only they understood.

The guests were completely silent; even the children stopped squirming and stared raptly. Lani would hold the gourd high, her face following it, as if looking to the heavens, then she would drop suddenly to a very low squat and use the gourd as a paddle. She had told me earlier that it was telling the tale of how their ancestors came to the island on long paddle boats. As Kalei increased the speed of his coconut drumming, Lani stomped her foot as she swayed and turned, and as the drum suddenly ceased, she then dropped to her knees and offered the gourd to the heavens once again. The audience was on their feet, clapping, whistling, and hooting again. My grin was so wide that the tears that leaked down my face dropped upon my lips. I licked them and tasted the salt, reminding me of the vast ocean that was so near.

Lani and Kalei took a bow then and began to mingle with the guests. It was like one big happy family. There was lots of hugging and kissed cheeks. After a few minutes, some of the kids pulled Lani to them and asked to learn to hula. Of course she was thrilled to show them just a few basic moves, and they were so very eager to learn. A few of the adults joined them and soon it was one big hula class. I couldn't help but squeal and laugh with delight. Lani's show was a hit.

EIGHT

Maluhia

It was a bright morning, not unlike many mornings in the islands. I hummed a little tune as I went about my chores. Being Ming's day off, I was finishing up the laundry for the inn. I folded the sheets and towels and stacked them on the shelf in the small room off of the kitchen when I heard raised voices and pots clanging. I stood still, holding my breath for a moment in order to attempt a little eavesdropping, but it was too muffled through the wall. There was no mistaking that an argument was in progress, but I doubted it was between Lani and Kalei. They never seemed to raise their voices at each other, using only the soft words of a couple deeply in love, often detectable even when they were simply relaying kitchen info back and forth to each other. There had to be a third person in the kitchen.

I eased out of the laundry, took a couple of tight turns to the kitchen, and stood in the open doorway near the large commercial refrigerator. Leaning against the prep counter with his back to me was a young man about Lani's height. Kalei was ranting at him.

"Why you come back? You go! We not want you here." His manner of speech fell back to pidgin English which indicated Kalei's distress as he held tightly to his wife's hand. I could see that she was near tears and I moved to her side.

"Is everything okay here, folks?" I glanced quickly at the faces of my valued employees and then rested my eyes on the stranger. Something was familiar about him that I couldn't quite put my finger on.

"Not very," Lani answered quietly. "Miss Macca, this is my brother, Kimo." That must be it; there was a strong resemblance between them.

I extended my hand to shake Kimo's, but he gave me the shaka sign. I smiled tentatively and dropped my hand to my side. "Nice to meet you, Kimo." I turned to Kalei and repeated my question in a more direct manner. "Is there a problem here?"

"It's... a family matter," Lani spoke quietly, eyes downcast. "I'm sorry. He shouldn't be here; I know." She turned her face to her brother. "Go now. Don't come back. Please." The tears that had been brimming her eyes began to spill, sliding silently like hot lava down her lovely brown cheeks. She brushed them away with the back of her hand.

"Right on." His smile did not feel friendly, "I goin'. See you latah den, bruddah, sistah." He slouched out of the kitchen and I turned to peer after him, making certain he was leaving the premises. Kalei stepped forward.

"I watch. You no worry, Miss Macca." His face was dark with pent up... something. He followed behind Kimo until both of them were out of my line of sight.

I turned my attention back to Lani and put my arm around her shoulders. In a rare show of affection, she put her head on my shoulder and I just held her until she had regained her usual composure. I didn't know what had transpired between them, but I got the feeling that her brother was a source of contention between the young couple.

"I'm so sorry Miss Macca. Kimo has been away for a long time and that was a good thing. He's just trouble."

"Every family has its difficulties at times." I blocked the sudden memory of my own troubled times.

"He got in with the wrong crowd and has been living on the beaches on Oahu. He came back only for money."

"Do you need money, Lani?" I spoke softly and peered into her dark eyes.

"No. We're fine, Miss Macca. We wouldn't give him any money anyway. He would just snort it or surf it away."

Kalei returned and began to speak. "He's gone." His glance took in his wife's troubled face and he reached for her. She looked so incredibly small against his large frame, his massive hands enveloping her in one of those all-around hugs. I nodded at him and left them alone.

I told Davy about the incident at dinner that night as we sat on the deck sharing a big vegetable salad and white wine. He shrugged it off though. "Brothers and sisters often have issues at times. I'm sure it will all be fine for Kalei and Lani. Kimo, however, is another story." I wished that I shared his confidence, but never having had siblings myself, I had no basis for understanding.

As we were cleaning up the dinner dishes, Davy stopped for a moment and found a music channel on the television that focused on very old music, including Broadway hits. He did a little hop of joy and began to sing with the music as we cleared and washed the dishes. At one point he grabbed me in a sort of ballroom dancing pose and twirled me around, singing a lively tune.

I'm gonna buy a Paper Doll that I can call my own
A doll that other fellows cannot steal
And then the flirty, flirty guys with their flirty, flirty eyes
Will have to flirt with dollies that are real

He had me giggling so hard as we spun that I ended up with the hiccups. He stopped twirling me and deadpanned, "I've decided to move in with you full-time. I shall be at your side 24/7 and I won't take no for an answer."

I found myself holding my breath, chilled to the bone with a feeling of impending doom. Then I saw a grin slowly spread across his face. "Gotcha! But your hiccups are gone! You may thank me now," he so graciously offered, providing a very low and theatrical bow to match it.

"I'll get you for that!" I dipped my fingers in the soapy dishwater that still filled the sink and flicked a little bit at him.

"Oh!" He mocked being shot. "You got me! My life flashed before my eyes… then I realized it was a rerun. I wonder if there are residuals."

He wandered away and left me snickering while the water drained from the sink. I tidied up and then joined him on the deck. He'd brought out the bottle of wine and had refilled our glasses. We admired the colors in the sky as the sun called it a day. I can honestly report that neither of us were feeling much pain as the evening wore on.

"How do ghosts know how to do anything?" I asked him.

"How do humans know that fire is hot?"

I simply stared at him for a moment before we both began to convulse in laughter. It's amazing how a little wine can tickle your funny bone over the silliest things.

"Hey, tell me about when the Monkles met the Beatees. Beakles." I waved my hand, giving up on getting it right.

He stared at me a moment before clutching his stomach and guffawing. "The Monkles and the Beakles you mean?"

I collapsed in a fit of giggles again. "Yeah... them."

"In the words of an old friend of mine, I'm told I had a very good time."

I giggle snorted, which just made us laugh even harder.

I have no recollection of how long we sat there talking about nothing and everything, nor do I know how or when I ended up in my bed. However, the hangover the following morning is burned into my memory.

The next time I went to Hale Maluhia with food, I brought along one bag each of dog food and cat food. The last few times I'd brought meals I'd noticed several dogs and cats that were obviously a part of the camp. Chad came trotting up to help, grabbing both big bags first. He gathered a few of the kids together to bring the food bowls for the camp pets, then scooped out food for each. There was a whole lot of tail-wagging going on, and cats were rubbing kids' ankles. I just stood there with a big goofy grin on my face watching them all having fun. The kids were giggling and directing the animals, who weren't listening of course.

Out of the corner of my eye, I caught movement by a stand of palm trees. I turned my head and thought I saw a familiar face, but it was gone before I could be certain. I blinked a few times and wandered that way. I still had a pot of pasta in my hands and it was rather heavy to lug so I didn't go too far. Reluctantly, I turned back and set the pot on the picnic table that was used for food service. Back and forth between the table and R2 several more times and soon we were ready for the chow line. Chad, Makala, Joe, and Kai organized the lines and helped the children while I perched on an empty cooler, glancing back at the trees now and then.

I excused myself suddenly when I thought I saw movement again and wandered into the tight grouping of trees. This time I saw a figure in the distance.

"Hello," I called to him. He turned briefly, and I quickly pulled out my phone and snapped a photo. Then he faded away into thicker foliage, and I could have sworn it had been Lani's brother watching, but perhaps it had just been a trick of the light. Davy shimmered in front of me.

"What's up, Babe?" He turned to stand beside me, peering into the distance.

"I think I just saw Kimo."

He frowned and shimmered away, reappearing in the exact place the guy had been standing. He too disappeared into deep tropical vegetation, soon emerging again on the other side. He took my hand to lead me away. "Someone had been there, but I could only sense him, not see him."

"How did you know to come here?"

"I felt your sudden tension and just wanted to check on you."

Although secretly I was relieved that we had that connection, I was also irritated about having a babysitter. "I'm a grown woman, you know. I can take care of myself." Indignant, I tried to pull my hand away, but he held fast.

"Yeah, every grown woman hangs from the side of a cliff with some bad guy clinging to her dangling legs."

"One time! It was one time!"

"More than enough for me, thank you." As we neared the makeshift buffet table again he shimmered away.

Later that evening as I helped Lani with the washing up, I broached the subject of her brother again. "Lani," I began as she and I were organizing flatware for the dinner service that night, "does your brother Kimo have a place to live when he's here?"

She frowned up at me. "He usually stays with my uncle in Kahua. Why do you ask?"

I waved my hand then, as if to dismiss the idea. "I just thought I saw him at the homeless camp today, but whoever it was disappeared into the trees before I could get a good look."

"Oh." She turned back to the folding of the napkins. "I haven't had much reason to talk to him. We don't... see eye to eye on most things."

"That's too bad." I didn't want to pry, but I surely was curious. It didn't take long for her to confide in me.

"He left the family several years ago and went to live on Oahu. He camped on the beach, surfed, and basically did nothing but have fun and lay about. He would occasionally call us for money, but Mama was adamant that he should finish his education and get a job like everyone else. Now he shows up when he's broke and creates problems, demanding that Mama owes him. For what, I don't know. I think it's something he's imagined."

"Is that what brought him back here this time?"

She made a face of disgust. "Yes. Money, as usual. This time he has some stupid get rich scheme. I don't know the details, and I don't want to know either. Mama stands strong, and there is no money to be had. I'm just hoping he'll give up soon and go back to surfing on Oahu. I don't even feel like I know him anymore."

"That's too bad," I offered.

She shrugged. "It is what it is. There is blood family... and then there is chosen family. Of course, I wouldn't trade Mama for anything." She grinned up at me. Although I knew Lani's mother lived with the couple, I hadn't yet had the pleasure of meeting her, for she worked long hours just as we often did.

I had an impulse to hug Lani and so I did. Surprisingly, she hugged me right back. "I'm always available if you want to talk, Lani. Never forget, okay?"

She nodded. "Thank you." Her voice was choked. "And know that when I speak of chosen family, I include you." Then she quickly wiped her eyes while she ducked her head and went back to her tasks.

NINE

Doolittle

Sitting alone in my bungalow after Lani and I had finished cleaning up one night, I had a little bit of McCartney music playing just loud enough to satisfy the soul and fill the room without blasting out the nearby guests. Chester was snoozing on the sofa beside me, his purrs nearly vibrating the cushions. I idly stroked his silky orange fur while I read my book. I was becoming quite a fan of the nearby library. It gave me inexpensive entertainment and the ability to catch up on reading some of my favorite authors that I'd neglected when I lived in Los Angeles. At this moment I was tearing through the Alphabet Series by Sue Grafton; I was on *T is for Trespass* and enjoying the exploits of the private investigator Kinsey Millhone. Chester took a moment to stretch, blink, turn over, and yawn.

Oh, I had the weirdest dream just now...

My hand froze on his fur. That... was from Chester. That voice. Those words. I blinked a few times as if the batting of my lashes would clear my mind. He slow blinked at me before leisurely jumping down and ambling to his dish in the kitchen nook.

It's empty again!

Oh. My. Heavens. The voice I'd been hearing was my cat! I jumped to my feet, the book falling to the floor.

"Davy!" He shimmered into my line of sight.

"What's wrong?"

"I can... I don't know... I think I've been hearing Chester talking to me."

Davy looked from me to the cat and then back again. "Are you serious?"

"I'm dead serious... no offense."

"None taken." He smiled at me indulgently. "Chester, can you talk to me?"

The room was silent. Chester looked back and forth between the two of us. "Anything?" I asked Davy.

"Nope. Ticking clock, crashing waves, birds..."

"Chester..." I leaned closer to him. "What's happening?"

I'm a cat. How would I know?

I gasped. "Oh my stars! This is just un-freakin'-believable!" I slid off the sofa and sat on my knees in front of my young furry friend. The world seemed to spin a bit more out of control. I say a bit more because, after all, I did have a ghost as my best friend. Was I dreaming? If so, I wasn't sure I wanted to wake up. I turned to Davy. "Why do you think this is happening after all this time?"

"I'm not really sure." He gave a very slight frown for just a fraction of a second and then smiled. "Could it be that you're a sensitive and that our friendship has opened you up to becoming more receptive to other beings?"

"What do you mean?" I felt heat flush from my neck up to my hairline. This was an awful lot to wrap my head around.

"Your friendship with me has opened you up to a part of you that may have been hiding for all of these years." He scratched his chin for just a few seconds. "I'll be right back. Keep him talking."

He shimmered away and I was left with just Chester again. He slow blinked at me. *I would never hurt you, you know*, Chester spoke in my head.

I sat back on my heels and felt a smile begin from my heart and reach my lips.

"I know that and I've always been fairly sure that you love me," I addressed the little orange guy, "despite your cat-like ways, aloofness, and all that. I would never hurt you either. We've been together through an awful lot, haven't we?"

Yep. And more to come.

I wasn't sure if I liked that idea and wondered what he meant by it, but before I could ask, Davy shimmered back in.

"Your mother never told you, she says, but she always thought you had a special something about you. You used to talk to yourself a lot. She believed you had a gift, but she never really knew how to cultivate that talent within you. Now she blames me." He chuckled, that raspy deep inside his throat sound that was so damned endearing.

I held my breath. This was all too much to comprehend at this moment. My head felt funny, my palms sweaty. I let my breath out in a whoosh. "Do you think it's only Chester that can talk to me?"

"I have no idea. We'll have to try out a few things and see what happens with Winston, Marley, and Susie. This could be fun!" He rubbed his hands together, a gleeful childlike gesture.

"Sure, fun for you. It's unnerving to me. How do I get them out of my head?"

"Why would you want to?"

"Because I didn't invite them!"

"But you didn't invite me either, yet here I am!"

"Exactly," I deadpanned.

"Oh pshaw," he mocked me.

"Pshaw? PSHAW?" I felt outrage growing until I realized how funny he sounded, and I burst into fits of giggles.

That night, once I was sure I was alone, I dragged my journal out.

Dr. Doolittle I'm NOT

*So, Chester talked to me yesterday. Yes. He said words — full
sentences with adverbs, nouns, verbs, and pronouns. His grammar was
surprisingly quite good. And he's surly, just like I suspected. His "voice"
is a little husky and somehow has a clipped British accent, but it only
sounds in my head. I think. I know Davy can't hear him, and he's a ghost.
Who knew, right?*
    So, now what?
    I haven't a clue.

And, true to form, a response to my entry appeared the next day:

Dear Macca,
*So, if we go to the race track can you have a little chat with the
horses? We could place a bet and win BIG!*

Love,
David
(a little horseshoe)

    It had been a long week today. I'm sure you have had those kinds of
days, where everything you touch breaks, everything you pick up falls, and
nothing goes as planned. Yeah. Those. And on top of all of that, my mind
was spinning with unwritten lists of things I had to do. I would walk into a
room and promptly forget why I had done so or what I had needed.
    It was nearing the cocktail hour for our guests when I actually began
talking softly to myself. I quickly finished helping with the set up for
cocktails that would then be followed by dinner, and then I made my
escape to the privacy of my own bungalow. A soak in a tub full of bubbles,
a glass of icy Pinot Grigio at my side, my Sue Grafton novel encased in a
plastic bag (yeah, I learned that the hard way) and the troubles of my
world, both real and imagined, drifted away... until I heard a certain
Mancunian accent at the closed door that is.
    "Oi! Macca! How much longer ya gonna be, Babe?"
    I slapped the wet wash rag across my eyes and sank further into the
bubbles. "Go away. No one is home."
    I heard his chuckle through the door. "Is that a recording then? 'Please
leave a message because no one is home?'"

I picked up the bar of soap and flung it at the door, creating a loud thunk. Soap flakes floated to the floor as the impact caused the bar to chip. Great. One more thing to clean up, and I only had myself to blame.

Picking up my wine, I took a long swallow and set it down on the little footstool I used as a tubside table. I picked up my plastic ensconced book and used the eraser tip of a pencil to reach into the plastic bag and turn the page. Ingenious, right? Hey, you make do with what you have.

Twenty minutes later, feeling refreshed and just a little tipsy, I strolled out to the kitchen in search of dinner. Davy was sitting at the small table, a beer in one hand and flipping through the pages of a magazine with the other. "It's about time." He didn't look up. "I really detest your rule of privacy in the bathroom, you know? All you was doin' was soakin', and I'm sure the bubbles covered up all the private bits. We could have spent that time talking."

I stopped in my tracks for a moment before a derisive snort escaped me. Yeah, that would have been a great way to unwind... Not. "Rules is rules," I muttered. "Hungry?"

"Stahving."

"How about a quick curry?"

"Not too spicy though?"

"No, just spicy enough."

"Right." He slapped the magazine shut and joined me at the counter, his beer in one hand and refreshing my glass of wine with the other. "I will help then."

I pulled out carrots, an onion, garlic, and a sweet potato. "Start chopping."

He gulped his beer. "Yes ma'am!"

I gathered my deep skillet and a small pot with its lid, a can of coconut milk, some lentils, and the Basmati rice. While I got the rice cooking, Davy had finished chopping the onion, so I dumped it in the hot skillet with a little oil. When the onion had softened, I dumped in a good amount of curry powder that I'd adapted to our tastes and let it "burn" a little. Not really burned, mind you, but the heat brought out the oils and flavors. When Davy finished mincing the garlic, he brought it over to the stove and unceremoniously dumped it in with the onion as I stirred. I added a small bit of vegetable broth and let it all cook for a bit while I moved next to Davy to help. He was chopping the carrot and I diced the sweet potato. I told him then about my weird day and how I had hardly been able to focus on tasks.

"You *are* rather scatter-brained at times, yes." He nodded as his knife went through the carrot again and again.

The sudden silence in the room was deafening. I swear, even nasty little crickets chirped, taunting me and scolding him. I turned and stared at him, his head bent over his task. The more I thought about his comment, the angrier I became.

And then he opened his mouth again and spoke. Big mistake. "But I love that about you." He lifted his head and turned to look at me, a Cheshire cat smile on his face. Until he saw my face. I swear there had to be steam escaping from my ears, otherwise I might have suffered spontaneous combustion and implosion at the same time. His smile faded quickly and his brows knitted together. "What?"

"You're not real." I turned back to my sweet potato. "You're just an imaginary friend."

He clutched his chest, moaning. "Ohhh, you got me right where it hurts!" Always the clown.

I scooped up the last of the chopped vegetables and dumped them into the skillet along with a good handful of lentils. Davy opened the coconut milk and poured it into the bubbling skillet. I put the lid on the skillet and began to clean up after our prep.

"Ooooh, not speaking I see. Or hear. Or don't hear," he mocked.

I grabbed my glass of wine and went directly to the deck to relax in my favorite chair while our curry simmered. I heard Davy open a fresh beer and then join me.

"I didn't mean to upset you, Babe." He sighed. I sipped. He placed his hand over mine and squeezed. It was impossible to stay mad at this man for very long.

"It's just been a rough day, and sometimes I feel all alone on days like this." I picked at an imaginary piece of lint on my tank top.

"And then I go and make light of it and isolate you even more. I'm sorry."

I turned my head to look into his eyes. He actually did get me sometimes. It was quite remarkable to me until I remembered that he often invaded my private thoughts. Cheater.

"Hey." He sat up straight as he spoke. "Did I tell you I started the beer diet?" He held up his bottle and gazed longingly at it. "I've already lost four weeks! Bum-di-bum."

A smile played at my lips.

"I only drink on two occasions: when it rains and when it doesn't rain," he added.

Now I was giggling.

"I've had six beers today! That's forty two in dog beers!"

I was chuckling now and he was off and running, entertaining me until our curry was done. How could anyone stay mad at this guy?

TEN

Project

The next day I had a meeting with Dylan Kimura, the former professor from Hilo Community College. As Alex had promised, the man was incredibly knowledgeable about the struggles of homeless people and veterans.

"Thank you for taking the time to meet with me, Professor Kimura. I really appreciate it." We shook hands and I took in his small and crowded office. There were stacks of reports, books, pamphlets, and opened mail dwarfing his small desk, with a fairly large photocopy machine the highlight of the room.

He motioned me to sit in the lone empty chair as he plopped back down into his own behind the desk. "The pleasure is mine, and please call me Dylan. Alex speaks highly of you, Ms. Liberty."

"Oh, please... " I chuckled. "I'm still trying to get the staff at the inn to call me Macca, and I hope you'll do the same. Ms. Liberty has always been my mother."

He grinned. "Point taken, Macca. I suspect that one of the main reasons I became a professor in the first place was so that I wouldn't be called Mr. Kimura because that's my father."

I was nodding in agreement and understanding as I glanced around at all the clutter. "It appears you are a very busy man though!"

"Yes, but you know the old saying. 'If you want something done, ask a busy person to do it.' I admit that most of this is due to volunteering though, so I have no one to blame but myself." He gave a wry smile. "But I do this because they need a voice and I can be one of those voices."

The hair on my arms stood up at that moment because I truly understood what he was saying. "I hope someday to be a voice too."

His eyes crinkled when he smiled then. "From what I hear, you're already a voice."

"Thank you," I blushed.

He handed me a folder and I flipped it open to see lists of names with notations next to them. "Now, about Project Peace House..." he began, and I grinned at the project name; it was perfect. "These are the people who have already volunteered to visit Hale Maluhia. There's a doctor, a teacher, and a representative from the local food bank. We know it's difficult to receive assistance without a permanent address, so they're willing to make arrangements. Also, the teacher on the list is working to expand Oahu's Project Feed Hawaii to our island. That project uses high school students to assist with food drives and volunteer work."

"Wow, you've been busy," I murmured, astonished at how much he'd accomplished already.

49

"Well, it wasn't difficult because my contacts are already in place." His smile had a way of putting me at ease. "It was just a matter of making a few phone calls. We just need to make sure they'll be welcome at the camp. Outside interference is not always looked upon in a positive light because these people have frequently been beaten down by society and therefore pull back inside their tiny community shell."

I had already discussed assistance with Makala, Kai, and Joe, so I knew this wouldn't be the case. "They assured me they'd be open to any and all help."

"Excellent. I'm also in contact with the Veterans Administration to see how they can help. I understand there are several Vets at this camp?"

"Yes, at least eight that I know of," for that's the number Chad had given me.

"Good! So give me a list of dates when you would be available to meet us there, and we'll check calendars and come to a consensus."

I found myself nodding like a bobblehead on the dash of a rickety old pick-up truck and made a conscious effort to be still. I perused the calendar on my phone and jotted dates on a pad of paper Dylan had put before me while he did the same. I went four weeks out, but hoped it wouldn't take that long. He then took my dates, swiveled to his computer, and began furiously typing at a fairly impressive speed. He took a moment to read what he'd typed and then hit the enter key.

"Email sent to all parties. Let me have your email address and I'll send you the dates."

I nodded yet again and jotted my email address on the same paper I'd written my available dates.

"I don't know how to even begin to thank you, Dylan."

"No thanks necessary! This is what I do, with the help of many, of course." And then he flashed a grin and it was contagious. I found myself grinning with him, and I grinned all the way home as well. It was so exciting to see all this taking shape, however early we were in the game.

That night I was making a type of gazpacho using my latest toy, a food processor. It was just a simple model, but I was tickled over finding it at the thrift store.

I hadn't seen Davy all day so I called out as I dumped some tomatoes, cucumbers, and peppers into the bowl of the processor which already contained minced garlic, jalapeno, and parsley.

"Hey Davy, you around here somewhere? Hungry?"

I felt his shimmer just moments before I felt his chin resting on my shoulder as he peered at my work. "Always hungry. Wot y'makin' there?"

"Gazpacho. Want some? I have some of Lani's taro rolls to go with it; they're still warm from the oven."

"Not quite sure what gaspotso is but I'll try it."

I set two places at the small table out on the deck and he sat in his usual spot, his feet up on the railing. I set the bowls down and ran back for the taro rolls. I flicked at Davy's feet on the railing.

"Oh, sorry Babe." He gave a guilty smile as he swung around in his chair and took his first bite of the soup. "You know," he pondered as he chewed and took another bite, "this would be really good if it was hot."

I snorted a little laugh and shook my head. "It's supposed to be chilled."

"Hmpf," he mumbled as he dipped some of the purple bread into his bowl. "Whoever thought of that is off 'is trolley."

I stopped eating and stared at him as he shovelled every last bit of gazpacho into his mouth, then wiped the bowl clean with taro bread.

"Didn't like it much then, yeah?"

He stuck his tongue out at me then. "It was fine."

I chuckled and ate my own soup and roll in a more leisurely fashion as I told him about my day.

"The Professor is a really wonderful guy," I ended.

"Yeah, but were Mary Ann and Ginger there?"

"Yeah, right next to the Skipper," I deadpanned. Out of the corner of my eye, I saw him grin and nod. He collected our bowls and carted them off to the kitchen; I could hear him whistling the theme song to *Gilligan's Island* and chuckled.

ELEVEN

Officers

On a hazy morning I had errands to run, so I hoofed it up the stairs to the torn up parking lot. Would this construction project never be done? I was growing weary of the trek down the road to the temporary parking lot that the county had allotted for employees of the inn. Whose idea was it to expand anyway? True, we were getting more and more guests with multiple cars. Families of traveling business people often preferred to have their own means of transportation while their spouse attended to business meetings. It had been a boon for the inn to advertise on a business travel website. However, this construction was going too slowly for my liking, and here it was a Monday and no construction crew in sight. I made a mental note to leave a message for the contractor... again.

Car keys in hand, I pushed the unlock, and my little R2 — the Smart Car with a heart — I swore, beeped a *good morning* to me as it unlocked his doors.

"Good Day wee R2. How fare thee last eve?" I put on a fake Renaissance Faire accent just for R2's enjoyment. True, I expected to see the men in white coats come and take me away someday with one of those out of style jackets. You know the ones — the sleeves tie in the back. Really not my style, but the more I hung around Davy, the more I found myself talking to inanimate objects as a means to disguise my talking to something — or someone — who was invisible to others. Yep, they're coming to take me away. I just knew it.

The nearly silent purr of the electric motor was music to me. Being cut off from the charging station I'd had installed in my nearly destroyed parking lot was causing me to make better plans for recharging and I had forgotten it yesterday. I would stop at the library on my way to run errands and give it a partial boost on their charger while I roamed the aisles for new reading material. I was sure R2 would thank me for that detour if he could.

As I pulled onto the road, I peered ahead and gently applied the brakes. There seemed to be a fairly large pile of discarded clothing just a few feet away. Leaving the motor idling and the door open, I trotted over to it and gasped before my stomach began to heave. I barely made it to the edge of the road before losing my breakfast, for in fact, the pile of discarded clothing contained a human body. He lay face down on the road with dirt across the back of his dark green jacket and mud crusted in his hair. I turned away again and ran back to the car.

"Where is it... where IS it?" I dug through my backpack for my phone but it wasn't there. A scene flashed in my mind; I'd left it beside the coffee pot when I was refilling Davy's and my cups this morning. "Damn!"

I turned the car around and headed back to the inn, parking among the rubble left by the absent construction crew. Taking the stairs a few at a time, I jumped down to the wooden walkway and headed to the closest phone — the inn's line in the reception area. Thankfully, only Bennie was present as I didn't want to freak out any guests when I called 911.

"911. What is your emergency?"

"I... I found a man lying in the road near my home." I took huge gulps of air and tried to ignore Bennie's sudden interest in my conversation. He was shrugging his shoulders and whispering, wanting to know details. I waved him away as best I could.

"Was he breathing?"

"I couldn't tell. It's about a quarter mile east of the Hale Mele Inn on the main road." Why didn't I think to check his pulse? Too freaked out, I guess.

"I see by your number that you are at that inn now."

"Yes. That's where I live."

"And your name, miss?"

"Macca Liberty."

"One of our units is on the way. Please stay at your home until they arrive."

"Okay. Thank you." I replaced the receiver slowly, gently, my mind racing and my stomach twisting again. "I'm going to be sick," I whispered to Bennie and headed for the restroom off the adjacent restaurant. Looking in the mirror took my mind off of my stomach; my face was flushed in areas, pale in others. I turned on the tap and splashed cool water on my cheeks and the back of my neck.

Stomach settled, I returned to the reception area. Bennie shyly opened his arms and I gladly accepted his hug. One more deep breath and I was able to give him just the basic details.

It wasn't long before I heard the squawk of a police radio up toward the parking area. Soon, two uniformed officers entered the building. For a brief moment my mind flashed on Abbott and Costello, for the first officer was tall and thin while his partner was short and stout. It's funny how your thoughts go haywire when the world seems to be spinning out of control around you.

And then it hit me: I had discovered yet another dead body. That's two within a two year period. I wondered idly if I could blow away the dark cloud that seemed to be following me around.

"Macca Liberty?" Abbott-Officer asked.

"That's me."

"Can you tell us exactly where you think you saw this body?"

Frowning, I considered this to be a very odd line of questioning. "It's in the road, left of our parking lot... less than a quarter mile."

He scratched his head. "We'll need you to come with us and show us exactly where this alleged body might have been."

Alleged? Might have been? What's next? Who's on First? I resigned myself to this tedious line of police work. "All right."

Costello-Officer led us back up the stairs and held the back door of the cruiser open for me. Oh great. My first ride in the back of a cop car. I sure hoped no one was looking. If only it were for something minor, like protesting animal testing or something. My mother would have been shaking her head and muttering my name over and over again in that universal parental show of disapproval... that is, if she were still alive. I glanced up to the sky and sneered at her yet again. I doubt she saw; she was probably busy frolicking with my dad.

From the back seat of the squad car, I directed Abbott-Officer just a few feet down the road. The... empty road. I leaned forward as they slowed down the car.

"Here!" I pointed to the spot where the body had been. "I mean... there! At least, it was there." I shook my head. Abbott-Officer and Costello-Officer exited the vehicle and Abbott-Officer opened the back door. I trotted to the side of the road and saw where I'd been sick. "See? I saw the body right there," pointing my thumb over my shoulder, "and then I tossed my cookies right here," redirecting my finger-point to the lovely bit of vomit in the grass.

"Cookies?" Costello-Officer raised his eyebrows.

I made an impatient gesture with my hands. "You know, tossed my lunch... vomited."

They both peered down at the very unattractive pile that had once been my breakfast. Even I felt sick looking at it.

We stood there, looking around us at absolutely nothing but trees, vegetation, farmland, and a road that was empty for miles in either direction.

Abbott-Officer made a few notations in his notebook and slapped it shut before slipping it into his chest pocket. His disgust for me was quite obvious. "Well, there's no body. You must have imagined it."

Not only did that statement infuriate me, but I didn't buy that as a solution either, yet I had no idea why the body was missing. "Maybe he was able to crawl to the side of the road?"

They seemed embarrassed that a mere woman had come up with an idea that they themselves should have had, what with all their training and experience. My irritation level was rising fast, soon to swallow me up.

"Stay in the squad car," Costello-Officer directed me. I barely had time to pull my legs in before he slammed the door. I watched them each take one side of the road, peering into the foliage. Abbott-Officer did a little dance, forgetting where my vomit was and stepping in it. If I hadn't been so upset about the missing man, I might have laughed as he scraped his shoe on the asphalt.

Costello-Officer spoke into the radio clipped to his shoulder and then beckoned to his partner. Both of them leaned against the front fender, ignoring me. After a few minutes I was sweltering in the squad car, my thighs sticking to the vinyl.

"I wonder how many criminal germs there are on this seat," I cringed. Davy shimmered in, settling beside me.

"Oi! What're they doin' keepin' you in here?"

"They think I'm nuts. I saw a body, Davy! I did! And now... he's gone." My brain momentarily thought of one of the running gag catch lines from *The Monkees* TV show: "He's GONE!" and I had to suppress a deranged laugh. Abbott-Officer and Costello-Officer would surely lock me up if they heard that!

Davy shimmered away and reappeared near the two cops. Within a few minutes he was seated beside me again. Well, I say seated, but he always seemed to hover about five inches above any surface; he claimed he was still trying to master "distance" in his current state. But I digress...

"They called for back-up, a search team, and a cadaver dog."

I shuddered. "Do you think they suspect I did the poor guy in?"

"Actually, they think you're nutters and that there never was a body, but their captain told them to wait here and they'd be joined by searchers, the dog, and — brace yourself — Detective Green."

I smacked my forehead. This day was going from awful to horrendous in mere moments. Detective Green was my nemesis from when I found the first body in my swimming pool last year. Thankfully, our paths had not crossed since he visited me in the hospital to let me know they'd gotten a confession from Mr. Sykes, my evil neighbor. And now, he was about to return to my life.

"All I wanted to do today was run a few errands and get my car charged. Was that too much to ask?" I heard the high pitch to my voice and so did Davy.

"You're whining. It doesn't look good — or sound good — on you."

I dismissed him with a light punch on his velvet-covered shoulder. As I began to chew my thumbnail, Davy swatted at my hand. "Bad habit. I used to chew my nails all the time. Don't get started."

"Yes dad," I sneered.

I heard a commotion behind us and turned to see two more squad cars and an unmarked sedan pull to a stop. One of the officers opened the back door of his vehicle and led a large German Shepherd dog over to Abbott-Officer and Costello-Officer. They had a brief conversation before the dog was directed to search. I craned my neck to watch, but both he and his handler disappeared down an embankment, then reappeared back on the road farther down. They repeated this process over and over until I had to stop watching. The stretching and craning of my neck had given me a headache.

Detective Green emerged from the unmarked car, and my headache took a turn for the worse. His eyes slid to me, seated in the back of the squad car like a criminal, before he joined Abbott-Officer and Costello-Officer, who stood up just a little straighter in the company of their superior.

It was like watching an episode of *Law & Order* the way they'd glance at me every now and then, suspicion in their eyes. One last nod from the detective to the officers and they rejoined me in their squad car. Detective Green sauntered off toward the search dog and his handler.

"We're taking you in for questioning." Abbott-Officer watched me from the rear view mirror as he turned the squad car around.

"But... why? I told you everything!"

"Detective Green has some questions for you."

"Of course he does," I muttered under my breath through clenched teeth.

"What's that?"

"Nothing." I sat back against the sticky vinyl. I sighed and looked out the window. Detective Green was watching, a curious expression on his face. I could almost swear he was smiling. I shuddered and tried to focus on the beautiful scenery, but it was just a blur.

Sitting on a plastic chair and leaning against a plastic table with a plastic cup of water in a plastic room at the police station was not how I'd planned to spend my day. I had no watch, no phone, no bag of tricks. I counted the pencils that had been tossed up into the soft cork of the drop ceiling tiles above me. Someone had a lot of time to kill — and a lot of pencils to waste — for there were thirty-three of them firmly embedded in the stained surface. After a while, my neck began to hurt from staring at the ceiling, so I turned my eyes to the far wall and squinted to play a game in my head to kill the time. The peeling paint chips took on various shapes — a whale, a house, a railroad car, and... Yoda?

My game was interrupted when at last the door opened. Detective Green slapped a file and a pad of paper on the rickety table causing it to wobble and slosh some of the water out of my cup. I swept the little puddles onto the floor in irritation.

"Sorry." But he really wasn't.

"Am I under arrest?"

He glanced briefly at me as he sat and pulled his pen from his shirt pocket and then proceeded to write on the pad. Upside down, I could still see that it was today's date, I assumed the current time, and my name. I turned my head to the door, hoping that Detective Elliot Stabler from *Law & Order: Special Victims Unit* would burst in and rescue me. I wouldn't mind being in Christopher Melloni's arms instead of at this plastic table with this rigidly metal man who was currently in front of me. The door remained closed. I really do watch too much television.

"No," Green finally addressed my question and I turned back to look at him, still keeping one eye on that door. "But with your history, I felt it was necessary to check your story."

"My history?" I felt my voice rising with the heat of the sudden adrenalin coursing through me. "I don't have a history! I was a victim, yes! Is that the history you mean?"

"You found a body floating in your pool last year." He crossed his arms on the table. "Could you be looking for attention? Publicity for your inn? Is business slipping?"

A low growl escaped my throat as I stood, knocking the plastic chair back against the wall behind me. "My business, which is none of *your* business, is doing very well, thank you!" I moved toward the door. "I'm leaving."

"Sit down, Ms. Liberty." His voice was firm, but without anger.

I stood rooted, trying to decide if I wanted to be bold and blustery or meek and mild. I decided meek might be the better option to get me out of here sooner.

"Fine." I turned on my heel and plopped noisily into my chair, arms crossed in front of my body. "I don't have a ride home anyway."

He sighed, a sound not unlike that of a weary father dealing with a petulant daughter. "We will arrange for a ride for you once we're done here."

Deep breaths, Macca. "Okay. Let's get this over with."

"You claim you saw a body in the road at approximately 10:10 a.m. Correct?"

"I'm not certain of the time. I didn't have my phone on me, I don't wear a watch, and I didn't think to glance at the dashboard clock in the car."

"Your 911 call came in at 10:15 a.m."

"Then why are you asking me?"

"Did you go straight back to the inn?"

"Yes."

He scribbled some notes. Davy shimmered in and hovered behind the Detective. He winked at me before leaning forward to watch the words appear on the paper. He gave me one of those thousand watt smiles and then a little wave of dismissal.

"Can you describe the body?" Detective Green continued, completely unaware of the ghostly guest behind him.

"There was mud on his head and he was wearing a dark green coat, a rather shabby one to begin with, but made worse by all the dirt on it." He scribbled a lot.

Davy nodded and smiled at me, shrugging. "So far, just the facts, ma'am," he whispered, trying to ease my fears. I rolled my neck to loosen the tension. Davy moved to hover behind me and put his warm hands on my shoulders. How did he do that? Nearly two years and I still questioned his otherworldly abilities. I felt the stiffness leave me as he kneaded my neck and shoulders. My mind began to blank, just drinking in the sudden comfort. Detective Green pulled me back to the situation.

"And it was then that you vomited on the side of the road?"

"Yes. I... couldn't help it. And I'm really hungry now so could we please hurry this along?"

"I could have someone get you a hamburger."

"No thanks. I'm a vegetarian."

Green crossed his arms on the pad of paper and leaned in. "Really? I've been trying but I just can't seem to give up fish. It's the only meat I eat, but living on an island it's just sort of a standard staple, you know?"

My jaw hung slack. Why was he telling me this? I blinked a few times to defog my mind. "I know a lot of pescetarians. They only eat fish and plant based food. It's a good start." Why was I telling him this?

His dark eyes were soft and I was looking at him in a new light. He was indeed an average looking fellow, average like me. Hair that was the color of a coconut hull was cut short against his head, the waves barely visible. His eyes were the deepest brown, even darker than Davy's, but perhaps it was just the lack of contrast with his smooth and darkened skin that made them appear that way. I peered down at his hands, twiddling with his pen; they were strong and hairless. He sort of had that Nick Stokes/*CSI* thing going for him — that is if Nick was just a little more average. I absolutely did need to watch less television.

"I'll take that into consideration and maybe stop beating myself up over it then." His dark eyes twinkled and I actually smiled. He too smiled in return. His cheeks flushed a little and he quickly turned back to his notes. "So..." He seemed to remember what we were there for. "You vomited and then drove back to the inn and called 911. What did you do then?"

"Nothing. I was upset. The 911 operator told me to wait there and that's exactly what I did. I followed her instructions. I didn't even leave the reception where I'd placed the call except to rinse my face in the loo." Oops, I'd been hanging with Davy more than I realized.

"The loo?"

Davy was snickering behind me, still touching my shoulders.

"Sorry. That's British slang for the restroom."

"I've always wondered," Davy whispered behind me, "why they call it a restroom. Are you meant to sleep there?" I shook my head to shut him up.

"Oh, I see." Detective Green continued taking notes. "And then what did you do?"

"I waited for Abbott and Cos... I mean the officers to show up."

"Abbott and Costello?" I saw the hint of a smile at the corners of Green's mouth.

"That's what I've been calling them in my head. Sorry." But I wasn't.

Green shook his head, light laughter escaping his lips. "That's what we call them here in the precinct too."

Now it was my turn to laugh. "I'm so sorry. I had no idea. That was just my first thought when they arrived."

"You're not alone. We all see it."

"Oh good. I didn't want you to think I was being disrespectful or anything."

"No." Green chuckled. "I completely understand." He read his notes for a bit before continuing. "We've found no body, as you may have figured out, but we'll keep the file open. I'm sorry if we've inconvenienced you."

Davy patted my back and kissed the side of my head before shimmering away again.

"You mean, I can go?"

"Yes, Abbott and Costello — also known as Officer Allen and Officer Charles — will drive you home. I thank you for your time."

He stood and extended his hand. A real handshake. Wow. I stuck my hand out and he grasped it firmly but still with a gentle touch. It was warm but calloused. I briefly wondered what he did in his spare time to cause the wear on his palms.

"Thank you."

Well this was unexpected.

TWELVE

Shovel

"Local police have reported a body was found in the North Kohala area. No further details are available at this time." The voice on the television cut through my thoughts. I'd turned on the local news while I was having a very late lunch, and the spoonful of pineapple and banana froze midway to my mouth. I pushed my bowl and spoon aside and pulled my laptop out to do a search; there must be more details! Was it my body? Wait, what? That didn't sound right even in my head.

I found the same short news item as I'd just heard, but giving me no further details. I hate it when newscasters are right. Deep in thought, I stared out the window, my finger tapping a beat in the area between my nose and upper lip. While my curiosity was definitely piqued, I didn't really want to open up the can of worms that was Detective Green. I opted against contacting him and went back to work.

Such plans for a normal day just never seem to pan out in my life. It was only two hours later that the man who had begun as my nemesis more than a year ago appeared at the inn. Bennie called my cell from the reception area and told me that my presence was needed.

The detective was sipping a cup of Bennie's Kona coffee, his other hand casually in the pocket of his khaki slacks.

"I heard it on the news. Do you think it's the same body I saw?" I didn't even start with the social niceties like hello.

He gulped the coffee that had been in his mouth and saluted his cup in Bennie's direction. "'Ono Kona, Bennie." He placed the empty cup on the counter before turning to me. "Is there someplace private we can talk?"

I led him to the empty dining room, for dinner service had not yet begun. Kalei and Lani were busy in the kitchen so I pulled the swinging door shut and we sat facing each other.

"It was, wasn't it?" I felt it in my heart. Davy shimmered in from wherever he disappeared to all the time and stood behind me, his hand on one of my shoulders. I reached up to pat his hand and then pretended I was brushing lint off my shirt since Detective Green was watching.

He pulled his phone out of his pocket, touched the screen a few times, and then slid it toward me. A close-up photo of a rumpled, discarded body made me catch my breath. Despite the additional dirt covering it, it did seem to be the same dark green jacket, the hair matted with caked mud and additional debris.

"I think it's the same," I whispered. "It seems... more covered in leaves and dirt and stuff though."

He nodded once. "We think he was buried and then unearthed and put back in the road."

60

"The road?" My words sounded raspy, even to me. I forced myself to look away from the photo as I pushed the phone across the table to return it to him.

"In the same vicinity that you had shown us last week."

"Oh," I whispered and sucked my lower lip under my upper to keep it from quivering. I'd seen a lot of death in my life, but to experience it like this was less common. Two murders in the lifetime of a law-abiding civilian was two too many. "Do you know who he is?"

"We haven't been able to identify him yet. I'm sorry." His face was soft then, and I truly believed he felt remorse for subjecting me to this.

"Thank you." I swallowed a few times. I desperately wanted to be alone. "Is there anything else?"

"No." He rose to leave. "We'll contact you if we have any more questions."

I simply nodded a few times, still trying to swallow the lump in my throat, and showed him out. A short wave goodbye and I was able to escape to my bungalow, Davy following behind me.

"Are you okay, Wee Wallaby?" He dredged up that old nickname he'd saddled me with the last time I'd found a body.

"No. I'm not. No more dead bodies!" I slammed my bedroom door just because it seemed the most rewarding thing to do. I knew he would shimmer in if he really wanted to. Mercifully, he left me to myself. I flopped on the bed and closed my eyes, shutting out everything except the sound of the wind and the surf, the light curtains billowing and creating a shadow that fell back and forth upon my face.

I must have fallen asleep, for when I opened my eyes it was very dark. I felt so out of sorts. Turning on my side to see the time, I stopped and watched the moonlight outside the window instead.

"I need you, Mommy," I whispered, hearkening back to my childhood when Mom and I would spread a blanket on the beach and watch the moon together, singing to it and just talking about the universe. I felt the bed shift and arms go around me. I could tell by the velvet sleeves that it was Davy. I closed my eyes and settled into the curve of his body. "Thank you."

"Shh." He squeezed me tighter, his warm breath against the hair on the back of my neck.

I slept again.

In the morning I was feeling less sorry for myself. Davy shimmered in.

"Feeling better this morning?" he asked and then shimmered for a moment before returning in his usual red velvet shirt with black pants and white boots.

"Yes, much. Thank you." I sipped a cup of tea. "Hey, I was wondering..."

Davy shimmered again and changed to jeans and a striped shirt with a collar. Shaking his head, he shimmered yet again and returned in red swim trunks and a light blue windbreaker.

"Stop shimmering for a minute!"

"What?" Sometimes he had the face of an innocent boy, but I wasn't fooled today.

"I'm trying to talk to you!"

"So talk." Davy sat on the arm of the sofa. The shimmering stopped.

"I just wanted to ask if you wanted to make dinner with me this evening? We haven't done that in a long time. Open a bottle of wine, sit on the deck, just enjoy the peace?"

His sudden grin was the answer, but he spoke anyway. "Yes! That's brill! Oh! And how about an old film?"

"You pick it. I suck at choosing; you always tell me that."

"It's a deal." And he shimmered away.

I put some kibble in the cat dish and sipped my tea to settle my stomach before hitting the shower. Ready to face the day, I opened the door and took a deep breath. Chester wandered out with me and headed for the back corner of the front porch. He alternated between sniffing at something and pawing at it.

"Whatcha got, big guy?" I moved slowly to see what had grabbed his attention. "It's just an old shovel. How did it get here? And what's..." I leaned closer to see and gasped. I grabbed the curious cat, backed away as quickly as I could, and then turned and ran to put Chester in my bedroom for safety. I hurried to the reception area and used the main phone to call the police... again. This was getting really old, and I now knew the number by heart.

Bennie had been uncovering Winston's cage and letting the bird out when I turned with the phone in my hand.

"What's wrong, Miss Macca?" he whispered, but I waved him off for a moment so I could concentrate.

Good morning world!

"Not now, Winston." I turned my back on the bird when I was finally connected to a real person and was able to report the shovel. "It appears to have blood, hair, and... other matter on it," I gulped.

"Stay where you are and I'll send an officer."

"Okay." Hanging up the phone, I blew my breath out in a whoosh. "Sorry, Bennie. When the police get here, can you hold the fort? They may want to ask you questions as well."

"Of course, Miss Macca."

I had noticed that he paled when he heard me talking to the police on the phone, and he was peering across toward my bungalow in suspicion. "Let's just stay right here and keep others away from my bungalow."

He nodded but kept his eyes on my front door.

Less than fifteen minutes later, not one but three squad cars and an unmarked car had swarmed our little inn. My heart sank and my stomach lurched. On the one hand, I was glad the cavalry was there, but on the other hand, I feared that a repeat — or worse — of the other day was imminent.

Detective Green began to head my way while the other officers milled around. Before I could even point to the shovel, Abbott-Officer shouted "Here!" and all attention was redirected; the detective veered toward them. I held my breath.

Over the tops of heads I could see camera flashes as they documented their "find." Bennie stood close to me, his modest way of showing support. I set aside my fears for a moment to give him what I hoped was a smile of gratitude, but his expression changed to sadness, so I suppose I failed horribly at the gesture. Instead, I reached out and gave his hand a squeeze.

"I'm fine," I murmured. Pasted-on smile in place, check. "Really."

He wasn't buying it, but Bennie being Bennie, he respected my privacy and turned to look ahead at the police activity creating chaos in the normally peaceful atmosphere of our inn.

It was nearly an hour before the police removed the shovel they'd wrapped carefully in a very large plastic bag. In groups of two, the officers slowly returned to the road above, leaving only Detective Green behind. Stripping off his latex gloves and stuffing them in his pocket, he strolled in my direction.

At this point, I was chewing my thumbnail as if it were a rack of baby back ribs — that is, if I'd ever had baby back ribs and knew what they tasted like. A wave of nausea washed over me. I heard Davy in my head and flashed back to the numerous photos he'd shown me; so many of them had captured him chewing or otherwise picking at his nails. I stuffed the offending hand into the pocket of my lightweight hoodie just as the detective reached me.

"Good morning, Miss Liberty."

"Good morning. And please call me Macca." Where the hell had that come from? My lips?

His face was unreadable in that scary police detective manner. "When did you notice the shovel on your porch?"

"When I came out of my bungalow to head over here to work. So... maybe 8:00 this morning?"

"Actually, you made your call to the precinct at 8:15. Did it take you fifteen minutes to walk from there," he pointed his pen to my door and then turned back to me, "to here?"

"Oh. No. I guess not. So it must have been 8:13 then." I resisted the urge to stick my tongue out at him.

"And you'd never seen the shovel before?"

"Not that I know of. I know we keep a shovel here on the premises, but I've never had a reason to use it myself."

"Where is that shovel normally stored?"

"In the garden shed." I pointed randomly behind me.

"Show me please."

I clenched my hand in my pocket to keep from gnawing my finger off to the second knuckle as I led him around the outside of the reception area to the shed near the laundry. I pointed and he motioned me to step away.

Standing just behind him, I was unable to see over his shoulder as he opened the shed and peered inside. He snapped a few photos, then noisily rummaged around. The thought struck me that I was glad he wasn't looking for a fragile wine glass in a cupboard but that these heavier tools could very well survive the manhandling.

"Miss Liberty." He was back in business mode, ignoring my suggestion to call me by my first name. This didn't bode well. This didn't bode well at all. "Could you please come here and tell me what you see?"

I see you acting like the ass I always suspected you were, I thought. Oh please tell me I didn't say it out loud. I poked my head inside the shed and looked around. "I see tools." Duh.

"Is your shovel there?"

I rolled my eyes. "No. You can see it isn't."

He nodded once. "I'll want to question your employees. Are they all present?"

"All but Lani. She stepped out to pick up some more produce at the farmers' market. She should be back very soon though."

We returned to the reception area. I stroked Winston's beautiful gray chest as I waited for Detective Green to question each of my team.

Rawwwk. Miss Macca with the lead pipe in the conservatory.

"Shut up, Winston." I wondered whose brilliant idea it had been to teach this African grey parrot to talk, and I suspected Davy was responsible for teaching him some of his more... questionable speech. But right now all I could worry about was this latest predicament and what would happen next. Marley flew in to join Winston on his perch and whistled a brand new Bob Marley song. I heard the distinct notes of "One Love" coming from her pretty little beak.

I paced the front porch area of the reception building and then increased my route to include a few feet of walkway, all the while singing a bit of Marley's tune in my head, the lyrics "let's get together and feel all right" repeating over and over again. It seemed like hours. I pulled my phone out of the pocket of my shorts and was surprised to see that it was nearly noon. There were still so many daily chores to do and I was beginning to get irritated. Just as I was contemplating barging into the dining area where Detective Green was doing his individual questioning, he emerged, slapping his notebook shut with a sharp snap. I jumped.

"I'll be in touch," were his only words, his face devoid of expression. I watched silently as he took the stairs to the road two at a time.

B'bye. Rawwwk. You said it, Winston. Marley reverted to whistling "I Shot The Sheriff" and I quickly shushed her.

My heart wasn't in the dinner we prepared that night, nor the film Davy had chosen for us. While I normally loved Gene Kelly, I just wasn't in the mood for dancing, singing, or anything else for that matter. A sense of doom and gloom had carried on throughout the day. Even the normally jolly Sam had felt it. Albert was upset that his garden shed had been ransacked and was equally irritated that his shovel was gone. I had dispatched him to the local supply mercantile for a new one and he seemed happy to escape the pervading sense of impending disaster.

The film was nearing the best part, the actual singing and dancing in the rain, when there was a loud rapping at my door. "Nevermore," I whispered to myself in wry humor.

Detective Green stood on my porch again, Abbott-Officer and Costello-Officer directly behind him.

"It's rather late for more questions," I grimaced.

"We're not here for questions. Please step out onto the porch?" I don't remember instructing my feet to follow directions, but they did anyway. "Macca Liberty, you're under arrest for the murder and..." the rest of his words faded away as my mind swirled, matching the churning of my stomach. Costello-Officer seemed almost gleeful as he instructed me to put my hands behind my back so that he could apply the handcuffs. He squeezed them tighter than necessary and I cringed. I tried to hold my head up high as they marched me off my porch. Kalei and Lani stood near Winston's cage. I could see Lani crying and Kalei squeezing her tightly.

"It will be okay, Miss Macca," he called to me. "I'll call Mr. Baldwin and the others."

I nodded, presuming he meant the others to be the rest of the staff. They would have to pick up the slack from my absence, which would hopefully be quite short. Ever the optimist...

THIRTEEN

Arrested

Having invoked my right to an attorney, I was taken to the precinct for booking. Sitting handcuffed to a bench in an intake area, I hung my head and let the tears come.

"Goldfish," I whispered. I felt his shimmer before he appeared on the bench next to me. He put his strong arms around me and just leaned his cheek on my shoulder.

"It will be all right. Just be patient and don't say anything."

I sniffed and gave one small, barely perceptible nod. *Don't leave me*, I begged in my thoughts.

"I won't."

And he didn't. I was taken to be fingerprinted, photographed, and to have my pockets emptied before I was searched and dumped in a holding cell. At least there they removed the handcuffs. The deep red bruising was evident like evil bracelets burnished into my skin. There was another woman in the holding cell with me, and I was grateful that she was either sound asleep or passed out from intoxication; the smell of booze was thick in the room. Davy and I sat huddled in the far corner. I fell asleep at last, leaning into his shoulder. I had stopped caring if anyone wondered why I was perched so precariously. Let them ponder.

Clueless to the actual time, I woke up to the sound of retching in the holding cell. My fellow jailbird was bent over the toilet in the other corner. How lovely. I pinched my nose shut and breathed through my mouth, averting my eyes to avoid that chain reaction that sometimes happens: you retch; I retch; we all retch together.

"She's done." Davy nudged me. I opened one eye to see he was indeed correct. She was lying on the bench, her shirt pulled up to cover her face. Lovely. I got a great view of naked breasts. My groan caused Davy to chuckle.

"Not funny," I whispered so quietly that I could barely hear it myself.

The outer door opened and a female officer about the height of a twelve-year old child but with the build of a fire hydrant stepped into the corridor beside us. I wondered briefly how she managed to find a uniform to fit; she barely topped four feet. Wasn't there a height requirement for the job?

"Hey, Sleeping Boobie," she nodded to my cellmate. "Wake up. Time to see the judge."

Sleeping Boobie pulled herself erect, straightened her shirt and wobbled to the open cell door. Officer Pint-Sized slammed it before turning to apply handcuffs to the lucky drunk.

66

"Oh my gosh, I'm so relieved she's gone." The corridor door closed behind them.

"How are you holding up?" Davy peered into my eyes as I sat up straighter and adjusted my rumpled clothing.

"Like I was just puked up into that toilet." He chuckled again and I glared at him. "It's so nice that you're able to laugh about this."

"Hey, just trying to lighten the mood. Remember... success isn't decided by the position you reach, but the obstacles you overcome."

"Huh?" I then realized he hadn't quoted it quite right, but I kept my mouth shut because it was easier. I was tired.

"What do you mean I didn't quote it right? Never mind," he scoffed.

"Get out of my head!"

"I know... I don't always get the words right." He was irritating in his ability to ignore my objections and yet he continued on. "But the sentiment is there." He never missed a beat. "By the way, I took your journal and stashed it in a plastic bag under the deck. I figured when they search your place you might not want them to see your comments about ghosts and all."

"Oh my gosh, thank you! I'd completely forgotten."

I leaned against him again, my head on his muscular shoulder. It was like a pillowcase stuffed with a boulder, but it comforted me simply in its familiarity. And smell. Have I ever mentioned how yummy he smelled? Like freshly laundered linens that had dried on a line in the breeze. It nearly covered up the less than enticing scent of the recently puked booze coming from the disgusting toilet.

"I wonder what happens next. To me, I mean."

"I know exactly what happens. Baldwin and another attorney will be here this afternoon and you'll meet with them. Then you'll appear before a judge. I suspect you'll be going home."

I sat up suddenly. "Really? How do you know this?"

"Well, I cheated and listened in on Baldwin's discussion with his colleague. As for the going home part, it's my best guess, based on that conversation."

Watching his face as he spoke, I held my breath and then threw my arms around him with so much strength that we fell back against the bench together. "Thank you!"

Chuckling, "You're welcome... although I haven't done anything yet."

"You'll be there, right?"

"I'll be there. I promise." He shimmered away, leaving me far too alone. I rubbed my face, trying to stimulate... anything. Awareness? Circulation? Grit that had dried on my face? Eww. I used the sleeve of my tee shirt to wipe some of it away. I lay down on the hard metal shelf they called a cot and closed my eyes. Within seconds I was asleep.

Vivid dream. Like Technicolor and a bad LSD trip combined. Well, never having tried LSD, it was simply my best guess. In the dream I felt my hands being held; it felt so real. It was my mother's voice I heard first.

"Hey Monkee Paw," she whispered in my ear. "Dad and I are here, but we're not supposed to be... so we need to make it fast."

"What do you mean you're not supposed to be? Where are we?"

"In your dream, sweetheart. We just want you to know we love you and you'll get through this. We know you will."

"Monkee Paw..." My dad used my childhood nickname as well.

"Everything is going to be all right. I promise."

"It will? You do? And why aren't you supposed to be here?"

"Because," he sort of hemmed and hawed, *"well, it was decided it would be too upsetting for you. That's why Davy came. Consider him our surrogate parent."*

Wait. What? I remembered the kiss we'd shared a while back. Eww. *"Um... no. How about a surrogate friend instead?"* I shuddered.

"Okay, Monks, surrogate friend. No... better yet," Daddy continued, *"your friend. True friend."*

"He's been taking such good care of you, sweetheart." Mom brushed the hair off my face. *"And we love you so very much. Never forget that."* They both smiled down at me adoringly and then began to fade. I reached for them, trying desperately to grasp them, hold them close, tether them to me, but they were gone.

I awoke panting, the room spinning just a little. "Whoa. Really weird dream."

Davy chose that moment to shimmer in. "Monkee Paw?" He could barely speak because he was laughing so hard, clutching his side, doubled over with mirth. Some friend.

Officer Pint-Sized came to retrieve me several hours after Sleeping Boobie had gone. I met with Alex Baldwin and another attorney, Mr. Rob Parker Kula, who handed me his business card. His deeply tanned and unlined skin fooled me into thinking he was in his thirties, but the wisdom in his dark brown eyes told me he'd seen much more in longer years. When I came closer to shake his hand, the fine lines were more obvious. I put him closer to Alex's age, in his fifties perhaps. Both men were dressed in lightweight suits and conservative ties, far different — more formal — than I'd seen so far on the island.

"I'll be assisting," Alex began, "but Rob here will be representing you. You're in very competent hands, Macca. Very."

"Okay." I know I didn't sound convinced, because I wasn't.

We discussed the facts surrounding my "case" as it were, although I was still unsure of how I, a completely innocent person, could be in this mess.

I suddenly remembered Dylan Kimura and all the dates we were trying to coordinate. "Alex, could you ask Dylan to go ahead and proceed without me on the homeless meeting? I don't want to be the one holding things up, and who knows how long..." I gulped, "I'll be in here."

"Okay, but I'm pretty certain we'll have you out soon," he responded. But I insisted. I didn't want to stall the progress.

Then Alex and Mr. Kula assured me they'd see me in court in just a few minutes as Officer Pint-Sized led me to the holding area. At least there was a clock on the wall. I watched the second hand go around and around until my eyelids began to droop. They snapped right back open though when Officer Pint-Sized returned and led me into the courtroom.

Alex and Mr. Kula were there, and I was told to stand with them facing the judge's bench. Bench. Why did they call it that? It wasn't a mere bench. It was a really scary, freaking-out sized throne of sorts. I began to shiver. Peering around the small but imposing room, I saw Detective Green and Officers Abbott and Costello standing to the side. I quickly looked away, feeling so ashamed. And then I felt ashamed at being ashamed. I'd done absolutely nothing wrong! Feeling the tears taunting me, I rubbed my eyes hard, forcing the traitorous waterworks away by sheer brute force. It was better to have bruised eyes than wet ones.

The sound of a heavy door opening beside the judge's throne made me jerk my head up. I squared my shoulders and let out a shuddering breath to find some semblance of calm. A small man took the throne; the incongruence of a minuscule slice of his Hawaiian print shirt collar peeked out from beneath the black robe. I was mesmerized by that small slice of color, for it was just a tiny bit of "normal" to hold close during this entirely surreal ordeal. So focused on this, I missed the opening comments, but I knew my presence was just a formality and that my attorneys would do the work for me.

"Miss Macca Liberty is charged in the homicide of Chad Stephens, no known address."

Wait. What? I jerked my head over to the assistant district attorney who had made the statement. Chad? Of the homeless encampment Chad? I felt the tears, stronger now and picking up steam as they poured down my cheeks. Poor Chad. Who would do such a horrendous thing to that wonderful young man, I asked myself. Mr. Kula put his hand on my arm, gently bringing me back to the proceedings.

"How do you plead?" he whispered, verbally nudging me to pay attention.

"Not guilty." My voice shook, and there was barely any volume to it.

"Speak up for the court," the judge demanded.

Clearing my throat and taking a deep breath, I repeated with strength and determination that I truly did not feel, "Not guilty, Your Honor."

And then Davy was beside me again. He put his strong arm around my waist, symbolically facing the judge alongside me. My hand hanging down by my side, I used my fingers to slyly give his trouser leg a little tug of thanks, but the emotions caused me to miss much of the rest of the proceeding until I heard the ADA again. I peered at her, a youngish woman wearing a navy knee-length skirt, modest heels, and a linen jacket over her sedate blouse. Her dark hair brushed her shoulders, the sides held back by small gold barrettes. Just another face in the crowd.

"The people ask for remand, Your Honor."

What? Why?

Mr. Kula spoke. "Miss Liberty runs a small inn that requires her daily attention. Remand would constitute a hardship, Your Honor."

"Her murdering someone else while she's free would constitute a hardship as well." The ADA's words were coarse, biting, and full of venom, and there were murmurs in the courtroom.

The judge rapped his gavel. "That will be enough, Ms. Jordan. Bail is set at $1,000,000."

I felt all the air whoosh out of my lungs. I looked wildly around me, my eyes finally resting on Detective Green's face. When I saw his expression I stifled a strong desire to scream at him. What did I see there? He looked so sad. All the noise around me fell away as Officer Pint-Sized handcuffed me once again. The last thing I saw was Alex Baldwin mouthing, "It's okay. It's okay."

But it wasn't okay. Nothing was okay. It seemed as if nothing would ever be okay again. Ever.

Clothes do not make the man. Or the woman. Especially striped clothes. In fact, I vowed I'd never wear stripes again as I sat there on the bottom bunk in a cold cell wearing really ugly stripes. I don't mean pin stripes. I mean big, wide, horizontal stripes, on faded and over-washed fabric. I'd been transported to a women's facility, forced to endure horrible invasions, and given these despicable clothes to wear along with black flip flops. Well, at least those were okay. Sort of. A million dollars was a lot of money. Bail could cost as much as $100,000 plus fees. Alex and Rob were working to secure the bail, using my inn as collateral. My inn. Well, I knew I wasn't a flight risk, so that should be okay, right? Right?

Davy took that moment to shimmer in, sitting so close beside me that our thighs touched. "Hi Jailbird Monkee Paw." He grinned, but when I burst into tears, he backed off with the lighthearted humor and took me in his arms. "Alex and Rob should have you out of here by tomorrow."

I cried anyway. It was all so humiliating, and I felt complete despair.

"Hey," he tried to soothe me, "did you know that Rob Parker Kula is related to the Parkers? I mean *the* Parkers. The ones for which Parker Ranch is named?" Taking deep breaths I held my sobs for a moment to hear what he was saying. "And 'kula' means gold. His lineage goes back to King Kalakaua."

"Really?" I sniffed and wiped my nose on the ugly stripes I was wearing; at least they were good for something.

"Really."

"Why does he work then?"

"He's wealthy, but he's also determined to help where others might not be able to. He's a champion of underdogs. He and Alex went to school together."

"How can I afford his services? They must be... oh my gosh, this is going to send me to bankruptcy court, isn't it? But I guess that would be the least of my worries if I'm sent to death row." I gasped, realization setting in again. "I'm in deep trouble, aren't I?"

He squeezed his arms tightly around me, his face so close to mine. "I prefer to be optimistic. The evidence against you is very thin. That's what I heard Rob say. And don't worry about the cost. He's doing this pro bono for Alex... and for your Uncle Wally."

"But why?"

"Apparently Alex, Rob, and Uncle Wally were poker buddies. Your uncle passed away before Rob could pay him the $111 he owed him. This is his way of setting that right."

"But... $111 can't nearly be enough, can it?"

"No." He shook his head and gave me a gentle smile. "To Rob it's the principle of the matter, Babe."

The cell was completely cold and silent, and then I burst into a fresh bout of tears. Davy rocked me against himself, saying nothing and just letting me cry it out. He pulled us down on the bunk and cradled me. The comfort was nearly unbearable in a most positive way, and emotions flooded, sending me into new bouts of sobs and hiccups.

Davy sang softly into my ear about loving me this year and next year and then forever. Oh, how lovely that sounded. Exhaustion took over and I slept long and hard.

I awoke as the sounds of clanging doors and heavy footsteps echoed around the facility. Peeking through the bars, I saw a quiet line of people exiting. A uniformed attendant was bringing up the rear of the line of women in stripes like mine.

"Where is everyone going?"

"They're going to the mess hall for breakfast. You're going home."

71

"I am?"

Her reply was a curt nod as she disappeared down the hall, the massive door clanging shut again.

Davy shimmered in so close beside me that we nearly shared the same clothing. His arms were around me, his head pressed to mine. And then...

"Monkee Paw?"

I smacked his shoulder and pushed him away, but it was half-hearted. I loved that he was right there with me even if he *was* laughing his fool head off and suddenly rolling on the metal cot beside me.

"Laugh now, old man..."

"Who you callin' old?"

"The ghostie sitting next to me. Yeah, the one with that cute sixties Davy facade."

"Yeah, but admit it... you like it fine then."

I grinned. "Okay. You discovered my secret. I always wanted to cavort with a cute ghost that no one else could see."

"Winston, Marley, and Chester can see me!"

"And I'm thankful that they cannot talk to anyone else about it. Very. Can you imagine?" We froze for a few seconds. I was imagining the world seeing Davy the ghost... and listening to Chester talk... and our eyes met and we dissolved into fits of laughter. Yeah, my world is not very simple.

We both sobered then as the heavy metal door clanged again. Officer Pint-Sized arrived and led me to a room similar to the intake room where I'd been brought yesterday. An attendant was waiting and handed me a bag; inside were my clothes. By now they smelled pretty ripe after my having worn them for more than a day. Still, I was grateful to be able to strip off the stripes and put my underwear, shorts, tank top, and hoodie back on. Sliding my feet into my own flip flops felt like home already.

There were few words spoken as I was led to freedom, but I swear a chorus of angels sang as I was let out through the final lock-down area and saw Alex and Rob standing in the vestibule to welcome me. Alex held his arms open and rather sucked me into his embrace like a giant vacuum cleaner. I laughed, I cried, I rejoiced, and I admit that I babbled a little too. Well... maybe a lot.

"Only one thing." Alex pulled away to look in my eyes. "You cannot go to the homeless camp until after the trial."

"And if the jury finds me guilty..." I trailed off, not wanting to dwell too much on the rest of that sentence.

It was only once I was safely locked in Alex's car that I turned to view the institution from which I'd just emerged. My limited time inside was more than enough for my lifetime.

FOURTEEN

Home

Even though I had slept so much during my... ahem... incarceration... it hadn't been the right kind of sleep. Upon arriving home I was feeling like I'd run a marathon, played nine innings of baseball, run another marathon, and finished off in a mud wrestling pit. Exhausted, sweaty, sticky, dirty, and shouldering a reduced self esteem, I still greeted my friends and let them hug me and welcome me home.

"We'll talk later in the week," Alex assured me as he and Rob left. I nodded, the smile on my lips feeling as if it might split my face in two. Turning back to the welcoming committee, I reveled in the sense of *ohana*, or family, we'd developed.

"We took good care of Chester, Marley, Susie, and Winston, Miss Macca." Sam was eager to ease my worries.

"No problems here with the guests," Bennie added.

"We cleaned your bungalow and refreshed the supplies in your refrigerator," Lani assured me as she and Ming held tightly to my hands.

Kalei and Albert joined in with their welcome home wishes too, but in their usual reserved manner.

"Thank you so much. You're the best family I could ever wish for. But now, I really need to clean up." I waved my hand in front of my nose and held the front of my hoodie out like it was stinky. "And I think I might need to torch these clothes." Gentle laughter had replaced the tension.

I gave Winston a little kiss on his beak and Marley a stroke of her feathers, and then I ran to my cottage and my Chester. The big orange cat had been watching from the window and leaped down to greet me. I picked him up and nuzzled his soft fur. "I love you big guy, and I missed you so much." He purred and rubbed his cheek on my chin. "But I need to slough off about three layers of skin, burn my clothes, and shave my head. Not really, but you get the idea."

I set him on the sofa and changed into my swimsuit, a green print one-piece. I grabbed a towel and headed down to the ocean. I needed the freedom and cleansing of the sea first; it was always rejuvenating to me. After swimming and splashing about, I sat on the sand and watched the horizon for a moment. The sun was comforting, and I felt warm for the first time since the day of *The Traveling Shovel of Death* as I had begun to think of it. How did it get there? Who put it there, because I certainly did not! Why did they put it there? What had Chad done or seen that caused him to be murdered? Or worse, was he just a tool to frame me for some reason completely unknown to me? What had I done to set all this in motion? That was the real question, because I had indeed been framed.

Gathering my thoughts helped me find some inner comfort again. I grabbed my towel and hit the outdoor shower that I'd had installed at the top of the stairs to the inn's main premises. We encouraged our guests to use it to reduce the amount of clogging of drains inside each bungalow. Sand had been a constant catalyst for plumber's visits, and the outdoor facility had reduced the amount of sludge in the pipes.

Inside my bungalow, Chester greeted me all over again. He then followed me into the bathroom and watched from the counter as I showered, scrubbing my body and my hair multiple times. The smell of that institution was still strong in my nose so I broke out my citrus shower scrub. The bathroom began to smell like an orchard, and the steam relaxed me. It was like a mini spa day in the privacy of my own home. Chester licked my damp arm as I combed my hair. "I promise I'm not leaving again anytime soon." I had a feeling I would be speaking those words to him a lot over the next few days, but could I really convince him if I wasn't convinced myself?

I tossed my dirty clothes into the empty hamper, making a mental note to wash them first thing in the morning. Twice. Maybe even three times. Perhaps I actually *should* consider burning them. But I really liked that hoodie... once.

Chester shadowed me. He followed me out the front door and to the main dining room. Guests had grown accustomed to seeing him all over the inn. I was so proud of his good manners, and he never jumped on counters or tables. Today, he wasn't letting go of me.

It was just nearing the end of the lunch period. The buffet that Kalei had created for both guests and staff had been picked over, but I was able to fill a fresh fruit and cheese plate before sitting down at a small table.

Chester hopped up on the empty chair beside me and rested his chin on my thigh, content just to be close, but even happier to be touching. I stroked his soft fur with one hand while I ate a light meal with the other. Bennie sat with me just long enough to inhale a spam sandwich. I resisted making a face at the sad spectacle on his plate. Most natives had grown up with the canned meat and considered it a staple that rivaled bacon, and while the scent of bacon cooking was not something that turned my stomach, the smell of spam was.

"I'm relieved you're home, but I am worried about you," he spoke between bites. I watched his eyes to keep from seeing the sandwich. "This isn't going to just go away on its own."

"I know. I need to figure out what's going on."

"Shouldn't you leave that to the police? I mean... you do remember what happened last time," he referred back to my near–death experience on the cliff.

"You sound just like..." I stopped myself before saying Davy's name and switched gears. "...a very concerned brother. But I'll be careful. I promise."

I could see the skepticism in his eyes; they screamed "famous last words," but he didn't actually say it, and for that I gave him what I hoped was my brightest smile. I slathered a bit of softened cheese on a hunk of warm bread. It tasted of the heavens, stars shooting before my eyes, the galaxy spinning down my throat, and I followed that bite with another and another. I had not eaten much in the past couple of days, but still, this was the stuff Thanksgiving feasts were made of.

"We had an interesting booking yesterday," Bennie got down to business. "A family of five. They will be staying for at least a month until their new home is completed."

"Really? That's wonderful! So they're building a new home?"

"Yes. One of them is apparently an architect and designed it himself, but there were some supply delays so they've already sold their home in California."

"Well then, we shall do our best to make them comfortable for as long as they need, right?"

He grinned and nodded. "I'm excited. It's always great to have kids around. It makes the place really come to life."

Again, he sounded just like Davy, who I knew would also be thrilled. "I guess this means we need a few extra pool and beach toys. Would you like to take care of that?"

He nodded emphatically, his mouth full of food. Once he'd swallowed and wiped his lips with his paper napkin he added, "I would love to. I'm still a big kid, you know."

I chuckled. "Most men are, Bennie. Most men are." I grinned, thinking of the biggest kid at the inn: Davy.

I stood to pour a mug of tea from the classic Brown Betty teapot that Lani always kept warm for meals. She brewed a local tea daily, a hand picked black tea grown south of Hilo; it resulted in a deep mahogany color with notes of dried cherry and caramel. Kalei used the same tea for his very special iced brew, adding some extra citrus and other secret flavors known only to him and his wife.

I took my seat again, sipping the unusual brew while idly stroking Chester. He'd only reluctantly allowed me to stand and retrieve my drink before reclaiming me immediately. Separation anxiety was going to make it hard to reassure my feline friend, and I knew it would take time and patience.

"He's not taking his eyes off you, that little one." Bennie smiled and nodded to Chester as he stood to bus his dishes and return to work.

"Yes. He'll be my next project I guess. Reassuring him I'm not going anywhere won't be easy."

"We all tried to tell him you'd be back soon, but he wasn't consoled at all. We'll help in any way; just say the word, Miss Macca."

"Thank you, Bennie. It takes a village..." We chuckled at my lame attempt at a joke about my cat–child and then parted.

I carried my tea back to my bungalow, Chester so close on my heels that my flip-flops actually kicked him in the chops a few times. "Sorry, Chet old buddy. Gimme some room, huh?" But I couldn't even begin to be irritated with the little guy. Inside the bungalow, I opened the *makai* (or sea-facing) windows to air the place out. I sat on the deck with Chester on my lap to finish my mug of tea, still basking in my return to freedom. There were chores to be done, sure, but the healing properties of peace and quiet had to come first.

My mug empty, I reached for my laptop and answered queries from our website, answered emails, and researched possible new products for the inn.

Hours later the sun was slowly beginning to head down to the horizon, Chester and I retired early. Exhaustion had taken its toll at last and I slept the entire night. Chester lay curled beside me, his paw resting on my hand. and just like the nights before, Davy shimmered in and snuggled behind me, his arms wrapped around the two of us, Chester and me. And then...

"Monkee Paw?" Davy loved to tease me about my childhood nickname. He dissolved into fits of laughter again until I elbowed him. "Ooof!" That shut him up.

Feeling drugged and hungover the next morning, I stumbled to the shower, my Chester shadow close behind me. He perched on the toilet seat the entire time I was in the shower, sometimes batting at the glass door.

"Everything will be fine, Chet."

Promise?

"I promise," admitting to myself that it might be a little white lie, but the poor feline needed reassurance.

I heard his purring then as he hunkered down on the toilet and sat sphinx-like until I toweled off and stepped onto the bathmat. I gave his cheek a gentle pat and was rewarded with a slow blink. I returned the slow blink and he leaped into my arms. "I love you, Chester." He always amazed me that he could leap like that and keep all his claws from slicing and dicing me.

In the kitchen, I put fresh food in Chester's bowl and made a pot of coffee. Three cups and two pieces of toast slathered with mango preserves did nothing to dispel the grogginess. I would just have to fight it every inch of the way. There were things to do.

Chester was my partner for the day. He "helped" me with the accounting books, the laundry, the ordering of supplies, and the returning of telephone messages. Once, when Winston and Marley flew over to join us, Chester hissed and chased them away. I was having none of that though and scolded him. He slunk a couple feet away, never taking his eyes off me.

"I promise I'm not going anywhere soon, big guy." I only hoped I could keep such a commitment. It was common knowledge that there were many innocent people incarcerated across the country, some even sitting on death row. The thought caused a little tremor to run through me, beginning at my toes and ending with that creepy crawly feeling on my scalp. I needed answers, but I needed to run my business as well. I could send in Sherlock Jones though.

I played the Goldfish card that night in the privacy of my bungalow. "I was wondering if you were ever going to call for my help." Davy shimmered in with that impish grin of his, dressed as — you guessed it — Sherlock Holmes.

"You could have offered, you know."

"But you needed to figure it out for yourself first."

"I really hate it when you're right," I sighed, causing him to chuckle in that endearingly raspy manner of his.

"Well, my darlin', I'm quite often right, and you should just accept that now. It will cause a lot less stress."

I half-heartedly smacked his arm with the back of my hand. "Nice costume by the way."

"From the show... I thought it was rather appropriate myself."

"So, Sherlock, what should we do?"

"I've been hanging out at Hale Maluhia, just listening... and watching. The police have only been there once, and not since you were arrested either."

"So they've just given up and are pinning it on me?" I felt my voice rising at the same rate as my blood pressure.

"That I don't know. I haven't visited the police, but that is my next step."

Rubbing my face as though it would erase this entire episode from my life, I groaned aloud. Davy grabbed both my wrists, but loosened his grip when I grimaced; the handcuff bruising was still tender. He whispered to me as he gently massaged my sore wrists, "Just give me some time, okay?"

"Okay. There's not much else I can do. If I go poking around I could end up back in jail."

"Yes you could, so you be command central right here. We'll discuss it all together and figure it out. Got it?"

"Got it." Sitting next to each other on the sofa, I peered into his sparkling eyes. I really did feel a tiny glimmer of hope. We could sail this ship with Davy Jones at the helm. That picture in my head caused me to start to giggle, which turned into near-maniacal laughter.

"What?" He was beginning to laugh with me, obviously without knowing why.

I had this picture flash in my head of Davy Jones at the wheel of a big ship, steering it safely through pirate waters.

"Arrrrr!" He grinned and shimmered from his Sherlock costume to a striped tee-shirt, bell bottoms, and pirate hat. I lost it and laughed so hard that I fell over on the sofa, my head and shoulders on his thighs. "Arrr, be careful there me lassie, or y'll see why me Roger is so jolly."

This only helped to make me laugh harder, tears streaming down my cheeks, and then suddenly there were real tears streaming down my cheeks and I was crying in frustration, fear, and fatigue.

"Arrr," he nearly cooed as he stroked my back in a soothing manner. "There, there me beauty. Ye be a fine salty cap'n o' this bloody inn. The murderous bilge rat be shark bait soon."

I'd cried all my tears out, and now he had me giggling again. I sat up and drank in his deep and loving expression as he pushed the dampened hair off my face.

"You're right. It will be fine. After all, I have the best secret weapon of all time: You."

He smiled and kissed my forehead. "You'd better believe it! And I have a fine sharp sword to prove it." He winked at me before getting one last jab in, "Monkee Paw."

I just shook my head, said goodnight, and crawled into my bed to escape for a few hours. Chester was curled at my side and Davy was spooned behind me. At that very moment I felt that all would be right in the world again someday soon.

FIFTEEN

Contrasts

One morning, just as I was uncovering Winston's cage and letting him out to stretch his wings and find his own perch to... well... *perch* upon, the young family that had booked with us for long term arrived, a load of luggage behind them.

"Aloha! Welcome to Hale Mele," I called to them, rushing to help with some of the luggage. "You must be the Morrisons?"

"That would be us," the taller of the two men responded. Both of them appeared to be fortyish, quite tanned, and very easy on the eyes. "I'm Rick," he continued, "and this is my husband Jack." Rick had close cut sandy blond hair and gunmetal blue eyes with a splash of forest green reaching outward from his pupils.

"Hello!" Jack smiled so easily. He was a few inches shorter than Rick and had a slender elongated body with broad shoulders, like that of a swimmer. His eyes were soft, with amber hues and flecks of green.

"Hello Jack and Rick! My name is Macca."

"You own this place, right?" Rick was juggling some suitcases and keeping tabs on two young children running about and hiding from each other in the foliage.

"Yes, I most certainly do," I responded, my usual pride evident in my voice. "And who are these little cuties?"

"That's Ella and Ethan." Jack pointed with his chin and the two children stopped what they were doing and greeted me with very polite manners before going back to their game of hide and seek. "And this," he indicated the sleeping baby in his arms, "is Noah. He's only ten months old, but into everything already, and the twins are five."

"I understand you're building a house nearby and it's not ready yet?"

"Yes. There have been some delays with permits and supplies." Rick grimaced, but it seemed half-hearted. "I'm the architect though, so I only have myself to blame; we should have come over much earlier to supervise better."

"Hawaii time is much slower than on the mainland."

"I knew this, and still I didn't take heed." He shrugged and Jack smiled.

"It's okay; everything will be just fine," Jack tried to assure his husband. The looks that they exchanged were so loving and warm.

"Well, let's get you all situated so you can unload." Sam began to cart much of the luggage off to the bungalow that was assigned to the family while Rick and Jack checked in. The twins stopped at Winston's perch.

79

"What's his name?" Ella was peering cautiously at the large African grey parrot. She and her twin Ethan both had soft curls of honey gold, with eyes bright and just a few shades darker.

"That's Winston. He's very friendly and usually talks a lot. Don't you Winston?"

Rawk. I'm a pretty bird. Hi there ho there let's go team.

Well that was new. I wondered who had taught him that.

"Hi Winston." Ella gently touched his talon.

Awk awk awk. Winston imitated a laugh. *Cootchy-coo.*

"He's funny!" Ethan cozied up to his twin so he could touch Winston's foot too.

"Just remember the golden rule, kids." Jack had such a soft and encouraging tone when he talked to his children.

"Do unto others as you would have them do unto you," they responded in unison.

"We don't want to hurt him," Ethan continued.

"I love him!" Ella was the pushover in the duo, I could see. Marley chose that moment to fly in and perch next to Winston; she didn't want to miss out on the attention apparently.

"And this is Marley. She's new to us, but Winston is showing her the duties of an innkeeper-bird. We also have a big orange cat named Chester and a big German Shepherd named Susie. Sometimes they hang around, and sometimes they hide or run off to have their own kind of fun, but," I turned to Jack and Rick, "they're all very friendly and extremely gentle with kids, adults, and other animals, so you won't have to worry."

"I think it's wonderful to have pets at an inn. It adds to the charm of this place. You chose really well, honey." Jack bumped Rick with the shoulder of his arm that was holding the sleeping Noah.

"Will you be needing a crib?"

"No. We have our own since we're actually ready to move in, but thank you."

As Rick completed the brief check-in index card, I rallied Kalei and Albert to help Sam move all of the Morrisons' belongings to their bungalow. Bringing up the rear of the human luggage train, I showed the family of five to their temporary home. Between all six of us adults present, we were able to get the travel crib set up and the correct luggage into each of the two bedrooms, with the boxes divided between the kitchen and living area.

I watched Kalei chatting with the twins, making them laugh. He even tried to teach them to hula. I nearly peed my pants laughing, but it was such a wonderfully warm gesture on his part that allowed the adults to get everything quickly organized.

"We can slowly unpack what we need, and when our furniture arrives we've got a rented storage unit ready for that and for the overflow from here too." Rick seemed to be thinking aloud, and I was impressed by the sense of organization. I couldn't even organize my bedroom closet.

"Perhaps I'll go live in the storage unit," Jack joked.

"Ha! I'm not letting you out of this adventure! Not on your life!" Rick teased right back.

"Well then, we should let you get your family settled..." My words trailed off as I saw Kalei on his hands and knees on the grass just outside the sliding patio doors giving the kids pony rides. Sam and Albert were shouting encouragement to the riders.

"*Paniolo!*" Kalei kept shouting to them, teaching them the Hawaiian word for cowboy as they shrieked in glee.

Jack turned to Rick. "I love this place already."

Rick grinned and nodded, slipping an arm around his shoulders.

"That," I pointed to Kalei, "is your chef." I batted my eyelashes as if trying to balance the image of him with his paniolos with that of him at the stove. All I could manage was to shake my head and chuckle.

"Well if he's even half as good with the food as he is with kids, he's a gem."

"He most definitely is a gem, and with that, we'll leave you." I called to Kalei, Albert, and Sam and heard the kids yelling "*Paniolo! Paniolo!*" at their fathers, prompting both men to get down on their hands and knees and take over the bucking bronco job.

As I strolled by later that day, I saw Lani teaching little Ella and Ethan how to properly dance in hula style. It was so adorable that I stood and watched for a very long time with a huge grin stretching across my face.

I knew we were in for a bumpy ride when our next guests arrived. Angelo and Zeta D'Antonio were a married couple nearing middle age, but it was obvious she was in denial about the "middle-aged" part. She'd been stretched, spray-tanned, spackled, and reconstructed to within an inch of... well, Disney, I'd say. Before Angelo could state their names at the reception desk, Zeta reminded him in a rather unkind way, "Hurry. It's time for me to moisturize." Bennie and I were speechless.

Angelo was unruffled and went about the business of checking in, inquiring about the facilities, arranging for a tour for himself and his wife, and asking about supplies for their mini-kitchen.

"I'm not cooking for you; you do know that," Zeta sniffed.

"I'll cook, dear," he spoke through clenched teeth. "Besides, it's just to have the occasional appetizers on hand when we have our cocktails in the evenings."

She turned up her nose. "As it should be. If you'd booked us into the Hilton Waikoloa like I instructed you to, we wouldn't be here in these… sub-standard living conditions." She glared around at the surroundings.

Angelo seemed to be exercising extreme patience. "I told you, it's quaint. And more importantly, it's near the offices I'll be working in."

"It's a dump." She was doing a great job of channeling Bette Davis with that line.

At this remark though, I stood taller. "Excuse me, ma'am, but this is no dump. You'll be quite comfortable here."

She looked me square in the eye, her espresso-tinted spiked pixie-cut hair on her head bouncing, emphasizing each word. "It IS a dump. Have you ever BEEN to the Hilton Waikoloa? It's the Eden of resorts. You don't even need to walk to your room; there's a boat to take you down the canal to your door. Do *you* have such amenities? No. You have rickety wooden walkways, where I am certain to break a heel or two." I glanced down at her three-inch platform heels. Who travels like that?

I slammed the registration book shut. "Perhaps you can change your reservation then. I'll be happy to call the Hilton and inquire about their availability."

"No, no, no." Angelo jumped into the conversation in a nearly flustered state. He turned and looked pointedly at his wife. "Here is where we will stay, and we will have a wonderful time. Of this I am quite certain. And I apologize for my wife's indiscretions," he said, turning back to me. "She's become quite… spoiled. But I have business here in the Kapa'ua area."

"I'm so happy to welcome you then." I pasted a smile on my face and reopened the registration book.

"Hmph," was all we got from Zeta, and believe me, it was more than enough. Once we'd completed the checking in ritual, it took Bennie, Sam, and me to navigate all of their luggage to the largest bungalow, where we stowed all the bags in the extra bedroom.

"Well, that's not right," Zeta whined. "Some of those bags belong in the master bedroom." She viewed the average sized rooms. "Such as it is."

"You point to the ones you need and I'll move them, until tomorrow when you're on your own. I have to go to work to pay for your extravagances." Angelo was gritting his teeth. We were getting quite a view into their relationship, and in that moment I thanked the stars for my unmarried status. Bennie, Sam, and I left them bickering to hurry back to the main reception area.

Heads together, we alternated between giggling and shuddering at the idea of Angelo and Zeta staying with us for an entire week.

"Auntie Uppity will surely test our skills of patience and decorum. I nearly lost it when she referred to us as a dump." I shook my head.

"I took it personally myself," Bennie chuckled, "but at least it's a very nice and friendly dump, yes?" He so rarely showed his humorous side that it took me a moment before I burst out laughing.

"It is that, yes. It is that."

Later that day, as I was making my rounds and checking for maintenance issues and anything that needed cleaning, I saw Angelo and Zeta sunning by the pool. I guessed Angelo to be in his early forties, with thick salt and pepper hair lighter than his wife's. Both were olive complected, but Zeta seemed to have a head start on a tan. By the color, I suspected a tanning booth or even spray on tanning solution. It rather fit her personality. She was wearing a black bikini and had all of her gold jewelry still in place. I always wondered how people could stand to wear that heavy stuff when playing in the pool or the surf. To each his (or her) own.

Zeta had some sort of tropical drink in one hand and a *Vogue* magazine in the other. The drink looked to be one of Sam's Mai Tais, complete with tiny umbrella and plastic monkey — the latter being one of my humorous touches as a nod to our own resident ghost Monkee. Angelo had a file folder open on the chaise and a pen in his hand, reading spectacles propped near the tip of his nose. All work and no play, poor guy.

"Angelo!" I heard her sharp voice as I was walking away. "I need lotion on my back."

I increased my speed and got the heck out of there before I blew a gasket. I was embarrassed for Angelo, as she treated him like dirt. But then again, he remained married to her, so she must provide something for him. Perhaps she was just a trophy wife, a few years younger than he, and I guessed she threw successful albeit tremendously expensive dinner parties for his business associates. Counting my blessings, I rounded the corner and walked smack dab into Sam who had been eavesdropping.

"What are you doing there?" I teased him.

"They're like a car wreck; I can't stop watching."

"I know. It's better than television, but there's no popcorn."

Sam blushed and whipped his other hand out to show he had a small box of Cracker Jacks, and I had to slap my hand over my mouth to keep from bursting out laughing and letting the couple know we were snooping.

It was nearly four in the afternoon when I had a moment to sit down in my bungalow. Chester had followed me almost everywhere I went and now he was exhausted. He climbed up on my lap and began to knead my stomach, purring loudly and drooling all over my shirt. I skritched the side of his cheek and he increased the speed of his knead, causing me to want to hug the stuffing out of him as if he were a teddy bear.

Davy shimmered in seated right next to me and already laughing without sharing the joke.

"I just saw your newest guests," he gasped. "You'll have your hands full with that one!"

"Don't I know it! I've already had quite the experience with her. I don't look forward to having her around for a week. Hopefully she'll go off shopping or something. Or maybe she'll be a day guest at her beloved Hilton Waikoloa."

"Oh, is that what she wishes? The queen wishes to stay at the palace then?"

"Something like that. Anything is better than this dump, as she called it."

He stopped laughing. "How rude of her!"

I shrugged. "Everyone is entitled to their own opinion."

"True, but they don't have to be so openly offensive about those opinions. If you can't say anything nice..."

"... don't say anything at all," we spoke the last line together.

It was altogether entertaining that evening in the dining room. The Morrison family was in attendance with their very well behaved children. Noah sat happily in one of our wooden high chairs, babbling away and munching on whatever his dads would put on his plate — bread, fruit, and vegetables. He was such a happy little baby and found much enjoyment in watching his older siblings; the twins' antics would often get him giggling. Jack and Rick were very attentive to their brood, making certain that they watched their manners and kept using their inside voices. When they had booked their stay, they indicated that they were vegetarians but would occasionally have a little fish. The kids seemed quite happy with their veggies, fruits, and grains and I found myself happily watching them.

And then there were the D'Antonios. Zeta and Angelo were on the other side of the dining room, sharing a bottle of red wine while they ate their meal. It appeared that Angelo was enjoying his meal, but Zeta only picked at her food, complaining all the while that there was no caviar on the menu. I had to laugh. We were a very modest little inn but promised excellent food and drink. I was certain that unless she were at her treasured Hilton Waikoloa she would never be happy, and if by chance we had included caviar on the menu, she most likely would have found fault with it.

It was then that Davy shimmered in and stood close to me near the doorway where I'd been watching. "How is it going?"

"As well as can be expected. We can do no right in Mrs. D'Antonio's eyes, but on the flip side, we can do no wrong for the Morrison family."

"Sounds like a good balance to me."

"The weight is on the Morrison family. I've fallen in love with them and they haven't even been here a whole day."

"I must be cautious around the kids. I don't want to freak their fathers out if they see them talking to an imaginary friend like me."

I chuckled but agreed. Davy loved children and played with all those who were able to see him, which I must admit were most children he met. Such purity and innocence they had. Davy was really good with them too. He joked as a friend but also made them mind as the adult in charge at times. I assumed it came from being a parent himself. He rarely talked about his children, but I knew he had a great and deep love for them. This was one of many things I admired about him. He always warmed my heart with his own sense of love and devotion. I hoped that someday I'd meet a man as wonderful as him and have a family of my own.

The next morning I heard the D'Antonio's before I saw them. She was complaining about something again.

"I hate getting up early to drive you to your meetings," she whined.

"If you want the use of the car for the day, then you need to drive me to work. We've discussed this."

"I don't know why you can't take a cab or something. Or maybe they don't have cabs in this remote hellhole."

"It won't hurt you to wake up a little early and do this."

"It's supposed to be a vacation. People relax on vacations."

"You didn't have to come, you know."

"Oh sure. I should stay at home while you enjoy the sun and sand? I think not. Besides, you'd probably meet some hula slut and have a torrid affair if I weren't here."

I couldn't hear his muttering, but I'm sure there were some choice words. She really was a disagreeable person. Their conversation trailed off as they took the stairs to the parking lot. I breathed a sigh of relief. She was gone for a little while, hopefully even for the whole day. Peace at last.

I had my Nikes on and took off for my morning run along the cliff path, using the route I took every day. However, I would always veer a little farther away from the cliff whenever I came to the place where I'd almost lost my life more than a year ago.

On the way back, I slowed to a walk and found Jack and Rick sitting with the kids on the grassy area near the whispering bench. They had a large plaid blanket spread out and the twins sat in front of their dads, baby Noah in Rick's lap. Jack had a book in his hand and was reading to them, then turning the book to show the pictures. I was impressed at how easily he seemed to hold their attention and couldn't help but smile as I passed. I loved this little big family. Rick beckoned to me so I wandered over and squatted down so that he wouldn't have to continue shading his eyes against the bright sun.

"We wanted to ask," he spoke quietly so he wouldn't interrupt Jack's reading, "is there a story behind this wonderful whispering bench? We had a lot of fun earlier whispering messages with the kids."

His words warmed me so I smiled widely and matched his volume as I replied. "The first owner of this inn had it made for the path, but she passed on before she could see it installed," I whispered. "Her husband dedicated it to her memory, and then I added additional dedicational plaques. It's become sort of a memorial to special people who have passed on."

"Oh, that's lovely! But tell me," he grinned, "who is David Thomas Jones?"

I felt my face heat a moment. "Oh, that's Davy Jones of the Monkees. He was a very important person in my mother's life."

He nodded and smiled. "That's beautiful; thank you."

"You're very welcome." I rose and watched the kids for a moment as they listened to the story Jack was reading, and then I turned and returned to my chores.

That afternoon, Rick and Jack sat on their patio, the sliding door open and the curtains billowing out with the occasional breeze.

"Hello Macca! Care to join us for some iced tea? The children are napping so we're getting the rare breather." Jack grinned, already pouring a glass of Kalei's wonderful tea for me, the level in the pitcher going down significantly.

"We have fallen in love with Kalei's iced tea!" Rick pushed his empty glass toward Jack.

"It's better than booze!" Jack laughed, filling his husband's glass after he handed a glass to me.

I chose one of the outdoor chairs and lowered myself into it. "How are you enjoying your stay so far?"

"I'm going to love it here. This area is beautiful, and your inn is so comfortable; thank you," Jack replied. "How long have you had this place?"

"Less than two years actually. Before that my uncle owned it. He left it to me when he passed away." I sipped the liquid gold. "I apologize for the mess in the parking lot. I'm always upgrading the place, and expanding the parking area has been at the top of my list of priorities for a while now."

"Aww, we don't mind a little dust now and then. We have plenty of our own when we visit our home-to-be."

"How is it looking?"

"It's looking like a big hole in the ground," Rick laughed.

"Oh wow, that far behind? Wasn't it supposed to be finished in a couple of weeks?"

"Yes, but we're looking at a couple of months, easy. Maybe even more. But that's okay. We're together, we're here in the sunshine, we have a wonderful place to stay, and the time will pass quickly. We'll be moved in before you know it."

"You should come with us one of these times to see the location," Jack enthused. "Rick found the lot and we bought it more than a year ago.

It's just the most spectacular spot with a view that will knock your socks off."

"I would love to see it!"

There was a sound of snuffling from the baby monitor perched on the coffee table, and they both froze for a moment, listening. When the snuffling stopped, they visibly relaxed again. "Whew. Too soon to wake up. Close call." Rick chuckled and pretended to wipe his brow. "If they don't get their proper naps, there will be three cranky pants running around."

"And cranky dads too," Jack added.

"I remember loving the sea when I was a child," I reminisced. "And my mother always said I slept quite well when there was a sea breeze."

"Our kids are the same," Jack joined in. "This is going to be such a fantastic place to raise them." He turned to Rick. "We made the best decision — ever."

Rick lovingly touched Jack's cheek and smiled. "We finally get our happily ever after."

"I'm so happy for you all." I felt like I knew them already. "And it will be such a treat to have you as neighbors!"

"Yes, and our lot is very close to the inn. You can visit us and come for dinner occasionally too."

"I would love that very much. Thank you."

At that moment, Chester strolled over and rubbed first Jack's legs then Rick's, and each man in turn bent to give the little guy proper pets and skritches. "Hi Chester, old boy," Rick purred to the feline. "How are you this fine day?"

Mraow.

"Is that so?" He gave Chester a gentle little chuck under the chin.

"We met Susie earlier this morning." Jack turned to me. "Such a nice boy! The kids have fallen in love with all the animals here, and may I repeat, it's a wonderful treat that you have them here on site. What a fantastic way to make a guest feel at home, you know?"

"It used to only be Winston, but Chester came with me from Los Angeles. Susie showed up just recently. He wasn't microchipped." Then I told a little white lie, not wanting to divulge his ghostly secret. "We couldn't find an owner so we just invited him to stay. Sometimes he goes off on his own though. He's actually more aloof than a cat sometimes. And Marley just showed up one day recently. We're still trying to determine if she's got people looking for her."

"You're an animal lover; we can tell." Rick nodded, accepting my odd explanation. "I think that's one of the things we really like about you. You're good people. You wouldn't hurt a fly."

Ha, I thought. *Tell that to Detective Green and the ADA and the judge, not to mention my occasional spider execution.* I simply smiled. "Thank you."

"But we have to ask... why is Susie a he?"

I had to laugh... to buy myself time to come up with an answer because I had yet to ask Davy for an explanation. I had to think quickly to come up with a plausible white lie. "Um... because we thought he was a she when he first got here?"

"Oh!" Jack slapped his leg. "We had that happen with a kitten for a long time. Named him Josephine... Had to shorten it to Joe."

Whew, dodged that bullet. I laughed along with them.

"We're taking the kids to the beach tomorrow," Rick jumped in when our laughter had quieted. "You're welcome to tag along, that is if you don't have work to do."

"And also," Jack added, "we'd love to have you join us."

"I might be able to get away for just a little bit, at least to splash in a wave or two. Are you just going down to the beach here?"

"Yes. No sense piling them all in the car when we've got a perfectly lovely bit of sand and surf right here," Jack confirmed, filling our tea glasses yet again. Kalei's magical potion sure went down easily.

"It's a nice little beach with some gentle waves. Not enough to surf really, except at dusk and dawn, but it's still a lot of fun."

"Well good, because I seem to have left my surfboard in my other pants," Rick teased and Jack playfully slapped his forearm.

I enjoyed watching them, envious of their devotion to each other and their children. We spent the next few minutes relaxing in the breeze until baby Noah began to snuffle again. This time it was a real wake-up call followed by a long wail. I excused myself, begging off for work, and they went inside to their little family.

The next morning I finished up my work around the inn and then later caught up with the Morrison family on the beach. When I got to the bottom of the steps and set foot on the sand, I could see Susie romping with Ella and Ethan in the gently lapping surf, while Rick held Noah by the hands so he could splash his tiny feet in the Pacific. Jack stood watching them all, a giant grin on his face when I stepped up beside him. "Good morning!"

"Oh, good morning Macca! It's so nice that you could join us. This is just beautiful." He swept his arm to encompass the water, the beach, and the deep foliage border.

"It really is. I wish I could take credit for it, but it's just a nice little semi-private spot that nature left for us. I come down here as often as possible, just to recharge."

"It must be a lot of work running an inn."

"It can be, but we've got a fabulous staff."

"A very warm and friendly staff, I might add. And the food is fantastic, just as you promised!"

"Oh, I'm so happy you're enjoying Kalei and Lani's creations. I think the lunch buffet will be perfectly suited for your family. We always have lots of fresh and local produce. And of course, Saturday night is the luau."

"The kids are excited about the dancing!"

"Lani will even teach them a little more."

He chuckled then and looked out to his family splashing in the foam. "Rick bought them all little grass skirts."

I clapped my hands in delight. "Oh, I look forward to seeing them!"

Rick joined us then, depositing baby Noah on the blanket and drying him off gently with a fluffy Sponge Bob towel. I felt Davy shimmer in behind me.

"I was on that show once, y'know," he whispered in my ear. I grinned and swatted at an imaginary fly, while swatting at him to shush him. I heard an "oof" as I connected with his midsection. My grin widened.

The twins turned to look at their dads and Davy quickly faded away in his usual shimmer. "Dad, look!" Ethan and Ella ran toward us with their hands outspread.

"Beautiful shells!" Jack knelt to inspect them and Rick leaned over his shoulder. "Should we take photos for the new house?"

"We should! But wait until we find more, okay?" Ella grabbed her brother's hand and together they ran back to the shoreline to continue their search.

"Instead of removing shells and rocks from the beaches, we told the kids we'd take photos and make a nice collage for the new house," Jack explained. "We want to raise them to be very respectful of the ecosystem wherever they are in the world."

"Oh, that's a lovely tradition to start." I was touched. "And the goddess Pele will be relieved, I'm certain." We chuckled together, our eyes on the kids. Noah was drifting off to sleep and Rick idly covered him with a lightweight cotton blanket. "See?" I reminded them. "The sea air."

"The best sleeping potion ever." Jack winked.

I wandered down to the water and helped the kids search for shells while splashing around in the surf just a little. As the sun rose higher in the sky, Jack and Rick began to pack their things up and called Ethan and Ella to come along. They laid out all the shells and rocks the kids had collected and took various photos. When all was done, Rick and the twins delivered the shells back to the water's edge. When it was time to leave, Jack led the way while Rick and I brought up the rear.

"Sunscreen is good for an hour or two, but when the sun gets too hot, we just call for indoor time… which eventually leads to naps."

I nodded, understanding the need for moderation in all things. "Too much sun can make you ill." I remembered a few guests getting overly cooked in the sometimes blinding reflection off the water.

We parted at the top of the stairs and I thanked them for their company. We waved and I washed the sand off of me at the outdoor shower that was by my bungalow. I saw the small family doing the same at the grouping of showers near the common area. I admired Jack and Rick's parenting styles; they were calm, encouraging, and loving, and reminded me of my own parents in many ways.

SIXTEEN

Adventure

I was wandering around my bungalow doing a little bit of straightening one morning. Chester sprawled on the coffee table, systematically knocking off one thing after another. *Splat.* A magazine landed on the floor. *Thunk.* There went a paperback novel. *Swoosh.* Three pens hit the rug.

"I would think that little game of yours would get old after a couple of times," I admonished him.

Plop. My empty tea mug landed on the magazine already residing on the floor.

But we're superior to you humans, he began, his eye on the little wooden hula girl that had been Uncle Wally's. *How would you know what games get old?* The hula girl rattled and rolled on the table, teetering on the edge, until an orange paw gave it the final smackdown.

"How can you be superior? You have no thumbs."

The only issue is that your kind designed a world that requires thumbs. He yawned, hanging his head over the side of the table to admire his handiwork. His tail thwapped a couple of times as he glanced back at the only thing left on the table: a leaded glass dolphin.

"Oh no you don't!" I swooped in and rescued the little replica of one of my favorite creatures in the sea.

Given another hundred years without human intervention, we would be filling your bowls twice a day.

I froze and glowered at the little feline before picking him up and tossing him gently onto the deck. "Go count birds."

Count? He mocked me with a little snicker. *Perhaps I shall eat one instead.*

"Fat chance. Looked in the mirror lately? Your hunting days have been replaced by lazy eating of scraps."

Are you calling me fat?

"No. I said fat *chance.*" I eyed him carefully as I stood in the doorway blocking his re-entry. "But now that you mention it, you could use a few trips up and down the beach steps." And with that I snapped the sliding glass door shut and cleaned up the mess he'd made around the coffee table.

With my chores done, it was indeed a day for rejoicing. The parking lot expansion work was finishing up, and tomorrow we'd have room for plenty of guest cars in the old main lot, with an extension that would provide room for the few employee cars we needed. We kept the charging station in the main lot but also added another charging station to the employee annex, not only for me but also for any future employees who switched to a clean energy source as I had.

Bouncing up the stairs to the parking lot, I was whistling a happy tune. My little R2 was happily waiting in his assigned parking spot, the charger having been lifted from his tiny hip last night as I'd returned from my run. Sometimes I ran in the morning, sometimes I ran at night, and many days I barely had time to run at all except to perform the chores for the inn. Last night had been one of the better times though. R2 purred as I stuck the key into his little starter. "Good morning, R2!"

"You do know that you're destined to meet with them men in white coats, right?" I looked up and Davy shimmered into the passenger seat. Suddenly my happiness was replaced with something akin to grumpiness, but I didn't give it much thought.

"Yep. And you'll be one of the main reasons they take me away." I put the car in reverse, looking over my shoulder to back out. "I hope that makes you very proud."

"Very proud indeed. I always wanted to be the undoing of a fellow human being," he deadpanned.

I braked suddenly. "You missed that boat, bud... no longer a human being... just a human was."

He clutched his chest. "Ohhhh, you got me. Right where it counts."

I took a moment to be sure he was just being Davy before I continued to back out of my parking space.

"Where we goin'?" He had recovered from his chest clutching moment.

"I'm going to meet with Alex and Rob."

"Rob? Like... attorney Rob?"

"That's the one, yes." I eased out onto the road and headed toward Hilo.

"Where *specifically* are we going?"

"I'm meeting Rob and his family just north of Hilo. Where are *you* going?" I put an accent on "you" just because I wasn't ready to be a free shuttle today.

"Rob? As in Mr. Kula Rob?" He annoyingly repeated his previous question.

"Mr. Robert Parker Kula has invited me to join in a mini-adventure today." I stopped at a traffic signal and turned to look at him. "I don't recall seeing your name on such an invitation though." I had to admit that I grinned. What can I say? My evil twin-that-never-was had taken control of my mouth.

"But that's the beauty of being me. In life, I could get in anywhere with the name Davy Jones or with a quick rendition of 'Daydream Believer.' And now? I can just get in." His face relaxed to show no emotion at all, which was un-Davy-like. "Anywhere. Anywhere I want," he repeated.

He turned to look out the front windshield as he absent-mindedly buckled his seatbelt. Why buckle a seatbelt? I shook the cobwebs and unanswered questions from my mind and pulled into the light traffic when the signal turned green, and I headed *makai* toward the ocean and Hilo, but not quite into the city.

"Could you give me just a tiny clue? Or shall I just invade your thoughts?" I could tell he thought he was being playful; I just felt he was being irritating and invasive.

"Do as you please." I turned the wheel slightly to avoid a bicyclist and came to yet another red light. Was I going to hit all of them today?

The small car was being jostled as Davy attempted to settle into his seat. I knew his curiosity would reach impact level at any moment. And then I felt it; he turned and looked at me, his eyes boring into my temple, his hands doing a little woo-woo gesture.

"Wait. Is that what you do? That's not even smoke and mirrors!"

"Can you do better?" He pouted. I mean really, pouting?

"Yeah. I can ignore you." I turned to him while the light was still red, because I knew it was a fate worse than death for him to be ignored.

"Green light," he calmly pointed out, and in the two seconds it took for me to react, five cars began honking at me from behind.

"You are annoying in so many ways." I flipped my turn indicator and edged the steering wheel around to the right, turning a corner.

"Until you want something from me..."

I glanced at him from the corner of my eye and saw that he wasn't joining in our usual repartee. I quickly turned my attention back to the road ahead and felt... what? Shame.

And it was just in that moment that I realized how much I used him, how much I took him for granted, and how little I told him — no, showed him — how much I appreciated him and his special spectral self. Some women wore Manolo Blahnik shoes or had a Jackson Pollock on their wall... while I had a Davy Jones original at my side. I crossed over lanes, horns honking all around me and fists waving at me, and parked at the side of the road. Then I turned to him. "Davy. David." I waited to get his eye contact, which didn't take long as he was a sucker for a camera or an eye. "I don't know why I get crabby with you lately, but I realize how wrong it is of me. So... why do you bring out my crabbiness? It's something I need to find within myself. I'm working on it."

And then he smiled, which irritated me more, and I couldn't even figure out why that was. I huffed and grumbled as I turned my attention to merging back into traffic.

Mercifully, Davy remained silent for a while so I could concentrate on my driving directions. I hadn't ever been to Honoka'a and I was following emailed directions on my phone. When I pulled into a short driveway, I thought I'd taken a wrong turn somewhere. It was such an unassuming home, sitting split level on a hill. I double checked the house number and it appeared to be correct. As I set the parking brake, Rob and Alex appeared on the deck above waving to me, and when I stepped out of the car I could see what made this very average looking house so very much above average in its location. The view of the ocean was breathtaking and incredibly close, and I could hear the waves breaking against the rocky coast below.

"Aloha," Rob called to me and I grinned.

"Aloha! This is spectacular!" I made my way up the stairs to the two men who greeted me with a kiss on each cheek, which I gratefully returned.

"Thank you. We like it. Come, meet our wives, please!" We entered through a bank of open floor-to-ceiling windows that had been slid to either side, creating a seemingly wall-less expansive view. "Momi..." Rob stretched his arm out to a petite woman with ebony hair cut softly about her rounded face. She was wiping her hands on an apron tied around her waist. "Macca, this is my lovely wife Momi." We shook hands and exchanged the usual pleasantries. I was mesmerized by her soft doe-like eyes. She wore little make up, and I guessed her age to be forty or so. Her skin was bronzed, but it was a natural tone born of island life and outdoor living.

"I am so very pleased to welcome you to our home." Her voice was musical.

"Thank you, Momi. I am so happy to be here. Thank you for inviting me!" I saw Davy shimmer in and move about the lovely home, admiring the view and the furnishings. He kept shooting me a "thumbs up" sign. Apparently he approved of the setting, and I stifled a giggle.

"And this," Rob turned toward a woman standing with Alex, "is Alex's wife Kate." Her hair was a platinum pageboy style, and she was nearly as tall as Alex and comfortably curvy in all the right places.

"Very happy to meet you after all this time." I extended my hand and we shook.

"I've heard so much about you, Macca." She smiled widely.

"Oh, I'm sure you have." I chuckled, and they joined in easy laughter. "That crazy woman from Los Angeles, right?"

"Oh, nothing like that, I can assure you."

"Would you like some tea or coffee before we head out?"

"Oh, no thank you; I'm just fine."

"Are you ready for an adventure?"

"I certainly am! This is the first touristy thing I've done since I moved here!"

"Well, stick with us and you won't look like a tourist. Momi used to live down in the valley. She's a true local!" As he chatted, he slid the wall of windows closed, and Momi shared a can of mosquito repellent around the group, each of us taking turns spraying and helping each other to get all the important spots. They had given me instructions on how to dress for the day, and I saw we all wore similar outfits: long sleeved cotton shirts, long cotton pants, and good hiking shoes.

Rob led the way to a carport. A medium sized four-wheel drive vehicle sat waiting for us. Kate and Momi slid into the back seat, giving me a window seat next to them.

"We don't want you to miss the views," Momi spoke excitedly. "We just love sharing these trips with friends!"

The two men climbed into the front and we all buckled up. Davy appeared in the back jump seat behind us and whispered in my ear. "I've never been to Waipi'o Valley. This is exciting!" He was decked out in a yellow-gold Hawaiian print shirt and a dried-out grass skirt over his jeans. I vaguely remembered this from one of *The Monkees* episodes where they were marooned on an island, and I had to cover my mouth to conceal a grin.

The drive to the edge of Waipi'o Valley was a short trip, and Rob pulled over at the entrance to the one road that would take us down to the floor of the lush valley. He put the vehicle into four-wheel drive and eased down the single lane road.

"This is about a 25% grade, but there are some areas where it's steeper than that." Rob's voice bounced with the bumpiness of the steep road while I held on for dear life. "In bad weather, it's just best to stay away," he continued as if this drive was his daily commute, "but we've had a nice stretch of sunshine, so this should be a piece of cake."

"It's 900 feet down to the bottom," Alex added. Rob pulled to the side and Alex continued, "Vehicles driving up, like the one coming now, have the right of way, as do hikers."

"Hikers?" My eyes grew wide at that thought.

"Yeah, it's only about a half hour hike down. Coming up? Well, I'd never try it." Rob laughed. "It's one mile down and three miles up!"

"Oh, we used to do it all the time in my youth," Momi teased him. "You're just out of shape."

"It's all that good food you cook for me, Momi," he teased right back, and she gave him a loving pat on his shoulder.

When the vehicle coming uphill passed us, I closed my eyes, waiting for that awful sound of metal on metal, but we were in the clear. I hadn't realized how long I'd been holding my breath and let it out in a relieved and very long sigh.

"He's a pro at this so don't you worry." Kate patted my knee and I shot her a grateful smile and nodded.

I marveled at the view out my window though. It was lush and green as far as the eye could see. There were waterfalls and rivers, and I felt a happy tingling in my stomach knowing how lucky I was to be able to enjoy such a trip.

While the trip down seemed quite long, it was really only a few minutes. Much of the flattened out road at the bottom was covered by trees, creating a tunnel effect. I found myself alternating between catching my breath and softly exclaiming "whoa" at the magnificent beauty of it all.

"This area was quite populated in the early 1900s. There were restaurants, shops, homes, and farms." Rob seemed to love acting as tour guide, and I listened to him with wide eyes. "But the tsunami of 1946 saw people fleeing. They even left behind their livestock, and you'll see small herds of wild horses wandering as a result. They're a sturdy horse, better equipped for this terrain than many other breeds."

"My family settled here in the valley in the late 1800s and grew kalo, or taro, down here," Momi added. "After the tsunami forced them to evacuate, they returned and tried to make a go of it again, but it was just too difficult for them. As a child, my mother used to hike up and down that road to get supplies for the families who were trying to restart down here. One of my uncles and his family did stay behind. They're still growing kalo too, and also guava. Many of the other residents are completely off grid; there's no power or running water, just spring water. My uncle was able to capture and gentle a few of the wild horses though, and they have chickens too. We'll meet all of them a little later."

"Oh! Horses!" Davy exclaimed from behind me. I smiled at both him and Momi.

"Tell me more, please," I begged. "The history fascinates me!"

"Kalei says Macca is fast becoming wahine," Alex chimed in, turning to address the two women beside me. I felt my cheeks burn.

Momi smiled, her voice full of enthusiasm. "Waipi'o Valley is full of history! This is the birthplace of the great King Kamehameha, and there are still many *heiaus*, or temples here, although they're just in ruins now. Too many floods." She shook her head, a fleeting shadow of sorrow washing over her like a paint brush of soft feathers. It was gone in an instant though, and if I hadn't been watching her so intently, I would certainly have missed it.

"Momi is very Hawaiian," Rob spoke proudly. "I think that if she had her way, they'd still be living and practicing the old ways."

"There was nothing wrong with the old ways."

"I know, dear." He smiled at her in the rear view mirror, and she lovingly put her hand on his shoulder. Rob slowed the vehicle to a crawl as he prepared to ford a stream. He pointed out his window to the back of the canyon, and I could see several waterfalls. "Off in the distance there is Hi'ilawe waterfall; it's about 1,450 feet high."

"Can people hike to it?"

"You can, but it's rough terrain and a full day. Many people do it though. There's also a hiking trail from above, but I'd never attempt it."

"That's because you've gone soft," Alex chided his friend and they chuckled together, sharing some private joke that I really didn't feel I was missing out on. Hiking that high? That long? I don't think so.

As we emerged from the stream, the road ahead of us was blocked. "Rush hour traffic," Rob joked as a group of about seven wild horses came into view.

"They're so docile!" Even I could hear the childlike surprise in my voice so I dialed it down a notch. "But they're wild you say?"

"Well, wild by Waipi'o Valley standards." Momi chuckled and opened the door. "If you're careful and know your way, you can approach some of them quietly, but they recommend against it. Still, you're with me." She winked, opened a bag of cut carrots, and we all joined her. She eased ahead slowly, moving catlike while we remained behind. I could hear her murmuring as she got close to one of the horses, a mare whose ears were pricked forward, her stance relaxed. Momi held her hand out, offering a few of the carrot pieces. The horse was shorter than what I'd been used to seeing, and stockier as well.

"See how sturdy their feet are!" Davy whispered to me. "Perfectly adapted to this valley floor." I gave him a small nod and smile.

The mare nuzzled Momi's hand, seeking out the carrot pieces. I could hear the crunching from several feet away. Momi motioned to us to join her, and we moved slowly forward. Davy broke off and approached another horse whose ears perked, sensing his presence. When Davy placed his hands on her shoulder and back and began to massage her, the horse visibly relaxed and rested one hind leg, enjoying her little ghostly spa experience. He gave her several kisses on her nose and I saw her lips wiggle at his cheek. I pressed my lips together to stifle a grin and relaxed my body and mind to approach the horse Momi was feeding. Such a gentle creature, she allowed us to pet her. I was amazed at her glistening coat that probably hadn't seen a brush in an extraordinarily long time and yet still seemed perfectly groomed. Momi handed me a few carrots. I loved the feeling of the horse's lips nibbling at the morsels in the palm of my hand. The mare's ears were relaxed and forward, and her eyes were half closed, enjoying the treat.

"This is heavenly." My cheeks were tight from grinning so much. With my free hand I gave the mare a few long strokes on her velvety neck, and she rewarded me with a contented little sigh. She began to move away from us, however, as the rest of her little herd made their way off the road and into the lush foliage. "Bye!" I called to her one last time. I saw Davy suddenly shimmer away and reappear on the bare back of the horse he'd been "speaking" with. Off they rode with the rest of the small herd.

"I'll catch up with you," Davy called over his shoulder as they disappeared into the foliage. I put my hand to my mouth to cover the grin that finally forced its way onto my face.

And although I'd felt as if I'd already met the most interesting residents of Waipi'o Valley, having come upon the wild horses, we all climbed back into the vehicle to proceed to Momi's uncle's homestead where I would be contradicted.

"Uncle Koa is quite the character," Rob chuckled as we bounced slowly down the unpaved road. "Let's just hope he has some clothes on this time."

"He promised!" Momi shook her head. "We brought Rob's parents down here last year, and there was my uncle, tending his taro plants, completely naked. I was so ashamed!" She covered her face with her hand for a brief moment, but I could see her grinning.

"I thought it was funny." Rob was still laughing, and as infectious as laughter can be, we were soon all joining in.

Rob turned the vehicle to the left, and before us was an expansive area of flatland with a small home situated at the far corner. The front "yard" was nothing but a patchwork quilt of taro fields, the water catching the sunlight and glistening with hues of blue and green. Behind the dwelling was a scattered grove of guava trees, looking as if they had not so much been planned or planted, but rather fell from the sky and grew where they landed.

The home was far from grand; it was a simple wooden structure with fresh green paint on the siding and a tin roof that held solar panels. To the side of it was a small barn attached to two very large rickety-fenced enclosures, one of which contained several horses grazing. We pulled to a stop near the front porch and climbed out. A fully clothed man and woman emerged from the house, all big smiles and waving hands. Momi ran to them and gave them a kiss on both cheeks. I could hear chatter but was unable to determine the words, which had the musical lilt of the native Hawaiian language. I was able to pick out a few words like 'aina and 'ohana, which could very roughly be translated to homeland and family.

Momi pulled them both toward us and made introductions. "Macca, I am so happy to have you meet my Uncle Koa and Auntie Mirasol."

I extended my hand to shake theirs, but instead I was pulled into a big hug, first by Uncle Koa and then by Auntie Mirasol. "Welcome, welcome," Uncle Koa exclaimed, showing one front tooth missing. He turned then to Momi. "The aloha is good in this girl!"

"That just means you're full of the spirit of love, happiness, and good intentions," Momi assured me, placing her hand warmly on my back. "Uncle Koa is very good at determining the character of people."

"Oh." I nodded and smiled to him. "Thank you so much. Mahalo"

"Come in, come in." Auntie Mirasol spoke with an accent I couldn't quite place. I guessed both of them to be in their sixties. She was a small and rounded woman, with nearly smooth tawny-beige skin and the dark eyes of the islands. Her thick chocolate-brown hair had only a few streaks of gray, and she wore it in two braids that hung down her back. Uncle Koa was only an inch or two taller but was more wiry, with a slightly grizzled beard on his wizened face; the color of his hair and his skin were differing shades of a warm sepia tone you'd find on a vintage photograph. His hair was perhaps two shades darker and liberally striped with gray strands.

We all followed our hosts inside their small home. I was surprised to see two rocking chairs in the living room and little else. We were directed instead to gather around the dining table that held eight chairs, plenty of room for our group. Auntie Mirasol trotted to the kitchen and brought back a wooden tray with seven glasses and a pitcher of juice.

"Today I made fresh pineapple guava juice. I got pineapple from our neighbor up the road, *mauka*," indicating they were toward the mountain. I hadn't realized how thirsty I was until I took a sip. The peach-colored liquid was sweet from the guava and tart from the pineapple.

"Ohh," I sighed as I finally set the glass down. "That is a heavenly treat!"

She beamed. "Glad you like! I pour you more!" I didn't resist, and she poured it nearly to the top. Davy appeared beside me and slurped the level down in order to taste it while I distracted my hosts.

"Do you make that often? It's fantastic," I blurted quickly as I watched him lick his lips.

"That's bloody good," he exclaimed for my ears only, or so I hoped. I glanced around and none of them seemed any the wiser about his presence.

"She doesn't make it often enough for me." Uncle Koa grinned as he drained his second glass.

"So, you're completely off the grid here in the valley? Is that correct?" I inquired, sipping my juice.

"Yes, but I have slowly upgraded us here." Uncle Koa puffed up his chest with pride. "We have an underground water catchment that allows us to have an indoor toilet, a sink, and a bath. And maybe you saw the solar panels?"

"Yes, I did! We've just added solar panels at the inn. I'm quite pleased!"

"Very good idea," he nodded emphatically. "We also have a septic system. That was a lot of work to dig out the trenches!"

"No details, please dear." Auntie Mirasol patted his arm.

"Do the other homes here in the valley have such modern amenities as you do?"

"Some do," Uncle Koa answered as he drained his glass. "We all help each other with the work. But not everyone has the money for the supplies."

"We're very lucky," Auntie Mirasol added, squeezing her husband's hand and then pouring more juice in his glass.

As we finished our cool drinks, conversation turned to the animals in their care. "We have four horses," Uncle Koa began, "and Mirasol has her chickens, and we have some cats that are good for keeping the vermin in check too. Would you like to meet them all?"

There was a chorus of agreement so Uncle Koa took us on a tour of the outside, leading us through the back door in the kitchen. The chicken coop was just down the steps; it was a fenced in area with a nice shelter. There were about six beautiful hens pecking about and a lovely rooster too. "Perfect for Mirasol to pick her eggs up in the morning," he grinned.

He pointed out the grove of guava trees as he led us to the horse enclosure. We all leaned on the fence as he called to them. "King here is the boss man. And Lulu, Leilani, and Grace are his harem."

"Grace?" I chuckled.

"Mirasol is a Grace Kelly fan." He winked and I turned to look at the horses. They were all a lovely chestnut color with dark manes and tails.

"Hello Grace." I grinned at the one he'd indicated with that name. I could see Davy already having a chat with King.

"She's a good old gal," Uncle Koa continued. "They're all good. Great companions and hard workers."

"And so gentle," Rob added. He'd already made friends with Lulu, and she was letting him pet her.

"What work do they do?" I asked because I'm such a newbie.

He grinned. "They plow my small patches and fields and they haul material between homesteads here in the valley."

A small calico cat appeared from the barn and weaved in and out of Uncle Koa's legs. He idly stooped to give her a pet, and she let out a tiny mew of gratitude. Apparently this awakened others, for suddenly there were five cats vying for his attention. They paraded around us, each giving tiny mews of demand for attention. There was a gorgeous big black tom cat, nearly twice the size of the calico. He was just as needy as the rest of them, and we all regressed to childhood behavior and scrambled in the dirt to give them attention and talk with them.

"I see each of us is a sucker for a good cat, yeah?" Alex was laughing as two more cats emerged and the party was set in motion.

"There's nothing better for the heart than a good companionable critter." Uncle Koa grinned as he stooped in the dirt right alongside all of us. I noticed Davy simultaneously having a chat with a white and brown cat and the horse King.

"Have you named them all?"

"Well, we just call them by their coloring. There's Blackie, Multi, Pinto, Whitey, Blue Eyes, and then there's Twink." He pointed to a tabby snoozing in the grass several feet away, more aloof than the others. "She was our first and these are all from her one and only litter before we got smart and had her fixed. A kindly vet offered discounts on spaying and neutering. Had Blackie fixed too, so far. Can only afford the money for one at a time, you know?"

I loved this man. "Are there many cats here in the valley?"

"Some might think too many. Most folks can't get 'em fixed. That's why I promised Mirasol I'd get all ours taken care of, if it takes till my dyin' days." He grinned, and his love for his wife and his animals was so evident, so obvious in his eyes.

I made a mental note to discuss this with Dr. Josh.

All around us the chickens clucked, the rooster crowed, cats purred, horses nickered, and the sound of the wind in the trees and against the valley walls was enough to lull me into that state where all you'd like to do is sit beneath a tree and think about how wonderful the world can be if you only let it in. Also, a nap sounded great, but I knew that wasn't in the plans for now.

Reluctantly leaving Uncle Koa and Auntie Mirasol behind, we climbed back into the four-wheel drive and stayed off the main road, heading further *makai*, to the sea. We passed a sizeable pond.

"What is that?" I pointed to the body of water, still hungry for knowledge of this magical place.

"That is loko pu'uone, a fishpond fed by streams and springs. It's separated from the ocean by a sand dune," Momi the patient but happy historian responded.

"Are there really fish there?"

"Yes, and there are fishermen and women to tend to them. They trade the fish with the other residents for crops. Makes a fairly balanced diet, believe it or not. It's not necessarily the type of fish you'd find in a restaurant. The water can be quite brackish at times, but the people of the valley are used to it."

"Seems logical to me, I guess. Have you ever tasted it?"

"Oh yes, but it's not something I'd go out of my way to eat regularly."

"Momi has become spoiled by life outside the valley," Rob teased.

"Yes, and I blame you," she teased right back. "Now I can never go back to live in the valley." She shot me a conspiratorial wink. I loved these people too.

We trundled farther down and came to a slight bend in the off-road path. Curving around, our senses were assaulted by the sudden rush of sea air, the sound of waves, and an incredible sight before me: a black sand beach. My first ever!

"Ohhh myyy." The words escaped my lips in a hushed whisper filled with awe. There were only a few other people on the beach, and far enough away that it felt so incredibly private.

"You see now why the people here never wish to leave, yes?" Momi stared out to sea, a wondrously soft look of adoration in her eyes.

"I'm not sure I'd leave either," I confessed, despite the fact that the idea of living so isolated was a little off putting. "For this beauty I think I could learn to adjust to that life."

I felt her cool hand on my forearm and ours eyes met. "You do have a wonderful aloha spirit, dear." She spoke so kindly, the smile on her face extending all the way to her eyes.

Chalking it up to the magnificent assault on my senses, I felt tears build and quickly brushed them away. She patted my arm. "It's okay," she continued. "You are so moved by the beauty. It's what makes you a special wahine."

I was touched by her words and tone, beginning to feel accepted in my recently adopted homeland. "I could definitely never leave the island," I whispered, trying to find words around the lump in my throat, "and if I ever stayed here in Waipi'o Valley, I suspect I'd feel the same."

"I was a very lucky girl to have access to this valley. I still am, and now even luckier because I have Rob too."

"You are, and it's rare to find someone who understands how lucky they are. I see that so much more here on the island than I did in Los Angeles."

She wrinkled her nose and Kate chuckled. "Momi isn't fond of the mainland, especially Los Angeles."

"We had to be in L.A. for two weeks once." Rob smiled at his wife as he spoke. "Momi flew home early."

"Too much hustle, bustle, and grumpiness. And the air?" She pinched her nose. "Peee-yew!"

At this I had to laugh, for I agreed. "I grew up near the beach, but it's nothing, absolutely nothing, like life here on the island."

"Good girl." She patted my arm again. "You understand."

Rob stopped the vehicle in a sort of unofficial parking area where rocks had been smoothed. "Ahhh, this is my favorite place," he added, and I could see Alex nodding in agreement.

"Do you all come here often?"

"We try to come at least once a month, weather permitting. In the bad rains, much of the road is under water. It's not worth risking a breakdown."

We climbed out and Rob rummaged in the back of the vehicle. I saw Davy shimmer away from his little perch there. "Momi packed us a lovely picnic, you know." He pulled out an enormous blue cooler, and along with Alex toted it down to an area on the beach that was quite flat.

Momi and Kate pulled out some blankets and towels and at the last moment grabbed the can of mosquito repellent, waving it at me. "Reinforcements."

I nodded, for I could see the swarms of mosquitoes at times when the breeze lulled. The men chose a site where the Wailoa Stream emptied into the sea. With the blankets laid out and the cooler perched beside, we plopped ourselves down and removed our shoes. Momi began to roll up her pants legs, prompting Kate and me to do the same, and then she bounded down to the surf, waving at us to join her. Without hesitation we left the men on the picnic blankets and did just that, splashing in the small tide that ebbed and flowed upon the beach. "The current, the waves, and the rocky bottom are hazardous. Only the best of swimmers and surfers and the least informed tourists brave it. Many lives have been affected over the years."

"Good to know." I shivered not only from the cool temperature of the Pacific but also from the idea that the seemingly idyllic setting could be deadly. I saw Momi suddenly look to her right and smile widely, pointing. I followed her hand to see the most magnificent waterfall cascading off the southern valley wall and into the sea, and beyond it, yet another. I gasped, "What is that called?"

"Kaluahine Waterfalls." She grinned. "They don't always have water in them. I think the gods turned them on to honor your visit." Again, that sweet wink of hers. On impulse I reached over and hugged the small woman with the enormous heart. She nearly squeezed the air out of me, her return hug was so strong. I think I even squeaked. Just a little.

Momi reached out one arm and drew Kate into a group hug. Despite my average height, I towered over them both. We must have made quite the picture, and to prove it, Rob yelled for our attention and took a photo of us standing in the light foam of the surf.

"Did you get my good side?" Momi teased to him.

"Every side of you is your good side."

She turned to Kate and me. "He's such a good man. And a good liar too."

"That's what makes a successful marriage," Kate laughed.

"It does!" Momi turned to me. "Is there a special man in your life, Macca?"

"Not really." I saw Davy snap his head up from where he too was playing in the surf, suddenly dressed in red swimming trunks. My eyes widened; he really had a wonderful, compact, and powerful physique. I tried to shoot him a wink and he smiled. Was that affection I saw on his face? How does one even consider a relationship with a ghost? I shook my head to pull myself out of my reverie.

"Alex says Dr. Josh used to be a little sweet on you," Kate teased.

I sighed. I knew this to be just a little true, but I hadn't given him the opportunity to cultivate a relationship. I claimed that the inn took all my attention and all my time, but really, I had cold feet, and I had been conflicted. I mentally kicked myself. "And now he's engaged. He's such a nice man, so gentle and kind."

"And gorgeous," Momi added.

"There is that." We laughed. Well, they laughed; I giggle snorted and then covered my mouth in embarrassment, sending the ladies into gales of laughter. "And see? I have such class," I teased.

"Hey!" Rob and Alex called from the picnic blankets. "We're hungry!"

"Men and their stomachs," Momi mumbled, but there was a distinct lack of any venom in her tone. We sloshed through the foamy water, through the black sand, and sat down on the blankets to enjoy a local feast.

Momi began pulling out fresh fruit, steamed vegetables with a light lemony sauce, some ahi poke, pickles, homemade poi, and sweet Hawaiian rolls. "King's Bakery in Hilo." She pointed to the bread. "Best ever! Alex and Kate made a detour on the way to our house this morning to pick it up."

I'd sampled King's Hawaiian bread over the years, shipped in to supermarkets all over, but it wasn't nearly as good as this freshly baked version. The smell alone, despite the fact that it had now cooled, was nearly intoxicating. I kept pulling pieces off and stuffing them into my mouth, having suddenly realized I was famished. Kate poured mango iced tea into plastic cups and handed them around. We feasted, laughed, talked, and feasted some more. Then Kate pulled out dessert, a tropical rice pudding full of macadamia nuts and pineapple.

"Ohmygosh! If Kate and Momi weren't already married, I'd propose right now." I only half-joked for it was really that good and I was truly that full. We packed up all our trash and leftover food. I was surprised there were any leftovers since we'd all pretty much stuffed ourselves. We lounged on the blanket and rested, chatting amiably.

A few small birds with long curved beaks poked into the sand along the water's edge. "What type of bird is that?" I looked to Momi.

"Sanderling or hunakai. Many seabirds only stop here during migration, but the hunakai is pretty common."

"Is that why I haven't seen many seagulls lately?"

"Yes. You will see them later in the year though."

I had much to learn about my new homeland. A thought popped into my head as I realized that my entire existence could change in a few months, depending upon the outcome of the trial I was facing. I tried to shake it off and was only successful when Momi placed her hand on my arm.

"I think we should take a walk." Momi bounced to her feet, thus explaining her fit figure. "We don't want the food to settle into fat on our bellies, you know," she teased the men who had groaned at her suggestion. Kate and I joined her.

"Yes! I'd like to see more of this beach area and the temples you spoke of, Momi."

"Very well then. You heard the lady! Up, up, up," she cajoled Alex and Rob until they reluctantly rose and joined us. We walked along the sand to the northern end of the beach and then wandered up into the trees. It was lush and cool, creating a canopy of vegetation. Turning around and walking back the way we came, we approached the area where we'd picnicked, and then we waded the Wailoa Stream. "Sometimes the stream swells and makes it harder to ford, but this time of year it's easy."

The black sand beach continued, but we veered slightly inland, and Momi led us to what looked like a pile of smooth rocks. She knelt down and pulled something out of her pocket. As I came up beside her I knelt too, recognizing this was something important to her. She had extracted a small flower and a guava and placed them under some of the loose rock. We were all quiet, waiting for her to be the one to break the silence.

"This is the remains of Paka`alana Heiau, a temple of the gods." She arose and backed away, a smile on her face. "I like to think of it as a piece of my past. Our heritage is being lost in this day of modern technology and ideas. It's up to those of us left to keep some of the old ways and the history alive."

"I agree. I wish I could help."

She turned her face and smiled up at me. "You do, just by listening to the stories and being respectful. I told you, the aloha is special in you, just as it is in Kate, Alex, and my sweet Rob."

"Thank you." I returned her smile. "I am honored to be included in such a wonderful group of people."

SEVENTEEN

Ghost

The return drive back out of the valley was slow as there were a few more cars now on the small and barely paved road, but we were in no hurry. Just before he turned left to head up the steep grade, Rob took us on a little detour. He pulled over and angled the vehicle so it would be easy to head back, and we piled out again.

This time it was Rob who led the way to a flat and open section. He turned then and pointed up. When I saw the magnificent waterfall, I remembered him pointing it out on the trip down. "This is Hi'ilawe Falls. It's one of the tallest in Hawaii, but it often runs a little dry. This is because many years ago part of it was diverted for irrigation. Such a shame."

"There is much division over the ditch," Momi added. "While it's historical, it's also against nature."

I peered up at the top of the valley wall where the water began. "That's awfully tall!"

"It's about fourteen hundred feet from the top to the bottom pool," Rob responded.

"Wow," was all I could muster. Sometimes I was just so darned eloquent.

The drive up and out of the valley was faster than going down. We had the right of way, and everyone else was required to pull over to let us through. It was also less harrowing since we were basically hugging the side of the valley wall. Once on the flats above, Rob took the vehicle out of four wheel drive and we toddled down the road. It all seemed so banal in comparison to what we'd just come from.

We zipped past the turn for Rob and Momi's house and headed for someplace called Tex Drive-In.

"Have you ever had a malasada?" Rob asked, glancing at me in the rear view mirror as we waited at a traffic light.

"No. What is that?" Instantly I was intrigued. Rob and Momi definitely had a flair for knowing the good stuff.

"It's a Portuguese fried dough that's rolled in sugar."

"Oh, like a donut hole? Or maybe a beignet?"

"Yes, but far better." Momi grinned.

"And bigger," Rob added. "You'll love them."

We pulled into an unassuming medium sized parking lot adjacent to a similarly unassuming building of questionable architecture. Even at this rather off-hour, the place only had a few empty tables, and we quickly pulled two smaller ones together to accommodate our sweaty and sandy crew.

Rob and Momi took our orders and stood at the counter while Alex saved our tables. Kate and I, with Davy hovering beside us, watched through a large window as huge batches of the malasadas were being made. They were much bigger than I expected, about the size of a sandwich. My mouth watered as I watched a variety of fillings being piped into some of them. The choices were mango, guava, strawberry, chocolate, apple, and Bavarian cream. I had chosen the cream filling.

When we saw that Rob and Momi had our food we met back at the tables. There were trays of hot teas, coffees, and our freshly fried malasadas. I dunked my tea bag a few times before picking up my malasada. Biting into the large and still warm pillowy beauty caused my heart to soar; it was heavenly. While everyone else was intent on their own chewing, I took a large chunk and held it in my hand on my lap below the table level. Davy dipped his head below and took it from me. He came back up munching and grinning. "That is delicious," he enthused.

I smiled at him and then turned my head quickly so that it would appear I was smiling at my hosts. I briefly realized how much my other friends were missing out by not being able to enjoy Davy's friendship as well, but another bite of my malasada quickly took all such thoughts out of my mind. "This is a perfect end to a perfect day, and I thank you all so much for being wonderful tour guides, historians, and most of all... friends."

There were grins all around. "It's easy to love someone who is hungry for knowledge and history like you are," Rob spoke between bites of the doughy sweet treats.

We chatted about everything and nothing all at the same time. I was amongst family and felt Davy's hand on my hand before I saw it. He nodded knowingly. He was the one who had told me about Rob and his special background. What a down to earth guy he was, living in a very nice but not grand home, with a loving wife and fantastic friends. Being put in the precarious position of being charged with murder and having only a small circle of friends and acquaintances who could point me to resources such as attorneys and bankers, I was highly fortunate to have Alex as my lead in so many ways. I smiled warmly at him as I watched him brush some sand off of his wife's cheek.

I felt like I was on an incredibly memorable family outing and I hated for it to end, but I had duties to return to at the inn. My day off had come to an end, yet the memories would stay with me forever. I also vowed to find a way to get back down to the valley now and then. It would indeed be good for the soul.

After saying goodbye to the Parker-Kulas and the Baldwins, I headed back toward home, with a slight detour to our local library. Davy and I had been comfortably silent in the car. "It was a fantastic day," was all he said, and I responded with a simple nod. At the library we wandered the aisles, peering at shelves until I found what I was looking for: local history.

"Oi!" I heard Davy yell.

"What?" I whispered, nearly shushing him in typical library zone fashion.

"'Oo's that?" He pointed and I saw nothing. "That bloke there!"

"I don't see anyone. What are you going on about?" I was whispering as I looked around, all the while hoping that no one was watching me appear to be talking to myself. It was times like this that I worried I'd be committed to an institution or something. *Really, occifer, I talk to ghosts... and aminals.* Sometimes my inner voice sounded drunk.

"Show yourself then," Davy demanded to an empty space. The air began to waver, like sunlight on asphalt on a hot summer day. An image began to appear, almost shyly. When he settled into a semi-transparent form, I could see a balding man, perhaps in his late fifties, with soft blue eyes the color of cornflowers. His skin was lined and loose on his frame. He twisted his hands nervously in front of the bulging paunch above his belt. "What's yer name?" Davy advanced on him aggressively at first, but backed up just a step or two when the man flinched. Davy was short but powerful even in spectral form.

"I'm..." he looked down at his twisting hands as if wondering what was powering them to fidget so. "I'm Mr. Pinckney." His voice was like soft taffeta, a whisp and a crackle. "I... I used to be a librarian here."

"What happened to you?" Davy questioned further, but in a more gentle manner. "It's all right, man; I'm a ghost too. This," he gestured to me, "is Macca. She won't hurt you. She wouldn't hurt anyone. You can trust us."

Mr. Pinckney's shoulders sagged in relief, and tears shone on his cheeks. "Oh good. I've met some very nasty ones. One must be vigilant in public places."

"I've never had a problem." Davy peered at him through narrowed eyes.

"That's because you're you." Mr. Pinckney cringed. "No one will bother you."

"Wot you mean by that?" Davy was on the offensive, I could see. I put a hand on his arm.

"Shh, relax," I warned him.

Mr. Pinckney's eyes darted back and forth between the both of us, cautiously sizing us up. "Because you're Davy Jones. The famous ones, the teen idols, the big Hollywood stars never get picked on in the afterworld."

I saw Davy's face soften then, always a champion for the underdog. "You're bullied?"

Mr. Pinckney nodded timidly.

"That's just wrong, man!" Davy stepped closer to stand beside the trembling apparition and put his hand out to shake. I saw Mr. Pinckney reach to grasp Davy's offered hand, but the gesture seemed milquetoast at best. Davy pumped Mr. Pinckney's hand in greeting. "Grasp it like a man, man!" But he was grinning amiably to Mr. Pinckney, trying to relax the poor ghost.

A very slight smile began to spread on Mr. Pinckney's face then. "Like that?"

"That's the way, man! Give it a grip!" They were both grinning now. Davy turned to me, chuckling, "My first human ghost on solid land. It's rather exciting, y'know?"

His idea of exciting and my idea of a nuisance were apparently one and the same. Just what I needed: another ghost. *At least this one is human* I thought to myself as images of Susie and Glory flitted through my mind. Or was human at one time. I stepped toward them though and offered my hand to shake as well. Mr. Pinckney seemed relieved to take it and grasped it firmly. I didn't pump though; I was never a pumper. It just seemed overly exuberant in the business world, and I had trouble separating the two sometimes. And suddenly I realized how odd this must look. "Excuse me if I don't join in much."

"She's afraid she's going to be sent to an institution for the infirm if she's caught talking to what people consider to be imaginary friends, but in private she'll talk yer blasted ear off." He winked and chuckled.

Mr. Pinckney relaxed a little more, offering a friendly smile my way. I turned back to the shelves and chose a few books on the history of Hawaii, mainly the big island and Waipi'o Valley. It was a good cover but also had been my reason for the stop.

"So, do you live here?" Davy engaged his new ghost friend in conversation.

"Yes, mostly."

"What happened to you?"

"I died in the basement here. Apparently I had a stroke."

"Oh, I'm sorry, man." Davy's face showed his concern.

"Oh, it didn't hurt. At least not that I remember."

"Well that's good. Do you ever leave the library?"

"I have, but that's where I find... mean spirits."

"Really? Well, stick with me, Mr. Pinckney. I won't let anyone bully you."

"He won't either," I whispered out of the side of my mouth, flipping pages in a book I planned to check out. "He's a scrappy little guy."

"Hey! Who you callin' li'l?" I loved it when he dropped his Ts.

"If the kids' clothes fit..." I teased him, smiling all the while, and he stuck his tongue out at me.

"Anyway..." He turned back to Mr. Pinckney. "Ya wanna come with us?"

"If... it's safe. Sure."

"Well, there's a bit of risk. You see, we live at Macca's inn. Lots of guests coming and going."

"Oh dear," the timid ghost fussed at his hands. "That seems stressful."

"Ha!" Davy did a little shuffle-dance. "Only for Macca!"

I grimaced at them and Mr. Pinckney cringed. "That doesn't seem fair to Macca..." He left his words hanging. Davy turned to peer at me mid-dance.

"Nah." He grinned quickly. "She's cool wi' it," he lapsed into his old Mancunian manner of speech.

"Gee, thanks," I muttered as I wandered to the checkout desk, my books in hand and my two ghosts following closely behind, chattering away with each other. I dug around for my library card, and soon we were on the way to the car.

"How do you all fit in *that*?" Mr. Pinckney stopped short upon seeing R2, pointing in horror.

"I'll show you." Davy shimmered, taking Mr. Pinckney with him. They ended up inside, Davy in the passenger seat and Mr. Pinckney hunched in the back. We ambled down the road toward home then. Davy used the time to advise Mr. Pinckney of the basic house rules. "No peeking at Macca when she's sleeping or bathing or doing anything personal like that, okay?"

Mr. Pinckney looked shocked. "I would never!"

"And there's a cat named Chester and two birds named Winston and Marley. They will probably be able to see you."

"I've noticed that with animals. They always know where I am. Are they... nice animals?"

"You'll never find any nicer. Although Chester's got some attitude, and Winston mouths off a lot."

"Mouths off?"

"He can talk. He's a parrot."

Mr. Pinckney grimaced. "I've never really liked birds except in the wild."

"This one is different. He's a really cool little bloke with a sweet disposition. And feathers."

"Okay then. Anything else?"

"Yes. None of the staff can see us. Occasionally we get a guest who can, and most children can see me. I'm not sure if that will be the same with you, but we'll see."

"What if I want to go back to the library?"

"You're perfectly welcome, man. I just thought it would be nice for you to have some friends, and Macca's a groovy chick."

Mr. Pinckney smiled widely for the first time. "I feel like I'm in a time warp. I remember the sixties vaguely."

"And I'm sure you're told you had a very good time," Davy repeated the old joke from The Monkees.

"Something like that; yes." Mr. Pinckney seemed to have a less than zero sense of humor, and Davy rose to the task of pulling it out of him.

"So tell us about yourself, Mr. Pinckney." I kept my eyes on the road, but glanced in the rear view mirror a couple of times.

"Well, I was a librarian for twenty three years." He grew quiet again.

"That's all?" Davy turned to peer over his shoulder at his fellow apparition.

"Twenty three years is a very long time."

"No, no, no," he grinned. "I meant, is that all there is about you?"

"Oh! Well, I never married, never had children or pets, and the library was my life."

We were all quiet while we pondered this tidbit. *How sad* I thought but asked instead, "Were you happy?"

He seemed to consider this for a long while before giving a single nod. "I was. I had routine, I had books, and I lived on the most beautiful island in the world."

"That you did, Mr. Pinckney." I nodded, smiling. "That you did. We're just driving back from Waipi'o Valley. Have you ever been down there?"

"I have! It's... magical."

I chuckled. "Yes. It is that."

We spent the rest of the trip home sharing our love for the valley. The conversation became animated, each of us reliving happy memories — Mr. Pinckney's from long ago, and ours from earlier that day.

Arriving at the inn, Mr. Pinckney was nervous again. "It will be fine," Davy assured him. I led the way down the steps and to our bungalow. Davy showed him around while I greeted Chester before jumping in the shower. Dressed in my usual shorts and tee shirt, this time red shorts and a yellow and red striped tee shirt, I found them sitting on the deck gazing out to the sea below us.

"This is beautiful," Mr. Pinckney whispered in a tone full of awe.

"I think so." I smiled. "I'm off to make a call and then check on Bennie and the kitchen. Make yourself at home. Davy will show you the ropes, so to speak."

"Yes. He's been a great host!"

"My favorite ghost host. And now this hostess must go off and... well... hostess."

"As in Twinkies or Cupcakes?" Davy teased.

"I prefer Little Debbie, thanks," I referred to another snack company. "Have fun, boys. Stay out of trouble." I opened the sliding glass door and

Chester wandered out, rubbing first my legs, then Davy's, and finally Mr. Pinckney's.

"Wow! He seems to like me!"

"He likes all good people, whether human or spectral." Davy beamed. "He's a good guy." He reached down and gave the big orange feline a few gentle strokes under his chin, directing Mr. Pinckney to do the same. And that's how I left them.

Sitting at the kitchen table with a cup of tea and my phone, I placed a call to Dr. Josh and relayed the information about the pets in need in Waipi'o Valley. In his usual manner, he was excited at the prospect of helping out less fortunate animals and promised to contact Rob and Momi about a trip down to the valley floor.

I was still grinning when I got to the reception area and Bennie greeted me with a big smile. "Did you have a good time?"

"I had a fantastically unbelievable time! Have you ever been down there?"

"Once, years ago. My friends and I hiked down and slept on the beach, hiking back up the next day. Brutal hike, but worth it one hundred percent."

"Well, I think I enjoyed it more using wheels to get down and definitely to get back up again." I laughed. "But I'd love to go back sometime. How have things been here?"

"Quiet, except for Auntie Uppity. She's bitching... I mean, she's complaining that the towels aren't big enough to sunbathe on."

I rolled my eyes. "I won't miss them when they leave."

"Oh." He looked nervous. "That's another thing. Auntie Uppity's better half has extended their stay by just a few days. His business is taking longer than expected."

"Oh dear." I put my hand to my temple, suddenly feeling a headache coming on. "I'm sure that won't make Auntie Uppity happy."

"No. You could hear her ranting from their cottage all the way to the dining room. I gave the luncheon guests complimentary drinks to compensate for the discomfort they may have experienced."

"Oh good. Great job as usual, Bennie." I patted his shoulder. "How are the Morrisons doing?"

"Great. They took the kids to Kilauea today. They're staying in that area until evening, hoping to find a good viewing spot to see the lava pouring into the sea."

"Well good for them! I'd like to do that too some day."

"I have lived here all my life, and the volcano has been erupting the whole time. I still find it awe-inspiring. Pele's anger is evident there."

I knew a little about the legend of the goddess Pele and was fascinated whenever I heard the locals speak of the myths with such respect. Pele, considered the goddess of fire, lightning, wind, dance, and volcanos, was renowned for her passionate and fiery temperament.

Later that afternoon I pulled out my journal and wrote about my ghost overpopulation issues. I snapped the composition book closed and held onto it for a moment. It seemed to vibrate in my hands, and when I opened it again I could see that Davy's response had suddenly and mysteriously appeared beneath my entry. How did he do that?

More Ghosties

So apparently I have become a ghost magnet. I've added yet another to my little ghostie family. Mr. Pinckney is a poor lost soul who had been hanging out in the safety of his beloved library for years, having been bullied by other ghosts. Two things come to mind:
1. Why am I getting so much ghostly attention?
2. Why is there still bullying in the afterlife?

Sigh.

Davy's reply:

Dear Macca,

singsongs Macca's got a boyfriend; Macca's got a boyfriend. Admit it. Mr. Pinckney is crushing on you.

Love,
David (hahaha)

EIGHTEEN

Love

I was working late one evening helping Lani and Kalei in the kitchen, leaving Davy and Mr. Pinckney to their own devices. Occasionally I would see the two of them wandering together, Davy pointing out things he felt were important for the meek ghost to know about how the inn worked.

Susie trotted out from behind a bush, and I marveled at his ability to be discreet in his appearances and disappearances, unlike his human counterpart who just shimmered in and out at will. I also still wondered why people could see him and not the aforesaid two-legged ghosts. Davy was of the opinion that animals are so guileless that they had no reason to hide. I also wondered if their undying loyalty had something to do with it. Further, I wondered if I'd ever get answers to these and other burning questions. But I digress... again. I do that a lot.

As I was clearing the bar of used glasses, I overheard Davy and Mr. Pinckney chatting just outside, perched on a couple of poolside chairs.

"So, are you and Macca... romantic?"

"Whoa! That's a little personal, don'tcha think?" I'd known him long enough now that I could recognize that Davy's laughter seemed relaxed though.

"Oh! I'm so sorry. Please forgive my indiscretion!" Poor Mr. Pinckney was such a timid fellow.

The shutters were mostly open so I peeked through the glassless window just in time to see Davy give his fellow ghost a little punch on his arm. "I'm jus' takin' the mickey outta ya there, mate."

"Oh." He looked unsure though, chewing his lower lip in thought.

"If I were me, the full me of the 1960s, in full flesh, I'd definitely have gone after her, but it wouldn't be very fair of me now, would it, in my present state?"

"I guess not. You're not as brash as you come off then."

"Brash?" Davy seemed taken aback. "You think I'm brash?"

Mr. Pinckney frowned. "I didn't mean that as an insult. Brash is defined as aggressively self-assertive."

"It also means arrogant and cocky, mate. So which is it?"

"Please accept my apologies! I only meant it in the most technical definition." Mr. Pinckney looked down at his hands, wringing them fretfully again. "I believe that's been my problem for as long as I can remember; I live in dictionaries and books. I'm not very good with actual... *people*."

Davy slapped him on the back, chuckling. "All right then. I get ya." He shook his head. "So, I may act brash, and I was definitely cocky in my younger years, but to get back to your original question... I am very fond of

Macca. I do love her, but I must tread carefully because I believe she could feel the same if I let it progress beyond our friendship. I can't do that to her. She needs to find her own way and not fall in love with a ghost, y'know? And I promised her parents that I'd watch out for her. I can't go back on a promise."

They were silent for a few moments which allowed me to let this sink in. I remembered our one and only kiss our first year here on the island. It had been... well... heavenly. And I had often wondered why nothing more came of it, never stopping to think of what the ramifications might have been. Now it made sense. Decidedly heart-rending sense.

"You have quite a kind heart then," Mr. Pinckney concluded.

Davy turned and smiled at his new found friend. I wondered if he caught me eavesdropping out of the corner of his eye then. I slowly backed away and carted the tray of bar glasses off to the dishwasher, a cloud of melancholy awareness engulfing me. I threw myself into the final clean up process before slipping back to my bungalow. I gathered Chester close in my arms and shut my bedroom door behind us. Stripping down to an oversized tee shirt I crawled into my bed, the cat still clutched in my arms. I buried my face in his soft fur. The rumble of his purrs brought on the tears. At one point he turned and licked my cheek, but thankfully no words from him invaded my thoughts; he was mercifully silent save for the purring.

Love

So apparently Davy loves me. I hadn't thought too deeply of our feelings for one another in a long time, not since that sweet kiss so long ago. I did wonder why nothing came of it, and it was rather dumb of me not to figure it out. I often forget about his ghostly status, for he is so real and warm to me.

I had a dream last night after overhearing Davy and Mr. Pinckney's discussion. Davy and I were together, but it was the sixties, and I wasn't really me but rather a version of me. Perhaps I was more of my mother in the dream since she was near his age back then. I don't know exactly, for dreams are hazy and the details are often forgotten within minutes of waking up. What I haven't forgotten though was the feeling, the emotions of the dream. It was warm, comforting, loving, and passionate.

And I awoke so much more mixed up than I was before.

Davy's reply:

Dear Macca,

This could be very embarrassing if it fell into the wrong hands. My reputation could be eternally marred. Oh... wait... nevermind.

Love,
David (heart)

Throwing myself into my work the next day helped dislodge some of the cobwebs I'd woken with after a fitful sleep. I was content to keep my head bent to tasks and not think too hard about anything. At lunch time though, I wandered back to my bungalow, fatigue tying my legs so that each step was a struggle. I had considered a light meal of yogurt followed by a nap, but when I opened the door, my two ghosts sat at the little dining table. Both heads turned at once and I purposely avoided Davy's eyes. I felt like my emotions were too visible at the moment, and I was not in the mood to deal with any conversations about... well, anything.

"Hello gentlemen." I offered a small smile to them both.

"Hello Macca." Mr. Pinckney smiled widely. He seemed to be settling in quite nicely.

"'Ello Luv." Davy's voice was softer than usual, but even without looking I could hear the smile in his tone. "Everything all right then?"

I sighed and nodded, grabbing a lime yogurt from the refrigerator and a spoon from the drawer.

"Cat got yer tongue?" He teased. "Chester? You got your mummy's tongue?"

Is he serious? Chester spoke and I heard it in my head. Turning to the cat, I shook my head at him and then turned back to Davy and Mr. Pinckney.

"No, just tired. I think I'll take a nap." I turned to head to my room and felt rather than saw Davy follow me. He shut the door behind us, took the yogurt and spoon out of my hand, and set them on the bedside table. He opened his arms wide and pulled me close. Although I resisted only slightly at first, I rested my head on his shoulder and let him hold me.

"I'm sorry, Luv. I knew you were there, but not until I'd already spoken the words. I wish I could have a retake of that scene, really."

I sighed, a long and shuddering sound. "It's okay. You're right, you know. And I'm a fool."

"You're not a fool!" He held me only slightly away from him for a moment to peer into my eyes. I couldn't ever resist the sparkle there. "Believe me, if things were different..."

"Just... don't finish that sentence, okay? 'If' is not going to give me any comfort. I just need to find myself again."

116

He cupped my cheek and pulled me close again. We just stood together like that, sharing warmth. After a long moment he began to sing about there being no day or night, dark or light, black or white, but that all is often gray. The words lent no comfort, but the melody and the baritone rumble of his voice were soothing. He rubbed my back. "You do need to nap," he whispered when the song died away. "And yer Mum and Dad send their love."

"Thank you." I nodded and crawled onto the bed, the yogurt suddenly unappealing to me. He pulled up the light afghan and covered me, kissing me on the temple before he took the yogurt away and left me to sleep.

When I awoke a half hour later, I felt nearly human again, but my heart was still heavy. I needed to spend some time conducting a little soul searching expedition. Or something. I decided to take the run that I'd neglected to take that morning.

Donning running shoes and raggedy shorts and a tee, I hit the trail that ran along the cliffs. After about twenty minutes I felt my muscles relax into that well oiled rhythm that allowed me to focus on my mind instead of my body. I was lost in thought when I came to the area again where I'd nearly joined Davy in his ghosthood more than a year ago, and instead of shying away like I usually did, I stayed right on the path, braving the feelings that had previously caused me to either turn back or veer far away from the cliff itself.

Feeling a remarkable sense of accomplishment upon conquering the cliff, I spurred on and ran all the way to the edge of the Royal Aina Resort, the Sikes' hotel complex, before turning back. This was the longest I'd run in a very long time and it felt liberating. I'd conquered my fear of the cliff and had settled into a comfortable acceptance of my relationship with Davy. I had come to the realization that I'd never really expected to have more than a close friendship with him, but that I'd allowed myself to sort of "crush" on him. I mean, millions of girls crushed on him for years and why should I be any different? Did it hurt that nothing could ever come of this? Of course it did. Any girl in her right mind would feel the pain. He was never mine to begin with, but I felt certain he would be in my life in some manner forever. That awareness was warming and encouraging. I loved that man-ghost, and that never needed to end.

Home again, I showered quickly and ran to catch up with Bennie on the tasks of the afternoon.

"Sorry Bennie." I stepped into the reception area. "I just had to clear my head with a run."

"Feel better? You looked a little... rough this morning."

"I do. I really do. Thank you." I was touched at his concern. "You run, don't you, Bennie?"

"I do! I try for three miles each day but it depends on my schedule."

"Wow! I'm lucky if I can get a mile in, but today I actually doubled it. I ran all the way to the Sikes' property line and back."

He turned his head sharply to look at my face. "The cliff?"

"Conquered it." I nodded, smugly proud of myself.

He lifted his hand and we high-fived. "You are one powerful woman, Miss Macca."

"Why thank you, Bennie! I never thought of myself as powerful. Of course, I was raised by four very dynamic people, so I guess it shouldn't surprise me that you think of me that way."

"I knew Mr. Wally was powerful, but it's good to hear you were surrounded by that."

"My Aunt Ruth kept Uncle Wally in line, if you can believe that!"

He whistled softly. "I'll bet she was a force to be reckoned with then."

"And she never put up with my teenaged tantrums and drama either."

He laughed, a friendly bark where he threw his head back. "Ahh, teen drama. I was full of that myself." He shook his head, grinning. "Poor woman. My mother was incredibly patient with all of us. I still don't know how she did it. She's amazing still today."

"I'd love to meet her sometime." I was touched that he was sharing some personal information. All of my employees had become family to me, but for a very long time they had still held me at arm's length. Now they were beginning to warm up, and as a result, open up to me.

"I would love to introduce you! She hears all about you and the inn. Would you like to have lunch with us on Thursday? Our family always gathers for lunch, but I can usually only get there on my days off."

"How does our schedule look for that day?" I peered over his shoulder at the monitor. The software that tracked our bookings was open as usual.

"No one checking in until the weekend."

"Great! I'm free then. Your family won't mind?"

"Mind?" He laughed again. "They'll be so happy that they'll finally be able to stop pestering me to bring you. I can come pick you up at 12:15 if that's okay?"

"Wow, a chauffeured event even!" I teased. "I'll be ready."

I felt an extra spring in my step the rest of the day. It had taken me so long to allow friendship into my heart, and here I was opening myself up to more and more. Life would be great if only I didn't have a murder trial looming before me in a few months.

NINETEEN

Build

The morning began as a typical Hawaiian day — a little foggy, then sunny, then overcast, then sunny again with a short shower of rain. Yeah, always keeping us guessing, but quite possibly the nicest climate I could ever imagine living in. Of course there were days when it was blazing hot and all I wanted to do was wallow like an elephant seal in the pool, but those times were few.

This particular morning though I had been invited to meet Rick and Jack Morrison at their build site for their soon-to-be new home. Our long-term guests had hired Bennie's younger sister to watch the children back at the inn so they could focus on the project and give me a proper tour. I had a quick breakfast and sat sipping my tea at the kitchen table. Chester was perched on the chair beside me, his front paws gripping the back as he stared intently out the window.

Ik-ik-ik-ik. He chattered at a bird hopping from branch to branch just beyond the deck outside.

"Think you'll catch him today?"

Chester jerked his head around to glare at me indignantly. I swear that if fur could blush, he would have turned a deep shade of red instead of orange. He grumbled deep in his throat, hopped down to the floor and stalked away, tail held high.

"Bye Chet! I'll see you later," I called after him. As his tail disappeared around the corner of the hallway, I got up and washed my cup. Setting it on the tea towel, I retrieved my purse and keys and headed out to meet with Jack and Rick Morrison.

Only a few miles away, I parked behind their rental car and saw both of them speaking with a man while gesturing at a large set of blueprints that Jack held open in his hands so Rick could conduct business. I stood quietly next to Jack and listened to the tail end of Rick's instructions for a slight change in the exterior of the construction that was behind me. I turned to survey it while we waited. It was still in the framing process, but I could already tell it would be quite magnificent. It was a two story building that backed up to a natural stand of trees along the road, thus creating a lush green privacy screen for the entire property.

I turned to face the same direction as the front of the building, *makai*, to the sea, and what a splendid sight it was! The view was expansive, encompassing both the Pacific Ocean and, to the north, part of the cliffs that our inn sat upon. I stood on a flattened area and gazed out to sea, imagining my old apartment in Los Angeles. The scenes in my mind felt as though they belonged to another person in another world in which there was no impending murder trial.

I jumped when someone touched my shoulder. Rick and Jack were beside me, the former with his hand at my elbow.

"Oops!" Rick smiled. "I didn't mean to startle you."

Waving it all away, I turned to face them. "No worries. I was just mesmerized by the sea." We took another moment to admire the vast expanse of blue before us, the brightness of the sky contrasting the dark depths below. I took a deep and cleansing breath, feeling only a little better as once again the realization of a murder trial was difficult to shake off.

Jack unrolled the blueprint one more time and held it up for us. "Right here will be the infinity pool." Rick pointed to the plans. "It's situated so that the water will appear to spill right over the edge."

He then moved his finger over to the driveway and showed a sweeping arc inside the gate that would give them privacy and security. "Jack always wanted a big curved driveway, and that will be made with stamped lava rock."

It was amusing to hear the excitement in his voice as he pointed out the various features on the plans. I admired the beautiful sketches of many of the detailed areas.

"Did you draw these?"

"Yes I did," he smiled, "but I wanted to show you this." He pointed to a sketch of the bank of windows on the sea-facing side of the building, both upper level and lower. "These will slide open and disappear into the framework to give the feeling of living in the open air."

I was impressed and told them so. "This will be lovely! You're very talented." I smiled at Rick in admiration and then turned to catch Jack beaming with pride toward his husband, an immensely endearing gesture.

Rick turned us all to peer at the framed structure and was waving his hands as he described the large kitchen and living area. On the lower level there would be only three enclosed rooms, a bathroom, adjacent laundry area, and office, while all else would be an open floor plan. Upstairs would hold the master suite and three bedrooms for the children, another bathroom, and a guest suite on the opposite end.

"There will be plenty of parties." Jack grinned "We hope you'll join us whenever you're able!"

"The kids have fallen in love with their Auntie Macca."

My heart swelled with love and my smile matched it. "Well, Auntie Macca would be quite proud and honored to attend!"

We all turned to look at the driveway as a large truck arrived.

"That will be the plumbing and electrical supplies," Rick murmured, glancing at his watch. "Only an hour late. Not bad."

"This is my cue to get back to work at the inn then." I gave them each a brief hug. "I'll leave you to your work. I can hardly wait to see it finished!" I left them as Rick was gesturing to the contractor and sub-contractor with Jack still holding onto the floorplans.

TWENTY

Sleuth

Although I was told to stay away from the homeless encampment, Lani and Kalei had still been handing out food at Hale Maluhia on Sunday mornings. I was itchy on this particular Sunday afternoon though.

"Whatever is wrong with you, Macca, stop it now!" Davy had grabbed my leg to keep it from swinging again as we sat on the deck. "You've got me all wound up with that jitterbug you're dancin'!"

"Sorry." I tried to still my legs and hands but stood up and paced instead.

"What is your problem today?" he demanded.

"Well, let's see. I've been incarcerated and am now awaiting trial for a crime I did not commit. How's that?"

"Why don't you go for a run then?"

"Because that does nothing to solve this mystery." I spun around and faced him. "I'm going to the homeless camp."

"I don't think that's a very good idea."

"Well I do. I need to ask some questions. I need to detect."

He snickered. "Detect? Well, I do declare." He put on a southern accent. "Decidin' to detect would definitely be damagin'," he alliterated.

"Drop dead." Yeah. Million dollar comeback it wasn't, but I was determined. "Are you coming with me or not?"

"Not."

"Fine." I grabbed my purse and keys and stomped away from the bungalow. As I jumped into my little R2, Davy shimmered into the passenger seat. I frowned at him. "Your unwavering support is astounding."

"Hey, I'm here now, aren't I?" He buckled his seat belt. "Let's go detect!"

While part of me didn't trust his sudden change of plans, the other part of me smacked me upside the head and ordered me to be relieved that someone, ghost or no ghost, had my back. As I turned to back out of my parking space, Mr. Pinckney shimmered into the small compartment where a backseat would normally go. I jumped and slammed on the brakes.

"Oh! Don't DO that," I admonished him, clutching my chest, my heart beating wildly.

"Oh dear," he pseudo-whined in his meek voice. "I did it again. I'm so sorry."

His pathetic demeanor momentarily melted my heart. I patted his fidgeting hands. "It's okay. Just... work on it, please." He nodded emphatically.

"Or maybe we'll just put bells on you like a cat," Davy teased.

Mr. Pinckney shook his head, his face drawn with worry. "Oh please, no!"

"I'm pullin' yer leg, man," Davy lapsed into his thick Mancunian accent. "Relax! Yer already annoying and bells would just make it worse." He nudged his fellow ghost in the ribs and turned to face the front again before pounding the dashboard. "Onward, fine maiden! T' the homeless!"

"I am not a horse."

"No, but just as beautiful as one."

I narrowed my eyes and regarded him for a moment. "I guess I'll take that as a compliment."

"And so you should. Horses are the most beautiful creatures in the universe, of the four-legged variety I mean."

"Nice save," Mr. Pinckney giggled.

"I've had a lot of practice. I've pissed off many a woman in my time," Davy playfully bragged.

I concentrated on navigating my Laurel and Hardy impersonators to Hale Maluhia while they chatted about things that were so "out there" that I tuned them out. I had one mind for the day: find out who really killed Chad. The problem was, I hadn't a clue as to how to gather... clues. But I had read so many stories where Stephanie Plum figured it out. Or China Bayless. Or Fortune Redding! But that would mean I needed a mini-gang of septuagenarians. Oh! How about a true P.I.? Kinsey Milhone! I could do this! I knew I could. Maybe. What was that lump in my throat, and why was it quickly moving down to the pit of my stomach?

A bit of the bizarre conversation between Davy and Mr. Pinckney was intruding on my thoughts, and then I did a double-take at the turn of their words. Davy was chuckling and having difficulty getting the words out due to his laughter. "So these kids were all sitting around with a Ouija board, and me and me mate were moving the thingy all over the board."

Mr. Pinckney's high-pitched giggle was shrill. "Oh my! I'd have loved to have seen that!" He was actually encouraging him!

"They were asking all sorts of personal questions, and we had no idea who the bloke was they thought they had contacted, so we were making stuff up left and right." Davy was laughing loudly at his memories now and finding it hard to speak. "Oh my. It was priceless."

I sighed, shook my head, and tuned them out again as I pulled into a makeshift parking area.

Hale Maluhia was buzzing with the usual energy. I wandered toward a group of adults surrounding my friends Makala, Kai, and Joe. The circle opened up a little as I approached, and I saw Makala open her arms to me, a huge grin on her face.

"Aloha *keiki*! Where you been, Macca-Roon?" She squished me to her massive bosom and I wrapped my arms around her in return. She smelled sweetly of flowers, and as I gazed over her sizeable shoulder I could s ee a pile of pikake, puakenikeni, and greenery that she had indeed been using to weave a lei.

"Well..." I began as she took my hand and led me to where they were sitting. Joe leaned over and kissed my forehead in one of those very fatherly gestures that I missed so much. Kai squeezed me in a big hug. "I was advised not to come here because of the upcoming trial... but when have I ever done what I was told, right?" This brought chuckles and more hugs from the group.

"Well, your obstinacy is a win for our team," Joe snickered. "And speaking of a win for our team, we had a meeting with your friend Dylan Kimura. Great things are in the works, Macca! How can we ever thank you?"

I grinned, feeling suddenly shy. "I don't need any thanks. I just need to know that you're getting the assistance you deserve. Just because society turned their collective backs on you once, or even many times, doesn't mean that there aren't people out there who care and want to help you."

Mr. Pinckney and Davy shimmered in, standing behind Makala and facing me, which reminded me of why I was really there. Eager to change the subject anyway, I pulled my phone out of my pocket and touched the screen a few times until I came to the photo I'd snapped that day when I swore that Lani's brother Kimo had been watching me. "Do any of you know this man?" I handed the phone to Joe, and they each peered at the screen before passing it on to the next person.

"He looks familiar," Joe commented, "but he's not part of the crew here."

Kai turned his nose up. "I remember him a little. He was a rude little creep."

But it was Makala who drew in her breath. "Chad said he once worked with him at the 76 gas station in Honoka'a and warned us that he's trouble."

"Did he mention his name?"

She put her finger to her bottom lip and tapped it a few times, giving it some thought before she replied. "A native name... Kekoa? Keona?"

"Kimo?" I hadn't wanted to prompt her, but she reacted in such a way that I knew I'd nailed the name.

"Kimo! Yes! That's him. No respect in that one. No aloha... no living *pono*."

"*Pono*?" I learned new words or ways every day it seemed.

"Living *pono* means you make a conscious decision to do the right thing in terms of yourself, others, and the environment. It is the way to happiness," Joe chimed in, coming to Makala's rescue as she struggled for a simple way to define the word.

I found myself nodding, thinking that 'living *pono*' perfectly described the way my family had raised me. I realized they were watching me, smiling.

"The *pono* is strong in this one though, eh Joe?" Makala began to chuckle.

"*Akamai wahine,*" Kai whispered conspiratorially, and Makala's chuckle turned into a cackle.

"He call you smart... He's right." Makala's smile touched the inner child in me, missing my mother.

I looked past them to see Davy nodding, still standing beside Mr. Pinckney.

"Ask them when they last saw Chad and Kimo." Mr. Pinckney nearly vibrated, almost jumping up and down like an impatient little kid.

"When did you all see Chad last?" I restated the question and saw Davy briefly frown, but I turned my attention to my three witnesses.

"On the night he died, he said goodnight to us around 11:00 and then disappeared into his tent," Kai volunteered.

"Yes, but I saw him leave again a few minutes later. I never saw him come back." Joe sighed sadly.

"Ask them when they last saw Kimo too," Mr. Pinckney nagged, but I was glad he did because my mind was stuck on the image of Chad's crumpled body.

I repeated Mr. Pinckney's question, and Joe shook his head solemnly. "Earlier that same day." Kai nodded in agreement.

Makala clucked her tongue. "I think I saw that Kimo when I got up to use *lua* that night." She waved toward the portable toilets on the other side of the encampment, pikake petals floating around her.

I couldn't help but gasp. "What time do you think it was?"

"No clock, but the moon was high. Early morning I think."

"Did the police talk to them about this?" Mr. Pinckney was still guiding me and I posed his question to the trio.

"They not ask right questions." Makala shook her head.

"I never even thought of Kimo until you asked," Joe added, Kai and Makala nodding their agreement.

My mind was racing. Mr. Pinckney was a better detective than Green. Now I had to figure out what to do next. I glanced at the portly ghost and saw him wringing his hands in the usual manner. He shook his head sadly. "I'm sorry. I don't know what else to ask right now."

Davy stood with his arms folded across his chest, his thick eyebrows knitted tightly together, and looking anywhere but at me. I only briefly wondered what that was all about for I had bigger issues before me.

It was Joe who put some of my ideas into words. "They stopped looking for the real culprit when they found you, didn't they?" He was shaking his head in disgust.

"It appears they did. Yes." I felt tears trying very hard to fall from my eyes, and I quickly rubbed my face, taking in a very deep breath. "Okay..." I blew out my breath. "I may be back if I have more questions. Well actually, I'll be back as much as possible as long as I'm not on death row." I tried out some of that self-deprecating humor but it fell flat this time.

"Hawaii abolished the death penalty way back in 1957," Kai offered.

"Well that's certainly good news."

"Macca, we will do some snooping around too. Don't you worry." Joe patted my hands tenderly.

"Thank you." The words came out choked. "*Mahalo.*" I got to my feet and said my goodbyes with accompanying hugs.

The ride back to the inn was quiet. I was so lost in thought that I had no idea what was eating my two spectral friends, nor did I care at the moment.

We were sitting at the kitchen table in our bungalow later, a pad of paper before me and a pen in my hand. Davy sat sullenly to my right, Mr. Pinckney to my left.

"We need to put some sort of timeline together." I drew a line and started writing down all the events leading up to Chad's murder.

"Also, keep a note of what your friends told you about Kimo." Mr. Pinckney tapped the pad of paper.

"Good idea." I wrote all that I could remember. Mr. Pinckney helped and Davy sulked.

I smacked the pen down on the table and glared at him. "What is your problem?"

"Nothing. Nothing at all." He left the table in a huff and slapped the sliding glass door open, stepped onto the deck, and shoved the sliding glass door closed again.

Mr. Pinckney and I looked at each other, shrugged, and went back to our task. After several minutes, we had a few pages of notes and times, and we sat back to admire our work.

"Now what?" I asked him.

"I think it's time to hit the internet and see if we can find out more about Kimo. Also Chad. Do you know his last name?"

"I do." I retrieved the laptop and we began to surf. It's not as easy as you'd think to get information on people without spending some money, and I really did not want any kind of trail leading the police to the fact that I had stuck my nose where they didn't think it belonged. Still, I was able to find the 76 station in Honoka'a where Chad and Kimo had worked. I picked up my phone and placed a call. Mr. Lewis was the franchise owner and apparently didn't have much concern for keeping past employee information confidential. He remembered Chad fondly, but Kimo not so much.

"That boy was nothing but trouble," he grumbled. "Chad tried to reason with him, but their work ethics were polar opposites and Chad finally gave up."

"How long did they work with you?"

"Ohhh..." I could almost envision him trying to think back. "Chad stayed the longest until I had to begin laying people off due to the economy. I ended up running the station with just my wife for quite a long time."

"I'm so sorry to hear that."

"Well, it's not uncommon. We eventually pulled things together and I've been able to employ a few local kids again. I tried to contact Chad and offer him an assistant manager position, but I couldn't find him anywhere."

"He apparently fell upon hard times as well and was living in a homeless camp until he passed recently."

"He died?" I heard sadness and regret in his voice.

"Yes." I tread gently here. "Suddenly."

"Well crap. I'm really sorry to hear that. He was a good guy."

"He was. I can pass your condolences on to his friends at the encampment for you if you'd like."

"Actually, I'd like to visit with them and maybe help in some way. Is it the big camp near Hilo?"

"Yes. The one with the buses," I confirmed. He sighed heavily and I felt bad about having shared such bad news. Before we ended our call, I promised to stop in at his station the next time I was in town and thank him personally.

"Wow Mr. Pinckney... You certainly missed your calling! You would have made an excellent detective!"

He wrung his hands. "Oh, no way! And talk to all those people... in person?" The look on his face as he vehemently shook his head caused me to giggle.

"You talked to people at the library though!"

He still shook his head "No. That was so very different. We always whispered, and the questions and answers were short, and there was rarely anything personal discussed." He shuddered and I placed my hand upon his arm, still giggling.

"Well then, you can just be my deputy. How is that?"

He screwed up his face and gazed out the sliding glass door. "No. I think Davy is irritated with me, and I suspect it has something to do with me helping you."

I felt my eyebrows rise. "Oh really?"

He nodded emphatically. "I don't want to irritate him. He's the only spirit friend I have."

I patted his hand and stood. "I'll talk to him."

"Oh no! Please don't!"

"I must. I need to clear the air with him anyway."

He put his face in his hands, and I left him moaning into his palms. I shook my head and headed for the deck where I could see Davy sitting in the sun dressed in his red swim trunks. I opened and closed the sliding glass door much more gently than he had and sat beside him, shading my eyes from the brightness of the day. I scooted my chair around so that the sun was behind me when I faced him.

"What's up?" I forced myself to sound casual.

"The sun."

"Har har har."

"It is." He wouldn't look at me; he just closed his eyes and sunbathed. I idly wondered if ghosts get tans or sunburns. I know I'd thought that many times before, but I had never bothered to ask. That is, until now.

"So, do ghosts get tans, sunburns, or anything like that?"

He snapped his head up abruptly and squinted at me, one eye closed against the glare. "Well aren't you the comedian."

I know shock registered on my face, so I smiled nervously. "Actually I have been meaning to ask you that for a very long time."

He regarded me silently for several hours. Actually it was barely a minute, but when he stared at me like that it was just a little unnerving for many reasons: he's adorable, sexy as hell, and just a little intimidating at times. That old "short man syndrome" certainly did not apply to him; he had both the natural confidence and power of a man well over six feet tall. Maybe it was just me, but hey, that was my story and I vowed to stick to it. And then I remembered that Davy was really a sixty-six year old man in a twenty year old body. It boggles the mind. Really. I felt a headache beginning behind my left eye as I waited for his response.

"No. We don't tan or burn, but I recall how I loved being in the sun, so it still brings pleasure." I heard a little softening in his voice then so I decided to charge ahead.

"So, what's eating you then?" I moved to the chair beside him.

He sighed, long and loud. "Mr. Pinckney is a better sidekick than I am."

I couldn't help it; I barked out a single derisive laugh. "You're joking, right?"

He turned his frowny face on me. "No."

Backtrack, Macca, I told myself. "Okay, first of all, you are not my sidekick, but my best friend in the whole world. Secondly, I love you with all my heart. Thirdly... Is that a word? Thirdly, no one can ever replace you. And... you don't have to be perfect for me to feel all those thin gs about you. Perfect is boring. And impossible. Just look at me." That got a smile out of him. "So, Mr. Pinckney is a good detective. You're a good friend. No, you're a great friend." I gently kicked his foot. He kicked mine back. Soon we were both grinning and having a foot fight. Of course I had flip-flops on so I was at a disadvantage and his bare feet won. Then we just stared at each other for a while.

"I'm sorry for being a grumpy ol' git," he murmured with a sheepish grin.

"Ohmygosh, I wish I had that on a recording."

He slowly and with much drama stuck his tongue out and gave me the longest, loudest raspberry I have ever heard. I nearly fell out of my chair laughing.

TWENTY-ONE

Generations

Bennie Abela's family home was a modest cottage about two miles southwest of the inn. Several smaller homes shared the long drive off the main road.

"The other homes all belong to my mother, but my brothers and sisters and I live in them. My dad, rest his soul, made sure the family could stay together, buying the land for a song and building six cottages on one plot."

"That's such a wonderful thing, to keep family together like that." I strained against the seatbelt to peer around at the nearly matching dwellings on the lot. They were all different colors, but built of similar construction materials. The main cottage was blue, while the others behind were green, pale yellow, dark red, coral, and the closest to the main house was purple.

"Purple?" My eyebrows lifted.

Bennie chuckled. "My sister Lea has had a purple passion for most of her life. That's her home. My father was not happy at her chosen color, but he accepted all of the quirks of his children. My house is the green one." He pointed to the cottage at the very far end as we exited his car.

"Are you the oldest?"

"Oh no. I have two older brothers and an older sister. Lea is my youngest sister."

I was surprised; his demeanor and his business acumen were that of an older sibling. "So, where did you learn how to be so... diplomatic and business savvy?"

"School. We couldn't afford university, but I did graduate from Hawaii Community College in Hilo."

"You never cease to amaze me, Bennie." My family — I think I'll keep them.

He actually blushed. "Nahh, I'm just me. Bennie on the inside, Bennie on the outside."

We slipped our flip-flops off and left them on the porch. Bennie held the screen door open for me and I entered a house full of happy noise. There were three children running about with an elderly woman shushing them as she dried her hands on her apron. Upon seeing us, she opened her arms wide.

"Miss Macca, aloha, welcome, welcome!" She enveloped me in the warmest hug, squeezing me tightly against her rather generous figure.

"Please, call me Macca. I keep trying to get Bennie and the others at the inn to drop the 'Miss' but, well, they're just so well-mannered." I winked very slightly at her and she beamed, putting one hand up to her son's cheek.

"He's a good boy, our Bennie, and I feel like Kalei, Lani, Ming, Sam, and Albert are family as well. And you? Oh heavens... I feel as if I already know you... but come in, come in! Join us and be welcome. Lunch is nearly ready."

Because the cottage was small, entering the kitchen was surprising as it seemed to take up most of the home's square footage, accommodating a huge family style table with benches around it. Bennie directed me to take a seat.

"Oh, Mrs. Abela! This is lovely!" I was admiring the woodwork of the highly polished massive table and benches.

"Please, dear, call me Akela. I know, I know... My parents were appalled many years ago when they learned I was marrying my sweetheart Eduardo Abela. Akela Abela I would be." She laughed and shook her head. I could only join her, for she was such a warm and welcoming woman. "My dear departed Eduardo made that table and those benches when our firstborn, Eduardo, Jr., came along. It's hand carved, the koa wood reclaimed from a barn he was hired to clean out and demolish. He was shocked to find it there, but the owners said, 'Take it! Take it, please!' and so he did." As she spoke, she stroked the table lovingly, as if remembering her husband's love.

"He was very talented," I smoothed my hand over the silken surface as I matched her tone, which had become quiet with respect and admiration.

"That he was." She flashed me a quick grin and then turned to the other two women in the kitchen. One had been stirring a pot while the other chopped fruit. "Please, meet my daughters Mana and Lea," she gestured. Lea turned from the pineapple she was slicing. She was a younger mirror of her mother.

"I'm so happy to meet you... finally." Lea gave her brother a look that seemed to say, "It's about time!"

Mana turned from the stove and added, "It took him nearly this long to bring Wally too as I recall." She shook her head at Bennie. "But I'm very happy you have joined us, Miss Macca."

At that moment, two men entered, dropping their flip flops on the mat outside the back door off the kitchen.

"Is this the famous Miss Macca? I'm Eddie." He extended his hand and we shook.

From behind him, the other man joined in. "And I'm Bertie. Aloha, Miss Macca!"

"Please..." I glanced around at my hosts. "Call me Macca." I then caught Bennie's eye. "And that includes you." I narrowed my eyes and grinned. He blushed again.

"Yes ma'am."

"Ugh! And no 'ma'am,' okay? That was my... grade school teacher or something."

He chuckled. "My apologies, *Macca*."

"There, was that so hard?"

"Mama, mama..." One of the small children, a boy of about four, was tugging on Mana's apron. "I'm hungry."

"Soon, baby, soon."

"These are my grandbabies." Akela gestured to the three toddlers. "Aliberto, Benito, and Clarita."

Davy chose that moment to shimmer in. I saw all three of the children's eyes latch onto him. "Whoops," he whispered and shimmered out again. I had to bite my tongue to keep from laughing.

"We named them in order of birth, A, B, and C. Triplets." Mana laughed.

"They are beautiful! Aloha Aliberto, Benito, and Clarita!"

"Aloha," each replied in that typical boisterous toddler manner, with seemingly little attention paid to or memory of the mysterious appearance and disappearance of the young man-ghost a moment ago.

At that moment, Akela clapped her hands sharply several times. "'*Aina awakea*!" She moved pots and serving dishes to the center island. "Lunch is served!"

Bennie directed me to begin the little buffet line. There was a beautiful spread of fresh local fruit, a broccoli salad that looked scrumptious, raw sugar snap peas with a dressing to dip them in, and baked tofu and green beans in a light sauce along with a tossed green salad.

"The green salad is the dividing line for vegetarian fare," he told me. "My sisters are vegetarians as well."

"Oh, thank you! That makes it easy!" I grinned and filled my plate. Akela and her sons went for the baked chicken and fried spam, along with potatoes and just a dabbling of fruit and vegetables. Bennie's sister Mana filled her children's plates before sitting down with her own. It was a lovely sight that all the family fit perfectly around the beautiful table.

Akela, at the head of her table, put her arms out, and one by one we all grasped our neighbors' hands. I watched to keep up with them. They did not bow their heads but looked around the table at all the smiling faces. I couldn't help but join them.

"Thanks to the earth for the soil," Akela began. "Thanks to the sky for the rains. Thanks to the farmers for the harvest. Thanks to our friends for the love."

"*Mahalo*," they intoned to finish. I was so moved by the closeness of the family and the sentiment of the words that I could only sit and smile. I could find no words myself to describe the atmosphere except pure contentment.

The food was wonderful, the discussion animated, and the mood close and friendly. And... I had made yet more friends.

TWENTY-TWO

Breaches

Being awakened by an early morning call on your cell phone is never a good way to start the day. My ringtone was still set to Davy singing "Daydream Believer," which I love, but having it blaring in your ear at not even crack of dawn o'clock in the morning is something else. The caller ID showed that it was a forward from the front desk's phone, and the time showed it was 3:00 a.m. I'm the only night staff except for special circumstances, so I cleared my throat, sat up, and tried on my most cheerful tone. "Front desk." It only came out as a froggy croak, but hey, they were lucky I even answered.

"I find it totally *hic* unacceptable that there is no twenty four hour *hic* bar in this dump you call an inn." Auntie Uppity slurred her words, burping and hiccuping in my ear.

"I'm sorry. Is there a *real* problem?" I had used my last bit of patience on her the first day she arrived, and each day thereafter I neared the point of a Kilauea eruption.

"Didn't you hear me?" She screeched in my ear like a banshee and burped. I heard ice tinkling in a glass.

"I heard you. That doesn't constitute a real problem at three in the morning. Are you bleeding? Shortness of breath? Is your bungalow on fire?"

"No, you silly twat. I am out of vodka. Fetch me some. Now. I'm a paying *hic* customer and I demand more vodka. How else would you expect anyone *hic* to enjoy their stay in this godforsaken place?"

I bit my tongue and counted to ten in my head. It wasn't working. "You're welcome to check out and find another place to stay." I knew I wasn't being very innkeeperly (I made that word up... just now) but she was on my last nerve.

"I am seriously considering doing just that tomorrow. For now, I demand more vodka!"

"Is Mr. D'Antonio there?"

"What? No. He went out on some stupid boat with his client and won't be back until tomorrow afternoon."

Well, that explained a lot. Mr. D'Antonio was smarter than I had given him credit for. If he jumped ship and swam to another island, I wouldn't blame him one bit. I sighed. "Fine. I will bring you a bottle of vodka from our *closed* bar. Expect to see a good sized bar tab on your bill though."

"Whatever." I could almost see her waving her hand at me as if addressing a mere peasant. "My husband will pay. He always does. He knows I'd *hic* leave him if he didn't. It's the only way I can stay in this

dreadful bedbug-ridden hellhole, which I'll have you know..." I ended the
call before she could continue. I threw on one of Uncle Wally's huge
sweatshirts over my nightshirt. It nearly reached my knees. I grabbed my
inn keys and headed for the bar, stopping on my front porch to slip into my
flip flops.

A quick view of our bar stock set my mind at ease that we had plenty
of vodka for Auntie Uppity. I selected a beautiful blue bottle of Ocean
Vodka, distilled right here in the islands and touted to be 100% all natural,
organic, and gluten free. Oh, and did I mention it was pricey? Not only
that, but there would be a hefty after-hours delivery charge added. There
was no excuse for her rudeness or her demands. I locked the liquor up
again and headed to her bungalow. My flip-flops echoed loudly against the
bamboo walkway so I tried to tiptoe. The last thing I needed was to
awaken other guests, especially the Morrisons with their young children.

I knocked quietly on Auntie Uppity's door, and she swung it open so
hard that it banged against the wall, the sound like a mallet against a
tympani, the reverberation bouncing along the walkway.

"Shh!" I caught the door before it could crash again. "You'll wake all
the other guests," I admonished her irritably.

"So *hic* what." She yanked the bottle out of my hand and stared
with bleary eyes at the label. "What the hell is this swill?"

"It's island vodka, organic. It's very good."

"I doubt that."

"Hilton Waikoloa Village was the first to stock it." I childishly
crossed my fingers behind my back as I told this little white lie.

"Oh... then that's different. I'll take it." She slammed the door in my
face. I stood there a moment, cursing softly under my breath. I had a few
choice names to call her, making me feel just a little better. I held my flip
flops in my fingers and jogged on tiptoe back to my bungalow. I was
within just a few feet when something caused me to stop in my tracks and
hold my breath.

In the pitch black darkness, a shaft of golden light spread from the
open door of my bungalow. I knew I had closed the door because it was of
utmost importance to keep Chester inside at night. I'd left my cell phone
inside. There was no way I was going in to retrieve it. I quickly turned and
fled to the reception area. I grabbed the cordless phone and rushed back to
the kitchen — the farthest point from that open door — and dialed 911
with shaking hands.

"911... What is your emergency?"

"I think someone is in my house."

"Are you also in your house?"

"No." I gulped, trying to moisten my dry throat. "I ran to the common
area when I saw my door was wide open. This is Macca Liberty. I own the
Hale Mele Inn and I live there too. I'm in the main kitchen."

"Miss Liberty, stay where you are. A unit is on their way now. I'll stay on the line with you."

"Okay."

"What were you doing outside at this hour, Miss Liberty?"

"Oh, I had to take a bottle of vodka to a very demanding guest."

The operator chuckled. "It must not be easy to run an inn."

"It's usually not that bad. I just get some crazies now and then." I knew she was trying to soothe me and keep my mind off of what was happening, but I just wanted the police to get here fast. "How much longer?"

"They're arriving now. They know where you are and they will come to you when it's safe. Just stay with me on the line."

I began to shiver, but not from the temperatures in the room. My teeth chattered and I held my breath when the door to the kitchen swung open. "Police," I heard someone say. I peeked from my hiding area on the far side of the work table. It was indeed the police so I stood up.

"They're here. Thank you," I told the operator and hung up.

"Are you okay, Miss Liberty?" the officer asked as he stepped closer, sweeping his bright flashlight beam all around the room.

"Yes, thank you." I shivered again.

"Come with us. Your bungalow is clear. The door was open, but only you can tell us if anything is missing."

He followed me to my doorway where his partner was waiting. "All clear, Miss Liberty," he repeated the other officer's pronouncement.

Stepping through the door and into my normally safe abode was a shock; it looked like a tornado had been through the place. Magazines and books were strewn on the floor, the sofa pillows were shredded, and stuffing still floated in the air. My hand flew to my mouth, complete and utter disbelief assaulting me with the scene before us. I stepped gingerly around the debris before realization hit me. "Chester!" I screamed for the little guy. "Chester, baby, where are you?"

"Who is Chester?"

"My cat. He's big and orange... and missing."

Both officers, bless their hearts, helped me look for my little feline buddy. All of us wandered, calling his name, but he was nowhere to be seen, and I began to cry. I sunk down onto the cushionless sofa and sobbed, my head in my hands.

"Is there anyone you can call?" one of the officers asked gently, and I simply shook my head.

"Not at this crazy hour. Who would do this? And who would take my cat?"

"Detective Green is on the way, Miss."

I silenced and looked up at him. "Why?"

"Because you're linked to an ongoing case and we have instructions to call him in the event something happens."

"Oh great." I wiped my eyes. "Just what I need." And right on cue, Detective Green stepped through my doorway.

He called the officers out to the porch and spoke with them for several minutes before returning to me. The officers stayed on the porch.

"I'm sorry." He actually did look remorseful. "I'm concerned that this is related to Chad Stephens' murder."

"But you think I murdered Chad. I didn't, you know."

"I know."

"What?" I was shocked. "Then why was I arrested? Why am I to stand trial then?" This night was getting worse by the minute.

Detective Green sighed and sat on the chair across from me. "Orders from higher up. I had no choice. We haven't stopped investigating though, much to my CO's displeasure."

I softened. "Really? You really believe me?"

He nodded. "I really do. And I am *so* sorry you're being put through this."

I held my breath for several beats as his words sank in. "Thank you."

He nodded again. "Is there anyone who can stay with you tonight?"

"No. I can't bother anyone at this hour. I'll just lock the doors and windows. It'll be dawn soon anyway."

"We'll have a patrol car in the area keeping an eye out then." He wandered to the door. "I'm really sorry about your cat." His words were softly spoken and I actually did feel his sorrow.

"Thank you. We might be able to find him in the daylight. He rarely goes very far. Maybe he was just frightened and is hiding out."

"I hope so. Good luck then." And he was gone. I locked the door, the sliders, and all the windows. I pulled shutters and curtains closed. I checked every room, every closet, and under beds. I was alone.

"Goldfish!"

Davy shimmered into the room, Mr Pinckney right behind him. "Wot's up, Luv?"

I burst into tears again and fell into his arms. "Chester's gone. Someone broke in. Left the door open. Or," I gulped, "took him."

"Oh Babe! I'm so sorry. We can find Chester. I know we can."

"What if... whoever broke in just..." I couldn't form the words, fearing the worst for my little baby.

"Oh dear." Mr. Pinckney was wringing his hands more aggressively than his usual. "This isn't a happy place today." He faded away.

"Did you call the police?" Davy hardly took notice of Mr. Pinckney's appearance or disappearance.

"Yes." And I explained all that had happened that night.

We fell asleep huddled together on the messed up sofa, having replaced the cushions as best we could.

In the morning things still looked bleak. I went through the motions of shower, teeth, and breakfast, my head in a fog. Bennie was the first to arrive with the others soon after. I put them on alert for Chester and also to watch for anything unusual after telling them of the break-in. They each went on their own search of the property for the cat we were all so fond of while I climbed the stairs to the parking area and searched there and beyond. I called Chester's name over and over, and finding nothing, I took to the road on foot. Something orange on the side of the road caught my eye and I took off running toward it. A bundle of matted lifeless fur lay partially hidden in the foliage. I wailed, crying out in a mixture of disbelief, angst, and grief. Bennie came running and Davy shimmered in behind him. All I could do was point. Bennie knelt beside the fur and I held my breath. Davy held onto me as Bennie stood, and holding the fur in his hands, walked back to me.

"Nooo!"

"No, Macca! It's okay! It's fake fur." He held it out to me. "See?" Reluctantly, I reached out and touched it. It was indeed that ratty fake fur you sometimes see in fabric stores. I dissolved into a fresh crying jag, relief overwhelming me. Davy faded into the background as Bennie led me back to my bungalow. "Oh my gosh," he whispered as he saw the wreck of my home. Ming was already in there, tucking books and magazines back into their places. She took over from Bennie and sat me down, then fetched a strong cup of tea for me.

Suddenly there were shouts outside. "I found him!" I heard Sam's voice. "He won't come out though."

"Where is he?" I followed the sound of Sam's voice and found him kneeling beside the laundry area.

"He's between the washer and dryer." He pointed and together Bennie and Sam disconnected the dryer and pulled it out. There, hiding in the very back corner and covered in multiple hues of lint, was my baby.

"Chester, baby," I cooed. He slowly edged his way toward me until I could grab him. I clutched him to my chest and buried my face in his soft fur. He was very much alive and purred directly into my ear. "I love you, baby. I thought I lost you."

I was scared, Mom, he said in my head.

"I know, sweetie, I know," I whispered back to him. He clung to me, his fat paws holding onto my shoulder and arm.

Bad man, Mom, really bad.

"I know," I repeated. Behind us there was cheering, and hands reached in to give the little guy a pet. "Thank you so much, all of you," I choked out the words before the tears came yet again. What a day.

"I'm calling Detective Green about the fake fur by the road. It seems very... suspicious," Bennie spoke between clenched teeth.

"Okay." I was too weary to argue, but definitely comforted by all the wonderful well wishes of my friends. I took my sweet cat back to our home. Ming continued to clean up, but now she was humming as she worked, happy for Chester's return.

I gave the little guy a big helping of canned food — chicken, not seafood — and once he'd finished every little morsel, we went to the bedroom for a little solitude and to let Ming do her magic without my watchful and probably annoying supervision. In the bedroom, Davy shimmered in and flopped on the bed next to us. He gave Chester warm hugs and admonitions to not scare his mummy like that ever again... or his Uncle Davy either. It warmed my heart and I decided a nap was in order. I slept deeply.

TWENTY-THREE

'Ohana

I joined Lani to assist with dinner setup in the dining area. "Miss Macca..." She turned her beautiful face to me. "Kalei and Mama and I would love it if you could come to our home and share dinner with us some evening."

"That would be lovely! Pick a couple of dates and we can see what works in the scheduling." I was so touched at the invitation. She threw out a few days that had been discussed with Kalei and her mama, and we settled on the following evening as there was no dinner service planned at the inn on that night.

That next evening I dressed in a light cotton skirt in hues of blue and green, the hem just above my knee and the fullness only enough to show some movement to the fabric without risking one of those embarrassingly breezy moments. My blouse was made of soft white gauze with short gathered sleeves, a scoop neck, and a blue cord tying in a loose knot in front. In lieu of my normal flip flops, I chose white and tan faux leather sandals with thin straps. I wiggled my toes, enjoying the shimmer of this week's polish choice: Ski Boat Blue. It was always the high point of my Sundays to change my toenail polish color. It had become a running joke. "What color will Macca's toes be this week?" The sparkling blue resembled the highly polished fiberglass of a spiff ski boat, thus the name.

I donned my usual earrings, my mother's sapphires, small silver hoops, and a single tiny diamond helix stud. The use of Bennie's suggested coconut oil upon my arrival on the island had made my hair a soft and fluffy halo of light brown, and I hadn't experienced the frizz of my first days here since.

I had detailed driving instructions in my hand and the coordinates programmed on my phone as I stepped to my front door. "Be good my little Chester. I'll be back after dinner, and I promise a game of Red Dot tonight, okay?" His yawn spoke volumes. "I love you," I added for good measure, and he gave me a delicious slow-blink that made me smile, warmed inside from his minimal show of love. Hey, he was a cat, and he was damned good at being one too.

R2 seemed to call to me to hurry up, but that was just in my terribly overactive imagination; not to worry — machinery was not yet communicating with me. I thanked the stars for that tiny revelation.

It was just before dusk and the light on the streets was at that hazy in-between stage — a little too shadowy with not enough moonlight or sunlight either. I drove slowly as I approached the lowlands that Lani had described in her directions. There were homes on stilts of sorts, as there was frequent flooding in the area. Carports dominated the ground levels of each, while all living areas were on the second floor and above. Many of the lower levels of the structures had lattice work around to provide a bit of a decorative touch, and the home with their number on it was no different except that their lattice work was of a natural colored wood instead of being painted like so many of the neighboring homes.

I parked behind Kalei's car and approached the stairs to the front door, which opened before I even got to the landing. Lani stood there, her beautiful dark hair free of its normal braid and flowing majestically down her back and in front of one shoulder. She was wearing a strapless orange cotton shift with matching tied belt. The dress was very traditional in that it had a fairly full skirt to show movement, especially during hula.

"Miss Macca!" She was all grins, her arms open wide, and we seemed to swallow each other in a giant hug. "Aloha! Welcome to our home."

"Thank you so much for this lovely invitation!" I saw a row of shoes just outside the front door on the wraparound porch and slipped my sandals off before stepping over their threshold. I was getting used to this quaint custom of bare feet inside and felt that it showed a sense of respect for their home.

Kalei rounded a doorway from what appeared to be the kitchen and spread his big arms out. "Miss Macca, aloha!" He squeezed me tightly to his barrel chest and then kissed both my cheeks. He was wearing long loose tan shorts and an untucked brown cotton shirt.

"Kalei thinks his two weeks in France make him part European," Lani teased about the kisses.

"Osmosis, my love... osmosis." He grinned at her. His hair was also loose and nearly as long as Lani's.

"I've never seen either of you with your hair down. So beautiful!" I admired them both and they spun around proudly.

An elderly woman appeared from the same doorway that Kalei had emerged from, wiping her hands on her apron. She wore a colorful muu-muu type shift with parrots and coconuts printed on it. Her hair was long too and hung past her waist, but with streaks of gray, creating the sort of highlight that many women pay huge amounts of money to achieve.

"Miss Macca, this is my Mama, Lehua." Lani beamed at the two of us.

Lehua dropped the hem of her apron and welcomed me with open arms. "Aloha, Miss Macca," she spoke in a voice devoid of the usual sounds of aging. If I'd had my eyes closed I would have taken her for a 20 year old.

"It's lovely to meet you at last, Lehua, and please," I implored of them, "everyone call me just Macca."

"Okay, Just Macca," Kalei teased, and I gave him a playful little poke in the chest.

Lehua ushered us into the room to our left. There were big brightly colored pillows scattered around the floor before a fairly large fireplace of sorts, the difference being that it was set up with a spit that could be turned with a crank. I could see a chicken roasting next to another piece of meat, perhaps pork, on the spit, and Kalei gave it a turn while the rest of us sat cross legged on the pillows. There was a sofa against the back wall, and two overstuffed armchairs flanking it, but it appeared the seating of choice were the pillows. I smiled, loving this little bit of charm and insight into Lani and Kalei's lives.

Lehua disappeared briefly and returned with a tray of drinks in tall bamboo cups, a straw bobbing in each.

"Kalei made mango papaya punch." She offered me one of the cups. When we were all seated with our drinks, I raised my cup to them all.

"*Mahalo* for inviting me into your home."

"Aloha," they all chimed. Then Kalei added, "You're *'ohana*." He gave me the greatest compliment: I was family.

"To *'ohana*!" We raised our cups again and then sipped from the straws. The juice was heavenly, and I detected a little bit of alcohol, but not enough to get soused on.

"A tiny shot of rum," Kalei confirmed. "Just a little to feel the happiness more."

"We have been wanting to have you join us for dinner for a long time, but you always seem so busy." Lani smiled, no hard feelings evident.

"I'm never too busy for you."

Lani disappeared next, and reappeared with a tray of *puu puu*, little bits of finger food. There were chunks of pineapple on skewers, the fruit slightly charred from the cooking fire, and rice crackers and hunks of white cheese were scattered on a plate. It was simple yet very satisfying, and just enough to tide us over until dinner.

"Lani has told me that you were helping at the homeless camp before... your unfortunate incarceration." Lehua broke the silence and opened up the subject of the elephant in the room that seemed to come up wherever I went these days. I liked to think my elephant was dressed in a pink tutu and ballet slippers like something Sandra Boynton might draw, but that's just my bizarre sense of humor. Go figure.

"Yes, and I will be going back to the camp once this whole mess is cleared up."

"I would be quite happy to help you. I have Sundays off and it would be my honor to assist," she added.

"Thank you! And I will take you up on that offer!"

She smiled a beautiful but older version of Lani's lovely smile. "Kalei and Lani told me all about it and I am eager to help."

"Mama is in charge of the cafeteria at the hospital," Lani spoke with pride.

"That's certainly a big job I would imagine!"

Lehua beamed. "I love my job. It is important to love one's work, don't you agree?"

"I definitely agree! It took my move here for me to enjoy my work, and I have such good friends helping me that it makes it a delight every day."

Everyone stopped speaking as we heard footsteps on the front stairs. "Who could that be?" Lehua murmured. She began to rise to check on their visitor, but Kalei motioned her to stay on her pillow while he instead went to the door.

"Kimo!" He bellowed this name and we all turned quickly to see. "What are you here for?" Kalei's normally calm demeanor had been replaced by something near to rage. A thought briefly flitted through my mind that I'd not like to ever be on the receiving end of that ire.

Kimo stepped through the door. He was dressed in surf shorts, a tank top with "Surf Hawaii" emblazoned on the front, and well-worn black flip flops. "Is that any way to greet your bruddah?"

"Kimo..." Lehua now rose. "I have nothing for you." Her voice was stern and her speech clipped. "I've told you this before. Go back to your surfing on Oahu."

"But I came to visit my *'ohana*." He was grinning as he advanced on us seated around the fireplace. "We meet again, Miss Macca Liberty. The new innkeeper where my sister and her husband work." The Pidgin English I'd heard him speak that one time in the inn's kitchen had faded, taking me by surprise. He sat cross legged between Lani and me, Kalei standing just behind, as if to guard.

"Yes," I answered his non-question quietly, picking up on the tension in the room and definitely not trusting this man. I followed Lani and Kalei's lead in keeping him at arm's length.

"I guess you trust them a lot, yeah? You named them in some will or something? They get the inn if something happens to you?" His expression was chilling.

"How do you know that?" My eyes narrowed in suspicion.

"I'm sorry, Macca." I could see the shame on Lani's face as she spoke. "He overheard Kalei and me talking about it with Mama."

"Well..." I turned back to her brother. "I do believe it's really none of your business."

"Macca is right." Kalei's voice was cold. "It's none of your business and you need to butt out. Butt out of this entire family. You're no good."

"Oh, I'm good all right," Kimo sneered. "You just haven't seen how good I am. Yet."

Kalei grabbed the back of Kimo's tank top and yanked him to a standing position. "Go now!"

"I'm going, I'm going. I just wanted to say hello to my family." He sauntered to the door, straightening his shirt that had been crumpled by Kalei's sizeable hand. "Aloha, bruddah, sistah, Mama." He waved the shaka, or "hang loose" sign at us. Kalei followed him to the porch and watched him go. It was several minutes before he returned to his seat.

"He's gone. I'm sorry."

"How did he leave?" Lehua asked.

"On foot. I watched until he was well round the bend."

She shook her head. "That boy is bad news. He wasn't always like that. Something changed him in all the years he spent surfing on the North Shore," she spoke to no one and everyone. I shivered.

"Come." Kalei tried to make his voice brighter. "Let's forget him and eat our dinner." He pulled the meat off the spit and carried it as we followed. To the right side of the front door was a small kitchen and a large dining area connected. On the dining table was a spread of fresh fruits, green salad, vegetables, and small side dishes of lychee nuts, poi, and little squares of baked tofu. There were poi rolls as well, a deep purple color visible when torn apart, and also purple Hawaiian sweet potato salad. Kalei carved the meat and served it on a large platter, setting it at the end of the table.

Lehua led the way, filling her plate with a little bit of everything. "Kalei makes extra dishes for us so we have meals the rest of the week," she beamed. "He's such a thoughtful son-in-law." I saw the big man blush and shake his head dismissively.

I followed her lead and took a little bit of everything as well, stopping short of the chicken and pork. My plate was quite full enough even without it. Lehua led us out the back door to a large section of the wraparound porch that was set with lit lanterns and a big table flanked by benches. "We prefer to eat outside when the weather allows," she explained. "Much aloha spirit in nature, I think." And I agreed.

The food was wonderful, of course, and I complimented them on the impressive spread. "I do believe I've gained at least ten pounds since first tasting Kalei's fabulous food," I teased.

"I'm so proud of his talents," Lani chimed in, gazing at her husband in adoration.

At that moment I felt Davy shimmer in behind me and touch my shoulder affectionately. Lehua caught my eye just before she focused on the space behind me. Davy simply froze where he stood instead of shimmering away. I could tell their eyes were locked. The look on Lehua's face was pleasant though, and comforting. She found no fear in his presence but seemed genuinely intrigued. I noticed that Lani and Kalei had stopped talking and eating and were watching Lehua closely.

"What is it, Mama?" Lani reached out and touched her mother's hand.

"We have a visitor." Lehua smiled and then she turned to me. "And I do believe he is a friend of Macca's, yes?"

I felt the heat spread up from my neck to my ears. I was speechless.

"Who is it, Mama?" Lani was smiling at her mother and glancing at me, a warm affection evident upon her face.

"You and I both know of him, Lani dear. I'm not certain Kalei will though." She was still smiling, watching Davy and me closely. I was frozen in my chair.

"Then it isn't Macca's Uncle Wally?" Kalei volunteered.

"No. As I said, it's someone you may not know." There was no rebuff in her tone, but clarification as if to a child. "He was famous at one time, was he not, Macca?"

I cleared my throat, trying to dislodge the lump. "Yes ma'am."

"Is he always with you?"

"Not always... but a good part of the time, yes."

Davy squeezed my shoulder where his hand had been resting then swept a deep theatrical bow to our hostess. "My name is Davy and it is a pleasure to be here in your lovely home."

She nodded, almost queenly except for the girlish grin. "Thank you. And it is indeed a pleasure to have you as well." I began to grin, for her own was so infectious. "I watched you as a child." She blushed.

"And I thank you for that." Davy put a hand to his chin. "I believe you listened to our music too."

She put a nervous hand to her forehead, a youthful embarrassment suddenly appearing. "Yes. You were my favorite Monkee," she giggled.

"Mama!" Lani was adamant now. She turned to me. "Mama has always been able to see spirits. I guess she is seeing one now?" Lani turned back to her mother.

"Oh dear." Lehua focused on her daughter. "I'm so sorry; how rude of me. There is a very handsome young gentleman standing behind Macca and his name is Davy Jones."

Lani gasped. "Of The Monkees?"

Lehua nodded, the shyness of a child suddenly so unlike the woman I'd been getting to know earlier in the evening. Lani searched my face then, and I could only smile and nod.

"This is starting to make some sense," Kalei joined. "There have been some odd things happening since you arrived." There was no sound of accusation or irritation in his voice, only admiration and astonishment.

"I'm sorry. I've tried... we've tried... to keep it a secret, but it hasn't been easy since we're all together nearly every day. Davy appeared when my Uncle Wally passed."

"He's here to help you, isn't he?" Lehua was fidgety. Clearly she was crushing on Davy something fierce, and I found it so enchanting.

144

"Yes. He's been my rock, frankly. It's not been an easy couple of years."

"Tell them to close their eyes," Davy spoke quietly to Lehua, and she nodded, her shyness melting away.

"Lani, Kalei, close your eyes, my children. Close them tightly." They did as she instructed. Davy shimmered away for a moment, then the air began to waver near Lehua and he shimmered back in a more elaborate manner, like there was more energy behind his actions. His hand rested warmly on the older woman's shoulder.

"They can open their eyes now." Davy smiled, and before Lehua could relay the instructions to her children, they did indeed open their eyes. They gasped in unison, and it was quite evident they could see Davy now, in all his red velvet shirted glory. "Hello." He offered his hand first to Lani for a shake, then to Kalei, and both eagerly returned the gesture. "And now I get the opportunity to thank you for taking such good care of Macca. You have my deepest admiration."

"You're... welcome." Kalei seemed in shock.

Lani appeared frozen with her hand over her mouth, nearly matching her mother's earlier reticence. I saw her blush and drop her gaze whenever Davy looked her way.

Lehua though, took her fangirlishness quite seriously and reached out to hold his hand, grinning like a kid who had won the grand prize at an amusement park. He turned and flashed a beautiful grin at her, squeezing her hand. I beamed. He was just a really nice guy. Except when he was annoying, that is. Then he was just an annoying nice guy.

"Mind you though, my presence needs to remain our little secret for Macca's sake and for the inn's as well."

"I like that." Lehua squeezed his arm. "It means I can keep you more to myself." And then she burst into a high-pitched giggle. Fangirl was definitely in the house. It was adorable though.

"Just remember, the more people who know about me, the more... unusual attention the inn may get. The Notorious Hale Mele Inn just doesn't have a very good ring to it, yeah?"

I had a sudden vision of ghost hunters clamoring to stake out our little paradise... and the ensuing fandom descending upon our quiet little inn. I shuddered.

"Please. It's important to me to not have that kind of publicity. I hope you understand," I added. I was also concerned that if the beans were spilled I'd eventually lose Davy. He wouldn't want to be a carnival act on display and neither would I.

"No worries, Macca." Kalei wore his warmest smile. "It's a secret."

"A wonderful secret." Lani's voice was just above a whisper in awestruck wonder. The five of us held hands around the table, Davy sitting between Lehua and me. Suddenly, Lani's shyness completely evaporated as she dropped her mother's and her husband's hands and clapped with glee. "Oh, this is so very cool!"

Any tension was now gone and we were just a happy group of people. Davy ate off of my plate.

"Would you like to make a plate of your own?" Lehua made doe-eyes at him, which I found utterly charming. The years seemed to drop away from her.

"No, thank you." He grinned impishly. "I prefer to annoy Macca as much as possible actually."

I rolled my eyes and the laughter surrounded us like music — the sound of family.

Lani and Kalei stopped me the following afternoon and asked if they could have a word with me. We stepped into the kitchen for a little privacy.

"Last night was amazing," Lani began. "I don't think Mama has come down off her cloud yet."

"You seem to have a solid spot on that same cloud, dear," Kalei teased his wife and then turned to me. "But we have something to tell you, Macca." He gestured for Lani to explain.

"I... we think that Kimo might be behind some of the troubles that got you arrested," Lani began hesitantly.

I nodded and gazed out the window for a moment before agreeing. "I think so too. I really hope not though, but it looks bad for him. I'm so sorry."

"Oh dear," Lani nearly wailed. "Please don't be sorry! It is we who are sorry! There is no love lost between Kimo and our family. He is *kapu* now; none of us want any contact with him."

I felt my eyes burn a little and held my arms out to them for a small group hug.

"Do you think we should tell the police our suspicions, Macca?" the big man inquired nervously.

"That's a good question, one I've been struggling with myself lately. If I turn over the information I have to Detective Green, will he pursue it or just consider we're sending him a red herring?"

"Red herring?" Their perplexed looks were nearly identical.

"Sending him a false bit of information to turn suspicion away from me," I explained. "A wild goose chase if you will."

"Oh! Good point. I hadn't thought of that." Kalei leaned against the counter, rubbing his face. "We have to do something though."

We stood staring at one another, none of us coming up with solutions. Finally I shook my head as I realized there was only one choice; we had to tell Detective Green. "I'll call him. Maybe he can stop by and talk to us."

Lani let out a whoosh of breath in relief. "Oh, thank you!" She gave me another hug then and I pulled my cell phone out. I left a voicemail for the detective, asking very nicely if he could take some time out of his busy day for us.

"I guess we wait now." But my phone rang before I could even slip it back into my pocket. "Yikes!" I saw the caller was indeed the detective.

"It's him?" Lani chewed her thumbnail and I idly pulled her hand away from her mouth as I nodded, as a mother might do for a child.

"Hello Detective Green," I spoke quietly into my phone. "Thank you for calling back so soon."

"Is everything okay?" he quickly inquired.

"Fine. I think. That is... well, we think we may have some information for you on Chad's murder."

I was met with silence on the other end until he finally sighed. "Okay. I'm over in your area so I'll be there in ten."

"Thank you," I spoke to dead air as he'd already ended the call. I took a deep breath. "I'm going to need a drink after this."

Nervous laughter bubbled up from the three of us. Kalei got busy setting up a pitcher of his wonderful iced tea along with a few of Lani's freshly baked cookies — fudge with macadamia nuts. My mouth watered but I resisted. We needed to ply Detective Green with as many sweet treats as we could get away with.

"Knock-knock." We heard his voice a few moments later and invited him in. I dragged the bar stools into the kitchen, setting them up around the big workspace in the center of the room. Lani poured iced tea for the four of us and pushed the cookies closer to our prey, the good detective, who eagerly sampled both.

I cleared my throat and took the lead. "Lani's brother Kimo may very well be behind Chad's murder. I was talking to my friends at Hale Maluhia and..."

He interrupted me then, fuming. "You were at the homeless camp? Didn't we tell you to stay away from there?"

Now it was my turn to fume. "We provide meals for them. I cannot expect Kalei and Lani to do it alone, so yes, I was at the camp. Now, as I was saying, Makala, Joe, and Kai are sort of the clan elders at the camp." I proceeded to tell him what I had found out about Chad and Kimo, including their history. Detective Green was busily taking notes.

When I was finished, Lani added her information. "My brother has been asking about the inn and insisting that it should have been left to us and not to Macca when Wally died. I..." She swallowed hard and shook her head briefly. "My brother is not a good man. I don't know what happened, but he changed when he returned from North Shore."

"Which," I added, "is interesting because my current will states that the staff will inherit should something happen to me."

"How do you think he could have found that out?" Detective Green directed his question to Kalei and Lani.

"We think he heard us talking about it," Lani pointedly responded, "and Kalei has caught him hanging out around here a couple of times."

This stunned me for a moment, for I'd only seen him here once, and by the look on Detective Green's face, he was equally surprised.

"I kicked his butt out," Kalei steamed. "Both times. I warned him I'd call the cops if I caught him a third time, but he hasn't shown up here, only at our house."

"Do you know where he's living these days?" Detective Green had his pen poised to write, but Kalei simply shook his head.

"His last address that we know of was North Shore, Oahu."

The detective leaned back and slapped his notebook shut. "This isn't a lot to go on. It's just basically rumor and hearsay and suspicion."

"Then perhaps you should go investigate it further, Detective Green." I was grinding my teeth to keep from lashing out at him. "Or do you just prefer the idea of me, an innocent in this case, going to trial for it? After all, as long as you clear a case, nothing else matters, right?" I slid off my barstool and faced him with my hands on my hips. "Good day then, Detective. We have nothing more to discuss."

I turned on my heel and returned to my bungalow where I proceeded to slam things. I picked up the throw rug at the door, slung it over the railing on the deck, and then beat the heck out of it with the broom. Sand and dust clouds formed around me until I was coughing but still spitting mad. I felt rather than saw the broom being removed from my hands and placed against the deck rail. A hand closed around my wrist, and as we walked out of the sand and dust cloud, I saw that Davy was guiding me back inside the bungalow and to the sofa.

"That was an interesting temper tantrum out there." He was grinning and still holding my hand, stroking my fingers with his thumb.

"I'm pissed off!"

He feigned shock. "Really? I never would have guessed!"

And that's when I dissolved into tears. I really hate that I cry when I get mad, but there it was. "That man makes me so mad!"

"Yeah. He's an irritating bloke, but I stayed after you stomped off and..."

"You were there?"

"Yes. I don't always have to be visible to be somewhere, Babe. Haven't you figured that out yet?"

"I never gave it much thought, I guess."

"So anyway," he continued so calmly, "I stayed after you left and I feel certain that Detective Green will pursue the matter. He talked a little more with Lani and Kalei, and I believe they convinced him that Kimo is shady as hell."

"Really?" I wiped my eyes on the hem of my tee-shirt and he watched my moves, a little grin playing on his lips.

"Nice view, Babe." His eyes were still on my shirt.

I punched his arm. "Shut up. And stop looking."

"Well, how can I not? You're flapping around there and showing everything off! If I were your father I'd be upset, but as it so happens, I quite enjoyed the view."

I punched him again and he began to chuckle. I heaved a deep sigh and leaned against him, letting him comfort me. "I need a drink."

"I can open some wine for us," he volunteered.

"No. This calls for something stronger. I need liquor. Gin. No! Tequila!"

"One tequila, two tequila, three tequila, floor! Party is on!" He chuckled as he recited an old joke and went to the kitchen to rummage around in my one little cupboard that held just a few bottles of alcohol. We were mostly wine and beer drinkers, but every now and then... well... I'd pay for it in the morning, but I didn't care.

"It's not a party. It's cheap therapy."

"Okay. Therapy's on! You lay on the sofa and I'll take secret notes and shrink your head."

His words tickled me and I began to giggle. I cry when I'm angry and I get giddy when I've been under a lot of stress. Yep, I could use the therapy.

TWENTY-FOUR

Onslaught

I was dreaming so peacefully, walking along in a grotto behind a waterfall, dunking my legs in the cool water, and then nailing a perfect swan dive into the deep pool around the bottom of the waterfall. I knew it was a dream because diving isn't really my thing. I pulled myself up onto the rocks around the splashing water and stretched out for a rest. It was then that a huge rock seemed to peel off the grotto walls and splash just inches from where I lay. But wait... the accompanying sound of breaking glass was out of context. I slowly pulled myself out of the deep sleep and looked around at my normally serene bedroom. There was indeed broken glass all over the floor, and the window was shattered. I scrambled out of the other side of the bed to avoid the glass and ran to the living room.

I screamed our emergency word, "Goldfish!" just as I realized Davy was already there. He sat me on the sofa and marched back into my bedroom. It was several minutes before he reappeared, a large rock in his hand. Tied to that rock was a note.

"Don't touch it," he spoke quietly. "Call the police. Now. I'm putting this back where I found it." His expression was grim as he tossed my cell phone to me.

"911. What is your emergency?"

I felt like I'd lived this scene before but I blundered ahead. "This is Macca Liberty at Hale Mele. Someone just threw a rock through my window and there appears to be a note tied to it."

"Have you read the note?"

"No. I didn't want to degrade any evidence. Detective Green warned me previously."

"Oh! Detective Green you say? One moment, and please stay on the line."

I did as I was told, hearing the tapping of keys on a keyboard.

"Detective Green will be there within ten minutes," she continued. "A patrol car will be there within three."

"Nothing like a good name-dropping to get some action," Davy sneered.

"Thank you," I responded to the 911 operator, pointedly ignoring Davy for a moment, and then ended the call.

"And you're okay? It didn't hit you?" He was checking my arms and legs.

"No. I'm fine."

"Are your doors and windows locked?"

"Yes. I'm all secure except for the gaping hole in my bedroom window where the rock sailed through. Not feeling too secure there."

A knock at the door caused me to unwind my crossed legs and get off the sofa to answer it, just opening it a crack. Abbott and Costello Officers at my service. I felt Davy's presence beside me.

"You should really look before you open your door," Abbott-Officer admonished.

"I don't have a peephole, but believe me, that's next on my to-do list." I opened the door wider to let them in.

"Where is the rock?" Costello-Officer asked, and I silently pointed down the hall to my bedroom. "You touched it?"

"Hell no! I didn't know what it was, but it sailed through my window. Would you have touched it?"

"No ma'am. I'm trained."

"Good for you," I mumbled under my breath.

"He's an arse," Davy grumbled and I waved him away, then turned the wave into a scratching of my head. Oh, I should have received an Oscar for my performances whenever he was around.

Both officers were in the bedroom for some time and I watched them from the hallway. Costello-Officer leaned down to peer at the large rock, his hands behind his back like he couldn't trust himself to not touch it. I followed Abbott-Officer to the living room and watched as he opened the drapes enough to unlock the patio sliders before he slipped outside. There was another knock on the door and Costello-Officer let Detective Green in.

Together they surveyed the mess... I mean, the crime scene in my bedroom. I nervously peered out the open front door and was tremendously relieved when no guests arrived to complain about being awakened by all the commotion. I took a seat in my comfortable rattan armchair, holding Chester close. He didn't seem to want to leave me, and I knew I didn't want to let him loose. He purred and I fretted, but occasionally I would gain inner strength by burying my face in his fur and reveling in his purrs. "I love you," I whispered into the soft orange fluff. He purred louder at first.

I will deny saying this, but I love you right back, he said in my mind. I gave a soft snort of laughter onto the top of his head. "Thank you." *Don't mention it. Ever. Like I said... I would deny it if asked.*

It was more than I could handle at that moment — the assault on my home, the police in my presence, the cat who was not missing this time. I began to cry, burying my face in Chester's luscious orange coat. I felt Davy beside me in the big chair, cuddling and whispering in my ear. I couldn't make out his words, nor could I comprehend the reason for such an invasion upon my personal life in the way of a rock through my window. What if Chester had been sleeping there?

"Oi." I felt his breath in my ear when I finally understood his words. "Think of this famous saying. I wish I knew who said it... 'A woman is like a tea bag – you never know how strong she is until she gets in hot water.'" He took a breath to continue.

I had to smile, even if it was the tiniest of displays of happiness or contentment.

"I'm not done," he admonished, but gently. "'Destiny is a name often given in retrospect to choices that had dramatic consequences.'"

I was silent, waiting for the name of the hero who had made this statement, and feeling quite inadequate.

"Tsk, tsk, tsk, you muggle," he teased. "That is someone you admire: J.K. Rowling."

I gasped, instantly recognizing my lack of attention to details of the literary world. "More!"

"'The day will come when man will recognize woman as his peer, not only at the fireside, but in councils of the nation. Then, and not until then, will there be the perfect comradeship, the ideal union between the sexes that shall result in the highest development of the race.'"

I stared at him.

He stared back and moved to sit on the sofa, plumping the pillows before settling back. "Come on. You don't know that one? Your mother would be appalled." I knew he was teasing but I could also see he was dead serious.

"Susan B. Anthony!" The words had popped into my head, did a little jig on my tongue, and flew out of my mouth before I could even think of the word "suffragette."

"'You may encounter many defeats, but you must not be defeated. In fact, it may be necessary to encounter the defeats, so you can know who you are, what you can rise from, how you can still come out of it.'" I knew now that he was only working to distract me, but it was a perfect ploy. There wasn't much else I could do.

"Oh, I know that one! She is one of my favorites and even spoke at President Obama's inauguration! Maya Angelou!"

"Very well done, you!" His grin buoyed my spirits.

"'I'll be scared later. Right now I'm too mad,'" he continued.

I frowned, not recognizing such a basic quote.

He shook his head at me, a twinkle in his eye. "Bugs Bunny. 'Th-th-th-that's all, folks!'"

I clapped my hand over my mouth to stifle a laugh when I saw him suddenly draw himself up and shimmer over to another corner. This was followed closely by Detective Green moving slowly into the living room and settling on the sofa Davy had recently vacated. I idly wondered if the cushions were warm when Green snapped my attention back to him.

"Were you just talking to someone?" he inquired.

"Chester. My cat." The laughter that had been bubbling up a moment before had suddenly dissolved inside me.

"Oh." He glanced at the cat and then turned his attention back to me. "What can you tell me about Chad Stephens?"

"What?" This just wasn't a question I'd expected.

"Exactly what I just asked. What can you tell me about Chad Stephens?"

I swallowed a few times before I found the words at last. "He was the friendliest man I'd met in a very long time, a veteran, a Marine, suffering from PTSD, and he was tossed aside by the Veterans Administration." I swallowed and rubbed my face. "He was the warmest, most caring person in the homeless camp where I've been helping." Hot tears began to slide down my cheeks — my first tears for Staff Sergeant Chad Stephens. I sniffed too hard and it ended in a choked cough.

He stared at me for quite some time before handing over a plastic evidence bag with a handwritten note inside that read:

I know what you did.
Sarge made advances.
You rebuffed him.
Then you killed him.
You'll pay. With your life.
A mere pittance, frankly.
Just like your cat. And your bird.
And the dog will be a challenge, but I'll win.

Something flashed in my memory and I attempted to hang onto the slippery thought. It was... almost there. I tried to hold tight to it all but it was like a greased pig in a muddy pen. I squeezed my eyes shut, as if I could push all the known stuff out and let the nearly-known things seep in. I shook my head. Nothing, but...

"Wait! No one would call Chad 'Sarge' and get away with it. Ask Makala or Kai... or more importantly Joe. He knows for sure."

Detective Green scribbled in his note pad. "And these people are...?"

I made a face. "Really?"

He squeezed his lips to the side. "I'm sorry. I'm on your side. I just need to hear from you how you know them."

Oh. OH! I perked up. "Oh, I see! Yes, Makala, Joe, and Kai are at the homeless encampment, Hale Maluhia. Makala is sort of thought of as the mother, so tread carefully."

I saw a flicker of recognition in Green's eyes, and just the hint of a knowing smile on his face. "And who is the dog he refers to?"

"That's Susie. He's one of our mascots."

"A new one?"

"Yes. Very loyal." I don't know why I said that. Perhaps I was worried about his actual status as a GHOST. Who knew that running a nearly haunted inn could be so complex.

"Did Chad Stephens make advances?" I saw something in Green's eyes that made me pause before responding.

"No. Never. We were friends. That's all."

"But can men be friends with women?" he pursued. I turned my head to look at Davy hovering in the corner nearly two feet from the floor. Could we? I stared at him, right into his eyes and through to the nucleus that was David. My heart was tugged hard and I felt this pull, like a suction. I gasped. A surreal scene played out in my head: I was being pulled toward him, but then the room dropped away and my body was no longer my own, yet it remained seated demurely on the sofa. Davy's eyes locked on mine. I felt my sternum rise to meet his, and when we touched there was a spark. Perhaps it was all in my mind, but it most certainly connected and zinged me right down to my toes. My face was numb, my tongue locked. I felt the pull through the core of my being. Davy and I would always be connected. I felt it strongly now. I swiped at the sudden moisture on my cheeks and realized I was still in my chair and Davy was still across the room. What was that? I shook it off quickly and found my voice again.

"Yes. Men and women can be friends." I didn't offer anything further but challenged Detective Green with my eyes. He backed off.

"We have some work to do on this in the lab. I suggest you stay somewhere else for the night."

"And where do you suggest that might be? I have guests who are depending on me, and I have a business to run."

"Then I suggest you get someone to stand guard." His sudden irritation caught me unawares at first.

"I... I'll make a few calls." I averted my eyes, suddenly feeling naked and unguarded.

Green exited, leaving his goons behind. To be fair, they weren't really goons, but friendly officers who left just a few minutes later. I was just feeling extremely unnerved by our local detective and his cohorts. Hell, I was feeling invaded. Period. And, being in this most vulnerable state, I took time to berate myself; I should be remembering the officers' real names and stop referring to them in my thoughts as Abbott and Costello.

"Did you do that?" I gazed into Davy's deep brown eyes. "Did you pull me to you in your mind or something?"

His face held a soft and beautiful smile. "Yes. You needed to see that we will be together as long as you want or need."

"That was one hell of a way to show it. Very surreal."

He chuckled and sat next to me; it was comforting.

"Where can I sleep?" I rested my head on Davy's shoulder.

"Right here; I'll be here."

"Am I safe?"

"Yes."

Why didn't I believe him? What was happening? Where had my confidence gone? Lying in glass fragments on my bedroom floor, I answered myself. He led me to the sofa and pulled a light throw over me as I lay down. He lifted my feet and put them in his lap as he sat. I fell asleep feeling his hand on my ankle like a security blanket.

Daylight came far too early for my weary mind and body, but the sun rose and spilled its warmth on my face. Davy was still sitting with my feet on his lap, watching me. He smiled with that radiance that melts women's hearts, and I couldn't help but feel comforted by his presence.

Chester placed his front paws on my chest and gave me the most pathetic mewling. "Hungry, big guy?"

I could eat a horse, but please, just chicken, thank you. I chuckled at his words invading my thoughts. Davy shimmered away.

"Chicken it is then." I got up and went through the morning routine after feeding Chester. I felt secure in the knowledge that this day would definitely be better than the previous night. It had to be.

After a long hot shower, a cup of tea, and some leftover fruit from yesterday's lunch, I opened my front door and stood peering out for a few moments. I knew it was silly of me to be fearful of the outside when my inside had been violated by a very rude rock and and an equally rude note attached to it, but there it was. Agoraphobia was beginning to make sense to me. I could lock my doors and have everything delivered to me, or... I could pull on my big girl panties and show the world — and the evil person with a great arm and a rock — that I was brave. Of course, it would be an act, but hell, I was getting to be good at this stuff. Oscar material I was, I was. I heard the Cowardly Lion in my head, "I'll fight you with one hand tied behind my baaaaaaaack." I knew my imitation was poor. A similarly cowardly whimper escaped from my throat.

I don't resemble him one bit, you know, that lion guy, Chester advised, his nose up in the air as he passed me and ventured into the bushes nearby. I stepped onto the porch. I mean, I couldn't let a cat show he was braver than I was, could I?

In the reception area, Bennie looked up from his work with his usual smile in place. Ahh, that was what I needed.

"Good morning, Macca!"

"Good morning, Bennie. Is everything okay in here this morning?"

He frowned briefly. "Yes. Perfect as usual. Why do you ask?"

I told him about the events of the wee hours of that morning and he stepped out from behind the desk and, quite impulsively, wrapped his arms around me in a bear hug. I matched it with my own, my head against his shoulder. "Thank you." I smiled, feeling both awkward and grateful. "I'm okay."

"Do you need one of us to stay each night?"

"No. Everything will be fine." I forced a brighter smile. "The police are increasing their patrol of the area."

"Okay, but if you need an extra person to stay, we can always pull the cot out and be here. You just say the word."

"Thank you. I will." I placed my hand on his arm. "And I really do mean thank you."

"Oh, you're welcome, but don't you think twice about us doing whatever needs doing. And we'll get your window fixed today. We're all in this together, sort of. I mean... we want to be." I could see he was a little nervous at the raw truth of his feelings showing in his words. I was touched and wiped my eyes with the back of my hand and nodded; words were stuck in my throat. Every day these people proved we were indeed a family.

It was nearing the lunch hour when a very angry Auntie Uppity stomped into the reception area. Bennie and I had been huddled together over inventory, and we both looked up when we heard her huff and stamp her foot.

"Someone has been in my cottage," she raised her voice unnecessarily. "Perhaps your maid has some sticky fingers."

"What?" Bennie and I responded nearly in unison.

"The book I was reading is gone, and so is a bottle of vodka I bought at the local store."

"Are you sure?" I was confused but asked the question anyway, despite realizing it was like putting gasoline on the fire that always seemed to burn in Auntie Uppity.

"Of course I'm sure, you addle-brained nitwit. I am calling the police!"

"Wait, please." I stepped out from behind the desk, my hand up to placate her. "Can you show me? Please?" I was putting on my nicest manners, trying to calm her.

"My word isn't good enough?"

"Oh, I'm sorry. That's not it at all. It's just that we've never had such a thing like this happen before." I backed off. At that moment, Jack Morrison stepped in and joined us. He looked a little concerned himself, and Bennie stepped up to assist. I overheard them though.

"I hate to complain," Jack began, "but someone has been in our cottage and taken two books. I know it seems trifling, but I was nearly done with one of them. I just need to know how it ends, you know?"

My mind flashed back to the rock through my window. These new developments were pretty suspicious to me. Within an hour, two more guests had complained of books being gone as well. I took down all the information on the missing items and promised that not only would I look into it, but I would also replace the items immediately.

I informed Detective Green by phone of the incidents and then told Bennie I'd be back soon. Armed with my list, I headed for the larger book store in Hilo, knowing that there was nothing closer that would all ow me to find each book.

A few hours and $103 lighter, I was back and delivering the items to the guests, with my fullest apologies.

Only Auntie Uppity was disagreeable. "It's about time!" I hurried away from her poisonous aura.

That night the dining room was full and I looked around at each guest, the usual happiness marred by the morning's uneasiness. As dessert was being served to some, I heard a shout outside. "Fire!"

Bennie was the first out the door, rounding the corner and heading toward the pool area where the voice seemed to have originated. There stood Sam, trying to use buckets of water from the pool to douse flames that reached higher than the roofs.

"Sam! No! Just leave it and back away. I don't want you hurt," I yelled as Bennie grabbed a hose and tried to put out the fire. But the flames were of bonfire proportion and there seemed to have been gasoline or some other accelerant used, judging by the acrid smoke. I was dialing 911 yet again, this time reporting a fire.

It wasn't long before we heard the scream of sirens. Bennie was using water from the hose to douse everything around the fire, to protect against it spreading any further. Sam was still bucketing water from the pool as well, but both men stepped aside as firefighters in proper h eat deflecting gear were advancing on the inferno. It was a very hot fire, the heat pushing us farther back. I watched nervously, hoping the structures would be safe. Bennie reached out and grasped my hand tightly; his face seemed to mirror my concerns.

While it was probably only ten minutes before the bonfire was a smoldering mess, it had felt like hours. Miraculously, the structures were untouched.

"Thanks to your good men here," the fire captain gestured to Bennie and Sam, "it was fully contained."

"Can you tell what was burning or what started the fire?"

"Definitely arson." He scratched his chin. "It appears to have been a large pile of paper, perhaps some books."

I groaned. The missing books. This had to be part of the rock throwing incident. "You need to report it to Detective Green. This sounds like part of an ongoing harassment issue that he's aware of and investigating."

The fire captain's face registered surprise, but he promised to give a report to the police. By now, all the guests had gathered around.

"I'm so sorry, Macca," Jack Morrison's voice was heavy with emotion.

"Thank you." I choked back the tears and the smoke.

Other guests who had reported stolen or missing items joined in. All except Auntie Uppity. I heard her hiss at her husband, "I told you this was a dump. Why we couldn't stay at the Hilton is beyond me. I hold you and that innkeeper bitch personally responsible for ruining my vacation."

Mr. D'Antonio turned on her. "No, Zeta. You are the only one responsible for your misery. You find misery wherever you go because you bring it with you. I'm sick of it. When we get home, I'm filing for divorce."

The look on her face was just enough to give me a little bit of pleasure, but then I immediately felt guilty for taking joy from someone else's misfortune. Still, I was surprised that Angelo had lasted this long.

I didn't sleep well that night with images of the ugly bonfire invading my dreams. In the morning, even a hot shower did nothing to perk me up. In the kitchen, I found I was at a zero energy level. I fed Chester and then opened a packet of oatmeal and dumped it in a bowl. My eyes rested on the cold coffee from yesterday. On a whim, I dumped it on top of the oatmeal and zapped the whole thing in the microwave. I was quite proud of my concoction as I sat down to eat it — breakfast and caffeine in one hit, and it tasted good too.

A quick wash of my dish and the coffee pot and I was ready to trudge to the reception area and begin the day. Well, I was as ready as I was going to be. First I stopped at the coffee pot adjacent to the reception desk and poured a steaming cup. I stood for a moment peering out the window at the edge of the pool area. The discarded pile of crime scene tape on top of the sooty sodden mess of burned books was still there. "I'd kind of been hoping it was just a bad dream," I spoke idly to Bennie standing behind me at the desk.

"Me too." He put more strength than necessary behind stapling a sheaf of papers together as he spoke.

I sipped my coffee in silence. I wasn't deep in thought, just completely blank of mind. Sam emerged from the far side of the building, dragging a wheeled garbage bin and holding a shiny new shovel. Involuntarily, my eyes shifted to the garden shed where a large industrial strength padlock had recently been installed. A ragged sigh escaped my lips as I set my cup down, retrieved a big dust pan from the cleaning supplies closet, and joined Sam. Together we faced the pile of putrid debris, scraping it up a little at a time and dumping it in the garbage bin. Soon Bennie joined, then Kalei and Albert. We worked in silence with makeshift tools. Kalei had brought several giant cookie sheets from the kitchen and we used those as well.

When all the rubble was scraped up and disposed of, the crew stared sadly at the muddy ground, now devoid of all green grass. Albert sighed, took the shovel from Sam, and began to cut chunks of sod from the edges of the landscaping. He placed them, patchwork style, onto the scorched and burned earth. One by one, the rest of us joined him, using our bare hands to pull the larger pieces of sod into smaller chunks and creating a mosaic of grass. Soon, it looked less like a crime scene and more like an art installment. Albert stood grinning down at it, shaking dirt off of his hands. He turned to me and the grin was contagious.

"Well done." Bennie's words were quiet but powerful. Albert pulled a hose around from the shed and began sprinkling water all over the area. We each rinsed our hands under the stream of fresh water, and then one by one we left to return to our regular work.

TWENTY-FIVE

Memorial

When the Medical Examiner was finally ready to release Chad's body, I used the last of my savings to provide for his cremation, for I felt a certain bit of accountability. He'd been nothing but friendly and welcoming and it had gotten him killed. Or.... "I" had gotten him killed. Either way, I felt the responsibility and acted on it.

On a particularly warm and sparkling Sunday, I joined the residents of Hale Maluhia and together we carried his box of ashes to the ocean. Makala, Joe, and Kai then took the box and stood in as family, as much family as Chad could have. A local outrigger canoe club known by Dylan Kimura had offered to assist and they took the makeshift family out beyond the bay to scatter Chad's ashes upon the sea, along with flowers and maile leaves.

It was several minutes before the paddlers brought the small group of mourners back, and I noticed that Joe in particular was struggling with emotion. I suspected it was that common bond of military life he had shared with Chad, and I slipped in beside him to put a gentle arm around his waist. He seemed grateful and rested his head on my shoulder as Makala helped the younger mourners to light just a few floating lanterns to send out upon the sea. I felt a sob escape from Joe as the lit tributes drifted off and two ukulele players began to strum and sing the beautiful piece written by Queen Lili'uokalani so many years ago, "Aloha 'Oe," or "Farewell to Thee."

Farewell to you, farewell to you
The charming one who dwells in the shaded bowers
One fond embrace,
'Ere I depart
Until we meet again

When the lanterns were but mere specks on the sea, we returned to the camp where our usual spread of food was waiting. As we ate, various people would share fond memories and even some hilarious stories about Chad.

Once the meal was over and cleaned up in the usual group effort, people began to bring out their battered musical instruments: guitars, ukuleles, and homemade percussion implements. We sat on the grass and sang songs of happiness to celebrate Chad's short life. Toward the end of the day we found ourselves swaying to the music, our arms around the people on either side. Davy shimmered behind me and rested his chin on my shoulder, singing along.

"What a beautiful memorial this has been," he whispered. I smiled and nodded, leaning my cheek briefly against his.

On the way home I reflected on my short but warm friendship with Chad. He had indeed been charming, open, and friendly, and he had brought me into the fold almost immediately. I vowed to remember him always, and I knew that by being a regular visitor and contributor to Hale Maluhia I could be part of the movement to shine a spotlight on the plight of dispossessed veterans and homeless and abandoned citizens.

TWENTY-SIX

Blitz

The following morning was bleak, the rain coming down sporadically in that tropical "I'm gonna mess with all your plans" sort of way. Ahh, the god Lono throwing his weight around yet again. I was out to visit the library again, to return a book and pick up another. I needed the comfort of going to a library instead of downloading to my Kindle or buying even more books. Besides, there's nothing quite like walking into that hallowed hall and having that smell hit you. You know the one: BOOKS. The written word. It was intoxicating. I could spend hours there, and I often did just that.

As a child, my mother was adamant that I needed to know the Dewey Decimal system. I thought about how she'd be disappointed to see how little it is used today. Granted, using the internet was easier, but the Dewey was just another one of those "arts" that seemed to be disappearing these days. Wow, I realized that I sounded like an old fart in my head just then and chuckled at myself.

This part of the road was narrow, and the eastbound side hugged the hill behind it with the occasional turnout dug out of the grassy face. Going the opposite direction was so close to the edge of the cliff that there were times I felt I was in Harry Potter's flying car with no road at all below. I made it a personal rule to never drive westbound at night, but today the rain was so heavy that it felt more like 10 p.m. than 10 a.m.

I glanced in the rear view mirror when headlights flashed behind me. Why was he telling me to move over? It's raining, ya fool! The road was slick as I gripped the wheel and saw the headlights pressing down on my little R2. I was going the speed limit and wasn't feeling safe enough to push the accelerator any further. I pulled to the shoulder when there was room and let him pass. It was a rental car; I could see the sticker as it passed.

I gave a little shudder and pulled back onto the road, continuing to the library. A golden glow spilled from its windows, welcoming me to pull into the small parking lot.

"Back later, R2." I patted his steering wheel, exited, and locked the car. Opening the heavy door to the library, I closed my eyes for a few seconds to inhale the fragrance of books as the air was pushed into my face. Letting out a happy sigh, I returned my book and then pivoted on the ball of my foot to the mystery stacks, going directly to the author I'd been wanting for this week.

Jana DeLeon wrote some humorous action mysteries that, after reading the reviews for the second in the series, I felt might buoy my spirits. The main character was an ex-assassin with the CIA who was

162

forced into hiding in a small town in Louisiana. I found the book and plopped on the floor, my legs crossed. I read the back cover info where it explained about her friends, two elderly women with a knack for getting into mischief. Oh, I thought, this was exactly what I needed. The title was *Lethal Bayou Beauty*. Perfect. I couldn't help but stop to read the first few lines. Pleased with my decision, I tucked the book under my arm and wandered the stacks some more.

Browsing through the selection of Janet Evanovich books, I made sure I was up to date on that series and then had a sudden feeling I was being watched. A glance over my shoulder proved there was no one else nearby. To my left, an older gentleman was snoozing in an overstuffed chair, a copy of *The Sun Also Rises* open on his chest as he snored quietly. *Yeah*, I thought to myself, *that book bored the crap out of me too.*

At a nearby table, two women were knitting, with pattern books open before them. On my right was a bank of computers. I shrugged and went back to my browsing. I ventured to the fiction section and checked on some older books. Miss Read was an English author who wrote of small villages and schools in England well back in the previous century. I had read only one or two of her books but enjoyed them during those times when I just needed soft and beautiful words to cling to. I hadn't felt much need for that since moving to Hawaii, but I checked out the selection anyway. When nothing grabbed me, I turned to another author whose words were like painted wordscapes, Rosamunde Pilcher. I hadn't read *Winter Solstice* yet so I grabbed it.

Again, prickling on the back of my neck caused me to whirl around and look for someone watching me. The sound of books being pushed along on the shelves in the next aisle caused me to peek around the corner, but no one was there. Okay Macca, I thought, you're losing it.

Several rows over I heard the sound of a book being slammed to the floor. Quick strides took me to the source of the sound; there was a book on the floor directly in the middle of the aisle. I moved closer to see the title: *The Valley of Fear* by Sir Arthur Conan Doyle. Squatting beside it, I gently opened the heavy front cover; the plastic dust cover protector was yellowed and cracking, the tape peeling. There was nothing unusual about the book except that the number of pages seemed slight against the heft of the hardcover surrounding it, but I began to turn the pages anyway. Just after the title page though, a loose piece of paper slid out. It contained two words: *You're next.*

I tried to scurry away but fell back on my haunches and then scrambled to get to my feet. My heart was pounding in my ears. I ran down the cross aisle, peering down each stack of books. No one was there.

"Is everything okay?" I heard a woman's voice.

I gasped and whirled around. The two knitters were watching me, kind and concerned. "Yes." I didn't even convince myself, but I forged ahead anyway. "I just... dropped a book. Sorry." I returned to where I'd left the suspicious book, tucked the paper back inside, and added Mr. Conan Doyle's novel to the stack under my arm.

"Did you find everything you were looking for?" the librarian processing my check out inquired.

"Y-y-yes," I stuttered. "Thank you." I handed over my library card for her to scan before turning to leave.

"Oh! Don't forget your books, Miss Liberty."

"Um. Thank you." I slid the small stack of books toward m e and then slipped them into the crook of my arm as if I were walking to junior high school once again. Before I opened the door to go outside, I carefully peered left and then right; there was no one else in the parking lot. I took a deep breath and exited the building, quickly using my key to access R2 and slip inside. The car was small enough that I could tell there was no one hiding inside it. I locked the doors and yelled at the top of my lungs, "Goldfish!"

Davy shimmered into the passenger seat. I hel d the book out to him.

"Your face is white, Babe." He shook his head, glancing between the book and me. "What's this? *The Valley of Fear*," he read the title out loud.

"Turn to the title page."

He did so and the sheet fluttered a bit. His head shot up and h is eyes were wide when he looked at me. "What does this mean?"

"There was someone in the library, hiding in the stacks. I heard him. Then he dropped this book, or... I should say, he threw it on the floor because it was really loud."

Davy thumbed silently through the rest of the book but found nothing else. "Maybe it was just a random note left by the previous person."

We stared at each other for a very long moment before both of us shook our heads, knowing that there are no coincidences such as this.

"Go ahead home," he continued after a moment. "I'm going to go look around the area."

"I'll see you there."

He shimmered away and I was left alone in the hollow silence that was R2. Turning the key, I muttered under my breath. "Okay R2, trusty steed, get us there in once piece, okay?" I was having that creepy-crawly feeling and just wanted to be safely tucked away in my little bungalow with my friends nearby. "Not that you're not my friend, R2, but I'd like a little human company." His motor simply purred in r eply.

The rain was coming down in sheets. I'd picked just the wrong moment to leave the relative safety of the library. I briefly considered pulling over to let the squall pass, but then I'd be a sitting duck at the side of the road, and considering the su dden drop off to my right, I wasn't fond of the idea of perching on the edge of a precipice with rocks and trees, and the waves crashing farther out. I slowed my speed considerably, crawling along with the wipers playing a heavy back beat.

Behind me, headlights approached faster than they should in this weather. I swore under my breath but was determined to keep below the posted speed limit. However, that creepy-crawly feeling I'd had was now like a hurricane of the heebie-jeebies. Something didn't feel right. My spidey-sense was never wrong. If only I really had such spidey-sense, but the intuition in me was strong and gaining strength the more I was around Davy and the animals who "spoke" to me.

At a straight part in the road, I pulled as closely to the right edge as I could. "Come on you idiot. Pass me if you want already," I muttered to the unhearing car behind me, but he didn't take the hint. I pulled back to the center of my lane and visualized the parking lot at home. Just let me get there in one piece. Please.

Suddenly there was a small explosion behind me, buffeting my car forward, and I glanced briefly in the mirror. But it hadn't been an explosion; the idiot had bumped me with his car. In this tin can (sorry again, R2), it had sounded like a bomb. The offending car dropped back and I kept going, ever the optimist. "He must have misjudged his distance from me," I tried to fool myself. But when I saw the car speeding toward me again, I knew it had not been an accident. The crunch of heavy metal was deafening. That is, his metal was heavy, whereas I felt as though my car were made of plastic. I felt the rear buckle and something, perhaps the fender, was rubbing on my rear left tire. I gripped the wheel, for my life did indeed depend on me staying in control. The creepy car dropped way back this time. I hoped he was done scaring me and would just toddle along on his way to go terrorize someone else.

I rounded a bend, only a mile from home now, and was relieved to see the road was empty behind me. But before I could sigh with relief, the same car came barreling toward me out of the mist, and without braking, rammed me from behind. The slick surface and the weight of his vehicle sent me flying over the edge of the road. I screamed and the echo was deafening. The car barreled through foliage and tropical trees, the contact twisting and pounding R2's body. Looming ahead was a huge tree, its shape oddly familiar. My brain wasn't connecting thoughts though, and there wasn't enough time to delve into that familiarity, but just as I made contact with a heavy branch it dawned on me. It was shaped like Davy... doing *The Davy Dance*. At that moment of revelation, my head hit something hard and the world went silent and dark.

Someone was rudely playing the drums on my skull, the pounding both painful and deafening. I suspected I was dreaming, but when I opened my eyes I was surrounded by deep green leaves and rough branches. The tree! The Davy Dance tree! I tried to turn my head toward the sound, but pain shot up my neck to the base of my skull. My face was sticky and, thinking it might be sap from the tree, I put my hand up to investigate. My fingers were covered in red... sap? No, must be blood. A face appeared at my crumpled window and I screamed.

"It's okay ma'am." The face had a voice, and his body was encased in yellow rainproof material, a matching helmet on his head, and ropes connecting him to a large winch of some sort. Oh! Firefighter? Rescue? Something like that. I squeezed my eyes closed as the drum playing resumed in my head. Huge machinery was tearing poor little R2 apart.

No! I thought I screamed, but it was only in my mind.

"Ma'am?" My rescuer was now talking to me from above, since R2's roof had been so viciously removed. I would have cried if I was of my right mind. "Ma'am, we have your vehicle secured now and I'm coming in to assist you, okay?"

Whatever, I thought to myself. *I don't even care at this moment.* I closed my eyes, but when I felt R2 bounce just a little I opened them again as Mr. Rescue eased himself into the passenger seat. Well, what was left of the passenger seat. It appeared to have been folded in half, like a jousting pole had rammed it. Mr. Rescue slipped a plastic collar around my neck, murmuring sounds of comfort the entire time. He took my pulse and checked my blood pressure as another face appeared at the now busted-out window. They tucked a silvery blanket around me and the drumming began again.

I heard the metal rip as they pulled the driver's side door off, and a sudden gush of sea breeze wet with rain pummeled me. I was jostled a few times and felt boards being slid beneath my body, but I didn't care. I opened my eyes just a little and thought I saw Davy shimmer before me, his face tight with fear as he perched on the hood of what used to be my sweet R2. He spoke no words at first but leaned in and kissed me warmly on the forehead. "I'll be with you, Babe. Everything will be okay."

I smiled and closed my eyes, secure in the knowledge that I was in good hands. Many, many good hands. I was pulled from the wreckage and then bundled and strapped into a basket. A shout from Mr. Rescue and I felt myself floating, swinging in the basket. Mr. Rescue was beside me, harnessed and attached to a rope that seemed to go up to the heavens. He steadied the basket as we rose, rarely taking his eyes off of me. It seemed days before I was on solid ground again, but finally that warm feeling of relief washed over me and I moaned. Mr. Rescue was right there, checking my vitals. I couldn't find the words to tell him I was okay. I knew I was though; I was just dazed, exhausted, and cold. The human body is an amazing machine. Machine. My poor R2.

Warm and safe in the ambulance at last, Mr. Rescue stabbed me with a needle, the bastard. Then I realized it was an IV and I immediately forgave him in my thoughts. The warm fluid began to course through me and I decided it was okay to sleep for a while, but they weren't having any of that.

"Ma'am, what is your name?" Stop yelling, I thought.

"Macca." Always the obedient girl. Man asked a question and I replied.

"Macca, stay with me please." He tucked another warm blanket around me. All was good and I was toasty. I tried to close my eyes again but Mr. Rescue was being his now usual annoying gnat-like self. I tried to swat him away but couldn't lift my arms.

"Sleep." I think I said the word out loud and he confirmed it.

"It's not time for sleep yet." He flashed a light in my eyes, one at a time. Gnat.

"Gnat." Oops, I knew I said that word out loud too.

"There are no gnats in here; you're fine." His voice was soothing. I chuckled, I think.

The hospital again. Same one as last time. Same people even. This was two times too many to be here. Buzzing all around me. A swarm of gnats again? Poked, prodded, and jostled. Very strong gnats with sticks. X-rays. Prodding. Pushing. "Does this hurt?"

Yeah, let me do that to you after you tried to fly into a tree and we'll see if it hurts, I thought. "No," I lied. I just wanted to go home.

I tried to open my eyes but the lights were too bright. Squinting, I could see Dr. Lee. Great, this was like a really horrific deja vu or something.

"No serious injuries, Ms. Liberty," Dr. Lee smiled. "Bumps, bruises, cuts, and scrapes. You'll be feeling it for a few days. I'd like to keep you overnight though."

"Home."

"Maybe tomorrow morning. Let's see how you do overnight. You've had quite a shock."

"Yeah." Such eloquence. Frankly, it hurt my head to speak more than a syllable at a time.

I was wheeled to a room soon after and placed ever so gently into a warm bed. Ahh, blessed sleep at last. But once I was left alone, I turned on my side, curled into a fetal position, and the tears came. "Goldf…" I didn't even get the entire safe word out of my mouth before Davy shimmered in, spooning behind me on the bed. His arms held me close, his compact body molded mine, and I felt his warm breath on the back of my neck. Sleep came at last, and thankfully without dreams.

Waking up in a hospital for the second time since moving to this island was making me begin to think I'd made a foolish decision to relocate here. But then I remembered the inn and all the important people in my new life.

Bennie arrived, his face dark with emotion. Anger? He had a cloth bag in his hand which he peremptorily slapped down on the bed. "This is a really, extremely, terribly bad habit, Macca." He *was* angry.

"I'm sorry. I didn't ask to be pushed over a cliff... again."

His face softened. "I'm not angry at you. I'm just... angry."

I couldn't help it; I began to cry. His face softened even more and he perched on the edge of the bed. He smoothed the few strands of blood-matted hair away from my face. "I'm sorry." He touched my cheek so tenderly that I was suddenly awash with comfort and warmth. He picked up my hand and touched his lips to my fingertips but then suddenly looked away. "I saw your car," he said to the window.

"R2." I cried some more.

"He's dead, Jim." Bennie quoted Spock and tried to crack a smile, but the attempt at humor was a little premature for me. "I brought you some clothes to come home in." He indicated the bag. "Ming collected them for you. Everything is fine at the inn, but the guests and all of us are anxious to see you home and safe." I nodded, swiping at the tears on my cheeks. Bennie jumped off the bed when the door opened.

Detective Green greeted Bennie with a nod before turning to me. "It took the crew most of the afternoon to winch up your car yesterday," he began. "That thing may be little, but it's solid. It seemed to be refusing to let go of the tree." He too was attempting humor. I just wasn't in the mood so I just gave him a slow half smile.

"R2," I mumbled. When I saw a frown on Detective Green's face I explained further. "My car. He kept me safe."

Green nodded once. "That he did." He sighed and I saw deep lines of fatigue on his face that I either hadn't noticed before or that had just recently appeared.

Bennie quietly left the room.

Green held up three evidence bags. The first was my Jana DeLeon book and I gasped.

"I really wanted to read that! Now it's going to be lost in evidence-land, isn't it?"

His smile softened his face. "I'm pretty sure I can release it to you before you leave. You checked it out, correct?"

"I did. I don't steal." I frowned, wondering if that's what he meant.

"No." He held up another bag. This one contained the Rosamunde Pilcher book.

"Yes. I checked that out too."

Then he held up the third and final bag containing the Sir Arthur Conan Doyle book. I'd nearly forgotten about it. "And did you check this one out too?"

"I did, but only because it..." my words trailed off, not quite sure where to start. I tried to think all the way to the beginning of yesterday, and when I found the starting line, I spilled the entire story about being watched at the library and about the threatening note that was inside the Doyle book.

When I was done I felt spent. Green didn't look happy, but I was fairly certain his ire wasn't directed at me. He tucked all three books under his arm. "Can you describe the car that ran you off the road?"

"No." I put a weary hand to my head. "The headlights were blinding. However..." I paused, pulling at a thread of memory. "If it's the same car that harassed me on the way to the library, it was a nondescript silver car with a rental sticker on it. Aloha Discount Rentals, I believe it was."

"Very good observation! We'll check into that."

We were interrupted by Dr. Lee and the nurse to inform me that I was able to go home once I signed some papers. Detective Green took his leave then, promising to talk with me later in the week. With the help of the nurse I was able to get dressed in the clothes Ming had provided through Bennie, and the latter then drove me home. I was short on words, short on energy, and long on wanting to crawl back into a fetal position.

TWENTY-SEVEN

Recovery

Bennie helped me navigate the stairs to my bungalow as my body screamed with each step. When I frowned from the pain, the steri-strips on my head pulled and ached. *Oh bed, where are you?*

Winston flew to greet me, landing on my shoulder, and Bennie gently redirected him to his own shoulder. "Not now boy... not now. Macca has had a rough couple of days." The bird's head bobbed as we walked, looking as if he were in agreement with what Bennie was saying. Marley sat on a nearby branch, watching her Winston. Chester must have heard us coming for he tore out of the bungalow and wound around and around my legs; we had to stop for a moment so I wouldn't trip over him.

"Hey Chet. Let's get inside." I couldn't help but smile at him. His purrs rumbled all the way up from where he stood on the walkway. He stepped to the side and we continued the longest hike of my life, or so it seemed. Chester ran ahead, his tail all jittery with excitement.

"Where do you want to be?" Bennie held tight to my arm as we entered the bungalow.

"Bed. Sleep. Lots of it."

"Got it. Good choice actually." Bennie smiled so gently.

"I won't break, you know."

"I know. You keep proving that. Stop it though, okay?"

I had to smile at that. "I'll try. I just seem to be a magnet for lunatics since I came here."

"Yeah, well, we need to find a way to fix that."

He stepped back once I'd flopped on my bed. "Thanks, Bennie." I could already feel myself fading to dreamland.

"Goodnight. Or good day. Whatever." He chuckled. "Just sleep well and we'll be around if you need." He set my cell phone on the bedside table and I closed my eyes. Chester snuggled against me and I pulled a light blanket around us both.

I was just falling asleep when I felt the bed being jostled. Warm arms surrounded Chester and me, and I felt the soft velvet against my cheek. "Goodnight, Babe," Davy whispered. I'm pretty sure I fell asleep with a contented smile on my face while Chester purred.

My dreams were vivid and surreal; I wasn't even entirely sure I was a player up on the silver screen of my poor addled mind. I slept long and hard and was surprised to see the morning already upon us. Any memory of the dreams had faded along with the luster of the full moon. Wait. Full moon? Oh, that explained a lot about the last day! I rubbed my hand gingerly over my face, avoiding the steri-stripped area but feeling little crusts of dried blood still in my hairline. More importantly, I smelled coffee. Dried blood would need to take a backseat for a while. I slogged my way through a single cat weaving in and out of my feet with each step. "If you trip me and I die, no one will be here to feed you," I spoke quietly.

You think? I think I've got Lani wrapped around my big orange paw.

"You're all talk, big man. I saw how you clung to me last night."

I will deny it to my dying day. It goes against the cat code of ethics.

Not surprised at this revelation actually, I rounded the corner and found Davy in the kitchen scrambling some eggs. Toast popped up just as he spoke, "Hello," and smiled.

"Hello." I stood behind him and gently rested my head on the back of his shoulder. He reached up with his free hand and gave my cheek a pat. "Ow."

"Oops." He jerked his hand away. "Did I hit a sore spot?"

"They're all sore spots. There's nothing on my body that... wait…" I touched my chest. "Okay... I take that back. My boobs don't hurt."

"I'll alert the press."

"You do that. And thank you. For coffee." I reached for a cup and poured myself some of the strong brew, and then I dumped a bunch of half and half in it to mellow it out. Cupping it in my hands, I sat in the nearest chair at the dinette table and sipped. And sipped. And sipped some more. The fuzzy cobwebs in my head began to thin. "Is some of that for me?" I was watching him turn the wooden spatula a few more times in the pan of eggs.

In lieu of an answer, he dished out two piles of eggs on a pair of plates and then added a piece of crunchy toast to each. When he placed one in front of me, I had to use my napkin to catch the drool on my lower lip. Sitting opposite me, he lifted his cup and saluted before we dug in. I had no idea I was as hungry as I was. As the last bit of crunchy toast was being washed down by my final glug of coffee, I began to plan lunch.

"Kalei is planning your lunch, so you can just stop right now." His impish grin was firmly in place as he took my thoughts right out of my mind.

"I hate when you do that."

"No you don't."

I sighed and admitted defeat. Although it was unnerving, it was also rather cute. At times.

"See what I mean?" His smugness couldn't even irritate me this morning. I was home, I was safe, and I wasn't going anywhere for a good long while. This was partly because I was afraid of the great world beyond our inn, but mostly because I had no car. "Checkmate," he added, and I stuck my tongue out at him. "Go shower. You look like hell, woman."

"Why thank you ever so much." My voice dripped with the honey of sarcasm, but I did as he suggested and spent a lot of time in the shower. I tried to keep the steri-strip dry, but it was a useless attempt, and I frankly didn't even care much. I'd slap a bandage on it after the shower. I'd had my fair share of steri-strips growing up. Climbing trees often resulted in falling out of them. Riding a bike... well, falling came naturally. Swingset, jungle gym, hopscotch... check. Nothing kept Macca Liberty off the ground. Except a certain tree that caught R2 and broke our fall. Hey! I had just remembered that. I dried off, patched up my forehead, dressed in blue shorts and a pink tee, and found Davy. He hadn't gone farther than the back deck, reading the newspaper and sipping from a mug.

I sat in the chair beside him. "I had the weirdest memory just come back to me."

"Yeah?" He was engrossed in something on the front page of the local paper.

"The tree we flew into, R2 and I..."

"What's it like to have a flying car?" he interrupted. "Did you feel like Harry Potter and Ron Weasley?"

"Yeah." I brushed off his question and forged ahead. "The tree looked just like..."

He folded the paper once and turned his full attention to me, a very slow smile beginning to light in his eyes. "Yes?"

"It was you, wasn't it?" I studied his face. "How did you do that?"

"I keep telling you that I have a lot of time on my hands. I couldn't stop the car behind you, nor could I stop you and R2 in mid-flight, but I found I could manipulate the tree to catch you. I had no idea it would look like me. Was it a good likeness?"

"You were doing your little dance."

He threw his head back with a laugh. "You do know that Axl Rose stole my dance, right?"

"Yeah, and Justin Bieber stole your hairstyle. I know, I know." I shook my head and smiled. "You amaze me. Thank you."

"You're welcome." So plainly stated, but I felt incredibly close to him at that moment. It didn't really matter that there were some emotional conflicts happening inside me; I simply felt loved and protected.

I kissed his cheek and then sat back to enjoy the glorious view beyond the deck... that someone had tried to take away from me. Davy shook the newspaper open again and folded it to a front page item. It was a photo of my poor departed R2 hanging from a winch as he was pulled from the tree that now just looked like your average evergreen tree. "Oh wow," I sighed as I read the article.

"You're front page news... again. You need to knock that shit off."

I chuckled. "I sure will try. Although I am not quite sure what I'm supposed to be doing differently since I don't even know what the hell is behind all of this."

I read all the way to the end of the article and handed the paper back to Davy. He pointed to something in another photo. "Do you recognize this guy?"

I peered at the fuzzy photo and could just barely make out a small dark-haired man. "It's hard to say. The photo isn't very good, but he does look very familiar."

He sighed. "Yeah. He looks a lot like Lani's brother."

I did a double-take and squinted at the fuzzy photo of a bystander in the crowd. He did resemble Kimo. I shivered.

He tossed the newspaper onto the small table between us and gazed out at the sea. I could tell something else was on his mind, but I waited for him to speak first. I didn't have to wait long. "So..." His hands were clasped, elbows on the arms of the chair, and he put his index fingers to his chin. "What's going on with you and Bennie?" He turned to await my answer.

I narrowed my eyes, a little confused. "What do you mean?"

"I saw him kiss your hand."

I picked up the discarded newspaper and smacked him with it. "You were spying!"

"Of course I was! That's what I do!" He fended off another smack.

"Well I don't like it." I punctuated each word with a newspaper smack until he snatched it away from me and held it aloft, out of my reach.

"What am I? A Labrador Retriever?" he inquired, a grin playing on his lips.

"No. More like a yappy little Pekingese."

He thwapped me with the newspaper a few times then and we began to laugh. "I am not a Pekingese, nor am I yappy!" When our laughter died down, I knew he was going to continue his line of questioning, and honestly, I didn't know how to answer.

"So..." an extremely pregnant pause for theatrics before he continued. "Bennie?"

"Yeah." I looked out at the sea, trying to find an answer in the waves. "I'm not sure what's going on."

"Do you have feelings for him?" He was picking imaginary lint — ghost lint? — from his red velvet shirt.

"I have always had feelings," I spoke casually. "We're all like family here."

He turned to me and frowned just slightly, knitting those heavy brows together even closer than they normally appeared. "You know what I mean."

"Yeah." I looked down at my hands. "I know what you mean, and the answer is that I don't know."

He gave one short nod and stared out again. I watched him in profile; it was a gorgeous profile by the way. When he finally spoke, he sounded so far away. "And here you were worried I would leave you, when in fact it might be that it's you who no longer needs me."

I gasped, and despite my aches and pains I moved to kneel before him, taking his hands in mine. "I will always need you. Always. And d on't you ever think otherwise!"

He smiled sadly. "Life and the afterlife." He shook his head. "Both can be cruel, yeah?"

I nodded, warm tears slowly making tracks down my cheeks. He used his thumb to brush them away and then suddenly grinned. "*B-b-b-BENNIE!*" He burst into song and all I could do was smile and hug him. He always knew how to lighten the mood when needed.

TWENTY-EIGHT

Crisis

It's amazing how good sleep, good food, good company, and a fresh Hawaiian breeze can fix a battered body. I awoke the next morning to the curtain fluttering at my newly repaired window. The rain was gone and the air smelled of peace, love, and happiness. What exactly do peace, love, and happiness smell like you ask? Well, they smell exactly like that fresh Hawaiian breeze.

I slowly crawled out of bed and gingerly stretched to loosen my muscles. It was definitely a day for a run, but maybe just a short one. I dressed in shorts, sports bra with a tank top over it, and my trusty running shoes. As I was lacing them up, Chester gave me a rub. *Don't go,* he said in my head.

"I won't be long. You could run with me you know." And I swear, he laughed. I'll bet you didn't think cats could laugh. Well, it was a derisive laugh, so I suspect cats are good at laughing *at* humans.

I could hear the usual Hawaiian music coming from the reception area as I approached, and when I passed the large perch for our two feathered mascots, I noticed both birds bobbing their heads and stomping their little feet to the beat.

"This is new," I muttered to myself as I crossed the threshold to the reception area. I grabbed a cup of Bennie's Kona and added a big dollop of milk. A little pre-adrenaline caffeine might make my run easier. Yeah, I doubted it too but it was worth a try.

"Morning, Macca," Bennie murmured, his fingers flying on the keyboard at the desk.

"Morning." I sipped and pleasantly seared my tongue, so I sipped again. "It's quiet today."

He looked up from his work with a slight frown on his face. "Kalei and Lani haven't gotten here yet for some reason."

I stopped and set my cup down. "That's not like them."

"No. It's not," he agreed. "I checked with Ming, Albert, and Sam, and no one has heard from them."

I pulled my phone out of my pocket and checked for texts or voicemail from them but there was nothing. I stooped down and checked Uncle Wally's ancient answering machine that no one ever used anymore but that we kept around the place for laughs and as a back-up. Zero messages.

I swiped through my contacts and put a call in to the couple but there was no answer, so I left a short message and then stuffed the phone back in my pocket. "Maybe they're on their way." I chewed on my bottom lip. "I'll check again after my run."

"Okay. Be careful, Macca." He smiled at me and went back to typing.
"I will. Thanks."

I went behind the building and did some gentle stretching near the imu oven before I hit the trail. As planned, it was a gentle run, but I could feel some of the kinks easing in my muscles, and the fresh air assaulted my senses giving me a sense of euphoria.

The feeling was dashed though when I returned to find Bennie, Albert, Sam, and Ming gathered together at the reception desk. There was still no word from Kalei and Lani, so I delayed my shower and we all jumped in to get the lunch preparation started. At the very least, we would have fruit, salad, and sandwich makings available. By mid-morning I was very worried and told Bennie as much.

"I'm going to drive over to their place and just see if the car is there."

"Want me to go with you?" he offered, putting plastic wrap over the cold cut platters we'd just arranged and sliding them into the refrigerator.

"No. You hold down the fort. I'll call you when I know what's going on."

He nodded and turned to cover the salads and slide them next to the platters.

I stopped at my bungalow to grab my purse and the keys to the rental car that I'd obtained after poor R2's demise, and then I headed to Kalei, Lani, and Lehua's nearby home. As I turned into their driveway, my worry became more intense when I saw that both vehicles were in the carport. The house itself was quiet and still. I turned off my rental car's engine and sat for just a moment before cautiously getting out and approaching the stairs to the living level.

I gave the front door a gentle knock and it swung open. It took me an hour to take in the scene before me. Actually, it was just a long few seconds. Lehua and Lani were sitting beside each other on a floor pillow, arms around each other. Lani's eyes kept darting to the area behind the open door. Kalei was on a separate pillow, lying on his side with his arms behind him and his ankles bound with a heavy rope. His eyes were closed and the hair on the side of his head was matted with blood. I stepped farther into the room as Lani and Lehua violently shook their heads. The door swung shut behind me and I whirled to face Kimo. With a gun. Of course.

"And our final guest has arrived." His voice was a block of ice, and his eyes were glassy and seemed unfocused. "So kind of you to join us, Miss Liberty. Now sit!"

I plopped down on a floor pillow; it was a good thing it was there because I just sort of folded my legs and landed on it. I thought of my phone in my pocket but knew there was no way I could get to it without

176

him seeing. I turned my head to watch the deranged Kimo. How on earth could he and Lani have sprung from the same parents?

My eyes met Lani's and she mouthed "I'm sorry." I shook my head and tried to tell her "It's okay" with my eyes. I'm not sure how successful it was because at that moment I was terrified. I saw her frequent glances at her unconscious husband.

"No talking!" Kimo waved the gun directly in my face.

"We weren't talking, Kimo." I heard the quaver in my voice but hoped he didn't because I was petrified yet desperate to get us out of this mess as well. "Maybe the voices in your head are talking, but we were not." I held my breath a moment and watched him closely.

He fidgeted and squirmed. "Who told you about the voices?"

My jaw went slack. Mentioning voices had just been an ploy on my part, but it sure explained a lot.

"You never heard voices before the drugs got to you," Lehua spit out the words. Kimo whirled and pointed the gun at his mother.

"Shut up old woman!"

"Who you callin' old, you little brat." Mama Bear Lehua rose to her feet to face her son, but he simply laughed and shoved her back onto the pillow with Lani. The two women clung to each other.

Kimo swung back to me and pressed the barrel of the gun directly to my forehead. "And if you'd just died in your car we wouldn't have to be meeting like this."

"Why are you doing this anyway?"

He gave me a shove with the gun. Great. That was going to leave a mark; I knew it.

"You're not too smart, little innkeeper, are you? Your inn goes to my sister if you die. Duh! Then we will be rich! Your millions will be ours!"

"Millions?" I couldn't help it. I laughed... loudly. "Why do you think there are millions?"

"Because... look at it! That inn is epic!"

"You moron," Lani spat. "It's only 'epic' because Macca works so hard at it."

"And there are no millions," I added. "There aren't even thousands at the end of each month."

"You lie!" He lunged at me again and then laughed. It was a frightening sound, for he was truly unhinged. He straightened up and pulled a tiny plastic bag from his pocket, dipped his finger inside, and rubbed the white powder on his gums. This explained a lot. He suddenly noticed we were watching him and tucked the bag away. "Stop judging me!" he shouted, looking pointedly at us one by one, the gun following his line of vision each time.

"So, what now, Kimo?" My voice didn't even sound like it came from me.

"We sit tight to be certain there's no cavalry coming after you, and then you will meet with an unfortunate accident." There was no remorse in his voice, and his facial expression was close to that of... I couldn't put my finger on it right away. Glee? I shuddered.

"I told the others back at the inn that I'd call when I got here. If they don't hear from me..." my voice trailed off when I realized the implications, for they would be in danger as well.

"I suppose you need to give them a call then." So much venom in his voice, on a face that reminded me far too much of Lani. "Where's your phone?" he demanded as he yanked my arm.

"In my pocket."

He yanked me by the arm again until I was standing. He dug in my left shorts pocket first, and I recoiled at his touch. He quickly found it in my right pocket and pulled it out. "Call."

I scrolled through my contacts and put the call in to Bennie. I was trying to think fast but terror was numbing my brain. Bennie answered on the first ring, "Are they okay?"

"They're fine. We'll be delayed though. I'm sorry." And then it dawned on me. "Could you finish feeding the GOLDFISH for me though? Thanks." I purposely put emphasis and volume to that one word, and then I sent all the positive energy into the universe that I could muster.

"Goldf..." Bennie sounded confused so I ended the call quickly.

"You're about to die and you're worried about *goldfish*?" Kimo scoffed and pushed me back onto the pillow, his laughter sounding frighteningly unbalanced.

But now I wanted answers. "Why did you kill Chad then?"

Kimo pulled up a kitchen stool and perched on it. "I thought he was my friend. I told him about the money and the idea I had. He underestimated me and threatened to tell the police. I found him walking to your inn that night and I knew he was going to tell you, so I bashed his head in. It was easier than I expected."

I felt my stomach lurch. Poor Chad, doing the noble thing yet again and was punished for it. "Why did you hide the body, then? I'd already called the police."

His laugh was harsh. "That," he scratched the stubble on his chin with the butt of the gun, "was just to mess with you. Let's call it entertainment value."

I was assured then that we were being held captive by evil, personified.

"Kimo," Lani called sharply to her brother. "You're sick! And why would you think I would share any of the inn with you if something happened to Macca?"

He thought this over for a while, rubbed at his red nose, and grinned. "Because if you didn't, you'd have to go too. I've killed once. I could kill again. I've heard it gets easier each time."

"What kind of trash do you hang out with that you would hear such a thing?" Lehua's face was a deep red of rage. "You're no son of mine!"

"That's no surprise, Mother," he spat back at her. "You've turned me away for years."

"She only turned you away when you wouldn't get help. She was trying to protect the rest of our family," Lani spat. "You don't deserve her!"

Kimo sighed and dipped back into his little packet of the enslaving powder. "Just shut up Lani."

I peered at the small clock on the wall; it had only been a few minutes since my call for *Goldfish,* but it had felt an eternity. I got Lehua's attention then and stared at her before giving a slow wink. Her brown face creased into a small frown but she remained quiet.

It wasn't but a few minutes later that I felt the shimmer before I saw Davy appear in the corner with Mr. Pinckney in tow. I saw a very slight movement from Lehua and knew she'd seen them too. She casually scratched her head to deflect any attention from her reaction to the ghostly guests. I gave her a slight nod of support.

"Oh dear." Mr. Pinckney wrung his hands and made that pitiful whine.

"Shh." Davy was watching Kimo closely. He was probably wondering, just as I was, if Kimo could see spirits like his mother did, but he didn't seem to notice any change in the room. I watched the two specters out of the corner of my eye; they were having a conversation about what to do. What to do? Really?

"I'll be back in a tick, Babe." Davy smiled broadly at me. "Mr. Pinckney will hang about and run interference if he must." He glanced at his friend. "Right?"

"Oh dear…"

Davy shimmered out and Mr. Pinckney wrung his hands some more. I was afraid that one day they'd just disintegrate and fall off his wrists from all the friction.

"Oh my," he whimpered some more.

I coughed quietly and glared at him; I wanted to shake him at that very moment.

"Hello," he addressed no one and everyone. "My name is Mr. Pinckney. My friend will be back soon."

We pretended to ignore him.

I let out my breath when Davy shimmered back in; I hadn't even realized I'd been holding it. He gave Mr. Pinckney a playful shove of his shoulder. "Are you able to move things with your hands?" he asked his timid friend.

"A little. I think I can."

"I know you can," he encouraged Mr. Pinckney. "Go to the back of the house and make some sort of noise."

"Oh no! What if he sees me?"

"You're dead, man. You're already dead!"

"Oh yeah." Mr. Pinckney disappeared with a bit of a blip, not unlike a sports show breaking for a choppy, low-budget television commercial. A few seconds later I heard a loud crash and the sound of breaking glass somewhere toward the rear of the kitchen.

"What was that?" Kimo demanded of his mother.

"I... I don't know. Something fell?" Lehua played dumb quite well.

Kimo grumbled something under his breath and waved the gun toward the three of us women. "You just stay here or you'll be sorry. Dead sorry." He wasn't a very efficient bad guy, thankfully, and off he went to explore the origination of the crash. I sprang into action once he was out of the room, grabbing a bandana that was on the coffee table and the broom that was propped in the corner by the door. I crouched behind Lani, hiding behind a part of the wall that jutted out into the kitchen doorway, and I handed her the bandana.

"Nooo," Lani whispered frantically and I shushed her, making a calming sign with my hand. Davy appeared opposite me and gave me a thumbs-up sign.

"I don't know what caused that vase to crash." Kimo was talking as he walked back toward us. Davy put fingers to his mouth and whistled shrilly. He was answered by loud barking just outside the sliding glass door. We all turned to see Susie scratching and banging on the glass.

"Whose dog is that?" Kimo exclaimed as he pivoted to point his gun at Susie. The loyal canine apparated through the glass and lunged at the gun, grabbing it in his fierce jaws while Lehua, Lani, and I sprang at the despicable man. Davy did most of the work, having mastered tripping humans for fun in his spare time. He knocked Kimo's feet out from under him so that the beastly young man fell face first onto the floor. I pinned him to the floor with the broomstick across the back of his neck and my knee in his back, and all the while Susie stood guard.

"Good boy, Susie," I praised and the dog relaxed as we pulled Kimo's hands behind him while Lani used the bandana to tie him up.

At that precise moment the front door crashed open and Davy, Susie, and Mr. Pinckney shimmered away with one last "oh my goodness" emanating from the timid librarian. The room was suddenly swarming with police officers. Well, I counted four. To me, that was good enough to constitute a swarm. Lehua jumped into action then and, in no uncertain terms, declared that this was her house and that her son had held us all captive for hours. The police took over for Lani and me and restrained Kimo in a more professional manner.

"We need an ambulance," I shouted over the noise and pointed to poor Kalei, still unconscious on the floor.

Kalei was loaded into the ambulance just a few minutes later, and Lani had to beg the officers to let her ride along and not stay behind to answer their questions.

"Why not take my statement and Lehua's first?" I offered to Abbott-Officer. (I still couldn't seem to remember their names.) "Then you can take Lani's at the hospital. You'll want to talk to Kalei once he's awake anyway, right?"

I was amazed, frankly, that they agreed to my suggestion, and then began the grueling task of telling our stories and answering questions. They separated Lehua and me, but we were still within view of each other. Every now and then we'd look at each other and send our silent support. Detective Green had arrived on the scene directly after the swarm of officers and he led the questioning. Davy and Mr. Pinckney shimmered in and out and about the home to listen in on the various conversations.

"Who called the police?" I asked the detective.

"Bennie did. He claimed your telephone conversation with him seemed off."

"Very off." I gave one little humorless laugh.

TWENTY-NINE

Resolutions

Kimo had been carted off to the hospital in police custody. Apparently we had done a real number on him. His nose was bloodied from falling on his face and his eye was already puffy and blackening. Tsk, tsk. What a shame. Not.

When we'd finished answering questions over and over again, I drove Lehua to the hospital to check on Lani and Kalei. The front desk wasn't going to let us back to see him until Lehua made a fuss and they relented, most likely because of her position there. Very important rule: Never piss off someone who makes your food. We wound our way around the maze of curtained beds in the emergency room until we found the big man sitting up in bed, a bandage on his head and Lani snuggling beside him. Lehua rushed to him, murmuring in Hawaiian, and gave them both hugs and kisses. I was beginning to pick up a little of the language, but all I could pull from her non-stop speech was *keiki*, meaning child. Lani kept wiping tears from her cheeks and Kalei would sweetly kiss the tears from her fingers. Lehua gestured to me to join them, as I'd been standing back to give them a moment.

"You're *'ohana*; you're family." She wrapped one arm around me and I perched on Kalei's bed. With a tilt of her head, a small grin began to stretch across the older woman's face. "So, Susie is a ghost too?"

Feeling the heat grow in my cheeks, I nodded and turned to Lani and Kalei. "I'm sorry for any deception, but you can see why we had to act as if he was a stray who adopted us. He came looking for Davy one day and now they're nearly inseparable."

Kalei laughed and nodded. "I get it. I do. But one thing I really don't understand is why does he have a girl's name?"

Now it was my turn to laugh as I shook my head. "Believe it or not, I keep forgetting to ask Davy." Their laughter joined mine, filling the drab hospital room with a brief moment of mirth.

"Miss Macca…" Kalei began as our laughter quieted, then shook his head as if he was clearing cobwebs from his thoughts. "I mean Macca," he continued. "How can we ever thank you? Lani told me what you did. You'll make a wonderful *'anake*." He smiled as Lani squeezed my hand.

"*'Anake?*"

"Aunt." Lani smiled. "I'm pregnant."

And it was then that I realized she had been truly glowing lately. "Oh my gosh!" I wrapped my arms around first Lani, then Kalei, and then Lehua, congratulating them all.

This was wonderful news! On a pretty unwonderful day. But there you have it: the balance between dark and light.

Kalei was only in the hospital overnight and suffered just a mild concussion. Despite his protests, I insisted he stay home for a couple of days, but he showed up at the inn to work on the second day. I stood in front of him, hands on my hips, toe tapping the wooden floor.

"What?" He had the sense to look like a kid with his hand in the cookie jar. "Do you have any idea how boring it is at home all alone?"

I gave that some thought. I gave it a lot of thought actually before I responded. "As a matter of fact, I have completely forgotten what that feels like."

The big Hawaiian grinned. "See? *You* should take some time off."

"Yeah," I chuckled. "During our *slow* times, right?" And we shared a little snicker then because frankly there hadn't been too many slow times in a very long... century. Or so it seemed.

"I promise to work light. Lani won't let me do much anyway. She's practicing being a mama already. But I love that *makuahine*!" His dark eyes twinkled.

"And soon there'll be a *keiki* to love too, and for me to spoil. So take care of yourself, okay?"

He thought for a long moment. "I hadn't even thought of it that way. Whoa. I'ma be a *makuakane*." His face paled and his eyes were wide. I laughed and hugged him.

"Just remember we're watching you," I warned him.

"Our *keiki* will need a healthy daddy," Lani teased as she put cookies into the oven for the homeless camp.

Bennie pulled me aside that afternoon and pulled a piece of paper out from under the laptop. "Macca, do you have any idea who might have put this note on the desk after we talked on the phone?"

I turned the paper around and hid my smile as I recognized Davy's handwriting in the scrawled words:

Macca in trouble
Call 911

I felt guilty, but I had to hedge my way out of this one. "No. Wow! I must have a guardian angel or something."

I could tell by his eyes that he didn't buy it, but I was relieved that he didn't push the issue. He simply slid the note back under the laptop. I patted his hand and tried to give him a thousand watt smile, but I suspect it came in at only ten percent of that.

I decided to change the subject quickly. "When are our next guests arriving?"

"Tomorrow," he murmured.

"Oh, then I had best go help Ming get their bungalow ready. Thank you again, Bennie!" What I was thanking him for neither of us really knew for sure. Perhaps it was the fact that he didn't press me on the issue.

Over the next weeks we experienced a lot of both usual and unusual activity. Detective Green stopped by two different times to keep me advised that Kimo's motives had indeed been monetary; he said that his sister would inherit the inn with the others once I was out of the way. Then he had tried to frame me with Chad's murder. When asked about the other employees who would also co-own Hale Mele, he told me that Kimo had simply shrugged his shoulders. Detective Green also indicated that a mental health hearing was scheduled for Kimo; this didn't surprise me for he had seemed unbalanced, in addition to having a drug problem.

But the best news was that the charges against me had officially been dropped, which meant that my bail money had been returned as well. Davy and I celebrated that evening with a bottle of Uncle Wally's better wine — this time a 2006 Pinot Grigio from J Russian River vineyards in California. It was crisp and spicy, and we enjoyed it to the last drop.

"Congratulations on your freedom, jailbird," Davy ever so eloquently toasted. Was toasted too. Both of us were. Wait. I just realized that ghosts can get drunk, for this was not the first time he'd been intoxicated. I burst out laughing and let Davy think it was because of his rather lame little joke.

Despite the busy weeks that had passed, we still managed to take our food to Hale Maluhia each Sunday.

Quite often we ran into one of the Project Peace House volunteers that Dylan had arranged for. One day there was a mobile lab parked near the buses, and people who wanted to see a doctor were welcomed inside for a basic examination. I learned that the doctors had also brought a few mental health workers into the fold for those people in need.

Makala was still making leis and had actually received a couple of orders from local inns and restaurants.

"Wow. You've got quite the business started there, Makala," I marveled, eliciting a chuckle from the elder lady.

"I've had to teach some of the camp *keiki* how to make them so we can keep up with the demand." She put her hands in her lap without letting go of her tools. "Imagine that!" She gave me a sparkly grin with matching twinkles in her eyes. I folded my legs under myself and joined her on the grass.

"Congratulations!" I gently fingered the finished lei beside her. "They are beautiful, as usual."

"Hey!" Joe and Kai joined us, bringing Makala a plate of food from our buffet and then each planting a kiss on both my cheeks. "How is our superhero?"

I blushed. "You heard then."

"Heard? Not only did we hear," Kai grinned proudly, "we've been busy spreading the word! You caught yourself a bad guy!"

Joe was examining my back and shoulders. "Where's your cape?"

Makala laughed and gave him a playful slap on the shoulder. "Leave Macca-Roon alone old man." She grew serious for a moment. "How are Lani and Kalei taking it, with her brother being *kalaima*?"

"What?"

"Criminal," Joe assisted with the translation.

"Oh! Sorry about that. I'm still learning. They seem fine. The family was on the outs with Kimo for many years anyway. I'm just glad no one was seriously hurt."

"And they have you to thank for that, Macca." Kai touched my hand, a soft fatherly look in his eyes that made me blush.

"Thank you, but I didn't do any of it alone."

He nodded once. "We know. But you are brave *wahine*."

"Thank you." I shyly ducked my chin. "Oh! Did you hear about Lani though?" I was eager to change the subject. "She's going to have a baby!"

"Oh my! That's wonderful news!" Makala rocked back on her haunches in delight.

"Kalei a father?" Joe hooted. "Can you just imagine a tiny child in those huge paws of his?" Kai joined in the laughter.

"Ahh," Kai chuckled, "but Makala is right; this is wonderful news!"

"Please tell them congratulations for us," Makala spoke as she picked up her tools again. "Now you learn to say it… *ho'omaika'i*."

They proceeded to continue with my language lessons, something I looked forward to each week. My progress was slow though. With only thirteen letters in the Hawaiian language there were an extremely intimidating number of syllables and punctuation involved, but I had decided that if I was going to live here, I should respect their customs and learn to speak and understand their ancient and beautiful language.

THIRTY

Encore

Alas, it was time to replace poor R2 and my rental with a new Smart Car. Insurance paid for most of it, and I used some of my returned bail money for the remainder, including inter-island shipping. Ouch. My shiny new Smartie arrived at the port of Hilo, where I took possession and returned the rental. The new Smartie was very similar to my old R2, but with a few upgrades. This one was silver with black trim, and his name came to me on the drive home: Roomba. Yeah. Google it. That's what he looked like.

"You'll see, Roomba." I patted his steering wheel. "We'll become fast friends. I promise."

"Until you kill this one too." Davy shimmered in beside me, and Mr. Pinckney followed in the rear compartment. Startled, I neglected to avoid a pothole and we went bump. "See what I mean?" I could hear the smile in his voice as I kept my eyes on the road.

"You keep sneaking up on me like that and your prediction will come true."

"Oh dear," Mr. Pinckney worried in the back. "I think I'll meet you both back home." And away he went in a less than impressive shimmer. Actually, it was more of a blink. No one could out-star Davy Jones' entrances and exits. Wait. What did he say? Home?

"What did he mean by 'home' just then?" I inquired nervously.

"The inn, of course."

"Holy cow. He's going to be a permanent resident now?"

"Yeah." Davy looked at me like I was from another planet. "Sort of. I like him. Don't you like him?"

"Of course I like him! But now I have…" I counted quickly, "three ghosts at Hale Mele?"

"Four," he reminded me. "Don't forget Glory." His impish grin melted my heart.

"Yes. Four ghosts. You had all better behave yourselves."

"Don't we always?" The Pest, at his finest. But who could be upset?

Determined to take a few moments to myself in the peace of my bungalow, I curled up on the sofa with Winston on his perch and Chester in my lap. The latest Janet Evanovich novel I'd checked out at the library was balanced on the arm of the sofa and I held it loosely in my hands. A glass of Uncle Wally's red wine was within easy reaching distance and I enjoyed an occasional sip now and then.

Out of the corner of my eye I saw the shimmer first before Davy appeared in the arm chair across the room, dressed in dark slacks and a white Nehru jacket with gold brocade trim. My own personal ghost. Oh goody.

"Really?" I sighed heavily and buried my nose in the book, hoping he'd get the hint that I wanted some quiet time.

"Miss me?"

"Yeah, but my aim will be better next time," I deadpanned, knowing full well that sarcasm just bounced off him like hot oil on a non-stick skillet.

"Oh, you say that, but I know in your heart you missed me."

I sighed and continued to try to read, but I was just distracted enough that none of the words formed thoughts in my head.

"What are you doing?" he pried as usual.

"Knitting."

"No you're not; you're reading."

"If it was obvious, why did you ask?"

"Conversation starter?"

I shook my head and continued reading, or at least trying to.

"I wrote a poem for you," he continued, despite our lack of eye contact. I could hear the teasing smile in his voice though. He took a deep breath in a overly dramatic stage manner before he began:

'Twas the night before Christmas,
when all through the house,
not a creature was stirring,
except Macca and a mouse.

A mouse? I actually heard an "eek" in my head. Where the hell was he going with this? And there had better not be any rodents present. He continued.

The stockings were hung
on the back line to dry,
while Macca read her book
under Winston's watchful eye.

"I'm trying to read here," I reminded him.

"But my poem is better than your book, I'm certain! I'll continue…"

The mouse was all nestled

snug in his bed,
while visions of Cheddar
danced in his head.

"Did you know," he interrupted himself, "there's a town in England by that name?"

"Yes." I hadn't, but I didn't want to encourage him. It didn't work, for he continued reciting his poem.

And Macca with her book,
and her cat Chester too,
were staying up late
to read the night through.
When out on the roof
there arose such a clatter
that Macca called the cops
(as she hadn't a ladder).

I picked up the pillow beside me and threw it at him, hitting my target perfectly in the face. He caught it on the bounce and spent a few moments tossing it up in the air, catching it, and repeating over and over. It was dizzying. I turned my eyes back to my book and got an entire paragraph read before he started up again.

"Did you know I once met Santa?"

I looked up at him and frowned. What was he going on about? But I remained silent.

"I lied. It was just a store Santa."

I went back to my book.

"But I did meet The Beatles."

"I know."

He tossed the pillow more. I read more.

"Oh! How about this instead?" He began to sing.

Young MacMacca had an inn, E-I-E-I-O
And at this inn she had a cat, E-I-E-I-O
With a "mew-mew" here and a "purr-purr" there
Here a "purr" there a "mew"
Everywhere a "purr-mew"
Young MacMacca had an inn, E-I-E-I-O

Young MacMacca had an inn, E-I-E-I-O
And at this inn she had a bird, E-I-E-I-O
With a "ra-awwk" here and a "ra-awwk" there

Here a "ra-awwk" there a "ra-awwk"
Everywhere a "ra-awwww-wwwwkkk"
Young MacMacca had an inn, E-I-E-I-O

Young MacMacca had an inn, E-I-E-I-O
And at this inn she had a snobby customer, E-I-E-I-O
With a bitch-bitch here and a bitch-bitch there
Here a bitch there a bitch
Everywhere a bitch-bitch
Young MacMacca had an inn, E-I-E-I-O

"Very clever, but I'm trying to read here." I looked up and he stuck his tongue out at me.

"I'm bored."

"You sound like a five year old."

Still holding the pillow, he slunk out of the room and I breathed a sigh of relief. The peace was short-lived though as I heard rustling on the other side of the sofa. Beyond my feet I saw Davy's head slowly rise from beneath the arm level of the sofa. What now, I thought. His head lowered slowly out of sight again and there was more shuffling as he repositioned... somewhere. This was ridiculous. His head then slowly rose over the back of the sofa before sinking back out of sight again. I worked so hard to keep from laughing, but this typical pesky behavior of his was so endearing... most of the time. I heard the sound of his shuffling recede. I knew he hadn't given up, so now I was on edge waiting for his next assault, and before I could even think it, the pillow he'd been holding came sailing out from the dining alcove, smacking me square in the face.

"AHA!" He jumped out. "Three point shot and he nails it!"

I sailed the pillow back at him and grabbed another. "This is war!" We beat each other with the soft pillows, laughing and dodging furniture and a certain cat who thought this was quite bizarre human behavior, even for us.

Winded, I fell back onto the sofa and dropped my pillow. "Truce! I call truce!"

"I won!"

"Truce does not mean you won!"

"It does too! Because face it... After you rest you're not going to want to start again, right?" He had his hands on his hips and looked utterly adorable and infuriating at the same time.

"You're right," I gave in, but as he reached for my pillow I gave it a good swing and hit him smack in the chest. I just loved getting the last laugh, but with Davy around that wasn't necessarily a common occurrence; he was a clever little pest.

"Pretty groovy that Kalei and Lani are having a wee one, yeah?" He tossed a palm-sized seashell up and down, catching it and twirling; it was rather hypnotizing to watch.

"Yeah. I'm so happy for them!"

"Does that mean we'll be needing a replacement for her then?"

"No." I watched the shell go up and down, twirl, toss, up and down again. "I told her she can bring the baby to work. There are enough of us here to help, and Lehua's hours will allow her to take the child during busy times." He set the shell back on the coffee table and began to pick up the discarded ammunition from our pillow fight.

"I'm stahving," he moaned pitifully as we set the pillows back to their spots on the sofa. "What shall we have for dinner?"

"I was thinking of an egg sandwich; I'm feeling lazy tonight."

"Oh." He wrinkled his nose. "I'm a bit tired of eggs. What about some of the leftover pasta salad?"

"You ate that for lunch."

"Oh." He chewed on his lip. "So I did."

We were silent for a bit, staring out at the sunset as if a fresh menu might pop up upon the clouds. "We could have a pizza delivered," I suggested, and he responded with the same wrinkled-up nose that had shown itself over the egg sandwich.

"We could go to the dining room and eat Kalei's dinner."

"I don't feel like socializing tonight. You can go if you want. Just be careful no one sees food floating in mid-air."

"Nah. I don't want to take the chance."

"How about tomato soup and a grilled cheese sandwich then?"

His eyes lit up like a kid's on Christmas morning. "That idea is brill! Do we have Swiss cheese?"

"Of course. Would I ever deprive you of Swiss cheese?"

"You're too good to me. Except when you're attacking me with an innocent pillow. Poor pillow." He stroked it and I briefly contemplated throwing the other pillow at him.

Instead though, we focused our energy on recreating my favorite childhood food. While I prepared the sandwiches and heated the soup, Davy opened a bottle of white wine, handing a glass off to me. "My darlin'..." He nodded and then raised his glass. "To grilled cheese sarnies and tomato soup."

I chuckled and raised my glass as well. "I will definitely drink to that." We sipped. "Did you love grilled cheese sandwiches and tomato soup as a child?"

"No. Not really. Beans and toast were my favorites. I didn't learn to love grilled cheese sandwiches and tomato soup until I came to the States."

"Well, you were still technically a child then."

"Quite true. I still am as a matter of fact," he declared, sipping his wine while I grinned.

"Me too, at times," I replied over the rim of my wineglass. He winked at me, and there were a few seconds of silence between us then. Frankly, silence was rare when Davy was around, but I didn't mind. Most of the time. After all, I had my mp3 player and earbuds to fall back on if necessary.

"It's been one hell of a year, yeah?" He was the one who broke the silence, which was no surprise.

"It has. My one wish for the coming year and all years thereafter is that I never encounter a dead body ever again. Ever."

"Are you up to more ghosts though?" His eyes twinkled.

I gasped. "What have you done?" I nearly jumped off the sofa. His only reply was gales and gales of laughter. But it was then that my Davy became David. My friend. My confidant. The ghostified version of a very wonderful man. And nothing he could do would shock me anymore. Or so I thought…

Glossary of Hawaiian Words

Word	Pronunciation	Meaning
'anake	ah-nah-keh	Aunt
'ohana	oh-hah-nah	Family
'ono	oh-noh	Delicious
'aina awakea	eye-nah ah-vah-keh-ah	Lunch
akamai	ah-kah-mah-ee	Smart, intelligent, wise
aloha	ah-loh-hah	Hello, goodbye, love, affection, goodwill
'anakala	ah-nah-kah-lah	Uncle
auna (hula)	ow-nah	Native dance accompanied by chanting
hale	ha-leh	House
haole	hau-leh	Foreigner, Caucasian
heaiu	hay-yow	Ancient Hawaiian religious temple or area
ho'omaika'i-'ana	ho-oh-ma-ee-kah-ee-ah-na	Congratulations
hula	hu-lah	The dance of Hawaii that tells a story
imu	ee-moo	Underground oven
kahiko (hula)	kah-hee-koh	Native dance tells a story with music and movement
kalo	kah-loh	Taro plant
kane	kah-neh	Man, boy
kapu	kah-poo	Taboo, forbidden
keiki	keh-ee-kee	Child, children
kekui	keh-koo-ee	State tree of Hawaii, the nuts are often used for leis
koa	koh-ah	Native tree, often used for building and crafts
lei	lay	A garland of flowers, leaves, nuts, or shells
lomi-lomi	loh-mee-loh-mee	Raw salmon massaged and cured, with tomatoes, onions, peppers.
lua	loo-ah	Toilet, hole, cave
mahalo	mah-hah-low	Thank you

maile	mye-leh	Plant whose leaves are used for special leis
makai	mah-kah-ee	Toward the ocean (directional)
makuahine	mah-koo-ah-hee-neh	Mother
maluhia	mah-loo-hee-ah	Peace, safety (Hale Maluhia)
mauka	mau-kah	Inland, or toward the mountain (directional)
mele	meh-leh	Song
paniolo	pah-nee-oh-loh	Hawaiian cowboy
pikake	pee-kah-keh	Small, white, very fragrant flowers used for leis
poi	poy	A paste made of taro root
poke	poh-keh	A dish of diced raw fish with spices
pono	poh-noh	Righteousness
puakenikeni	poo-ah-keh-nee-keh-nee	Yellow to orange fragrant flowers used for leis. Name means "10 cent flower" because the leis used to be sold for 10 cents.
shaka	shah-kah	Pinky and thumb salute for hang loose or right on
wahine	wah-hee-neh	Woman, girl
wikiwiki	wee-kee-wee-kee	Fast, speedy

Place Names

Place Names	Pronunciation
Hi'ilawe (falls)	hee-ee-lah-veh
Hilo	hee-loh
Honoka'a	hoh-noh-kah-ah
Kahua	kah-hoo-ah
Kaluahine (falls)	kah-loo-ah-hee-neh
Kapa'ua	kah-pah-oo-ah
Kilauea	kee-lah-weh-ah
Kohala	koh-hah-lah
Kona	koh-nah
Oahu	oh-ah-hoo
Papakôlea	pah-pah-koh-leh-ah
Waimea	wye-meh-ah
Waipi'o	wye-pee-oh

Given Names

Hawaiian Name	Pronunciation
Kai	kye
Kalakaua	kah-lah-kah-oo-ah
Kalei	kah-lay
Kamehameha (King)	kah-meh-ha-meh-ha
Kimo	kee-moh
Lani	lah-nee
Lehua	leh-hoo-ah
Makala	mah-kah-la
Momi	moh-mee
Pele	peh-leh

Other	Pronunciation
Macca	MACK-kah (not Hawaiian, obviously, but I use John Lennon's pronunciation as my own personal guide)

ABOUT THE AUTHOR

Jerri Keele resides with her husband, two dogs, and three cats in Salem, Oregon. She has been a fan of Davy Jones since the age of nine, in 1966, when he first hit the scene as a Monkee. Since his sudden passing in 2012, she has worked tirelessly toward fundraising to help care for the herd of retired racehorses he left behind. The horses are under the watchful eye of his four daughters – Talia, Sarah, Jessica, and Annabel – who created the charity The Davy Jones Equine Memorial Foundation (DJEMF).

CPSIA information can be obtained
at www.ICGtesting.com
Printed in the USA
LVHW081351030719
623106LV00027B/305/P